KELVOO'S TEACHINGS

An Unwilling Ascent to Godhood

PHIL BAILEY

ISBN
978-1-7781024-7-9 (Hardcover)
978-1-7781024-8-6 (Paperback)
978-1-7781024-6-2 (eBook)

1. FICTION, SCIENCE FICTION, ALIEN CONTACT

To Cora, my lovely wife and the one who somehow puts up with the highs and lows of her husband's self-publishing journey.

My boundless thanks to those who made
Kelvoo's Teachings a reality.

Thank you to my beta readers for giving your time so generously, and for improving Kelvoo's Teachings through your corrections, ideas, and encouragement.

Sarah Bailey
Craig Becker
Peter Ehm
Dave Eisler
Blake Thurston

Thank you to my editor, Kevin Miller, for all the red lines, corrections, annotations, and other input that mangled my manuscript, but made this book, and the ones before it, so much better in so many ways.

Merci beaucoup, Alain Berset, who was somehow able to take my thoughts and my kindergarten-level sketches, transforming them into the 3D rendering of Kelvoo on the flying altar, which graces the cover of this book. Thanks as well for your work on the previous books in this trilogy.

Thank you, Jan Westendorp for working with Alain and me, and for using your professional layout talents to produce the cover of this book and its predecessors.

Gross External Kloormari Anatomy
Plate 1 - Anterior/Posterior View [1]

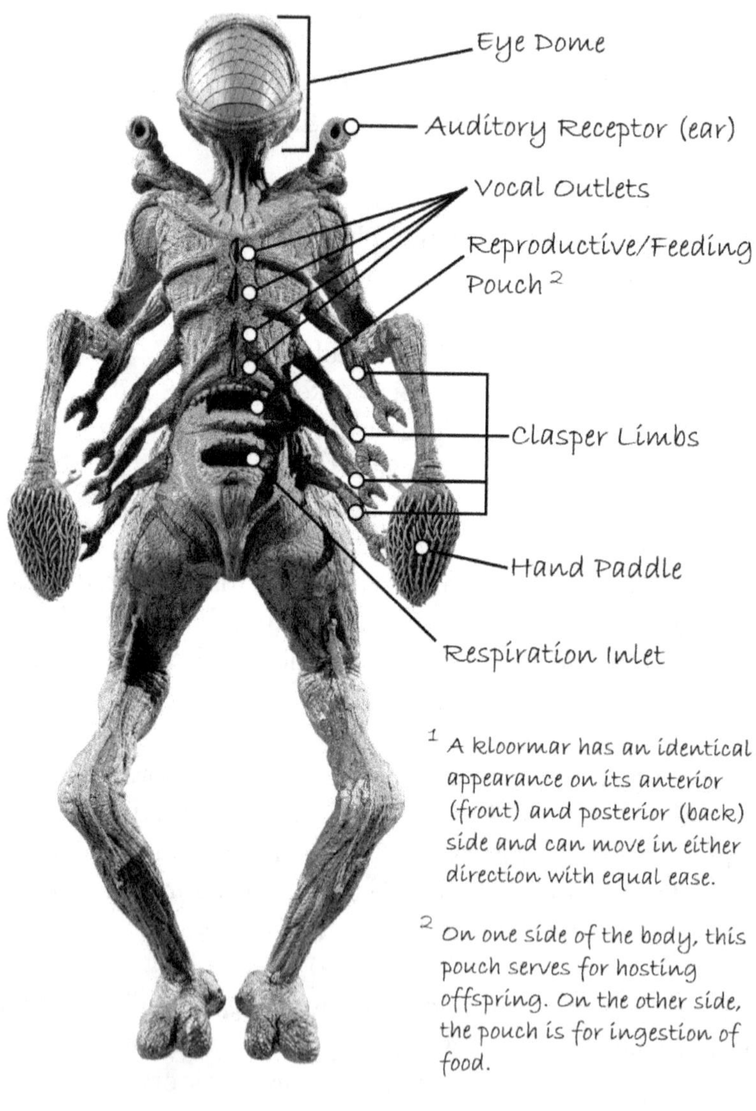

[1] A kloormar has an identical appearance on its anterior (front) and posterior (back) side and can move in either direction with equal ease.

[2] On one side of the body, this pouch serves for hosting offspring. On the other side, the pouch is for ingestion of food.

Gross External Kloormari Anatomy
Plate 2 - Oblique View

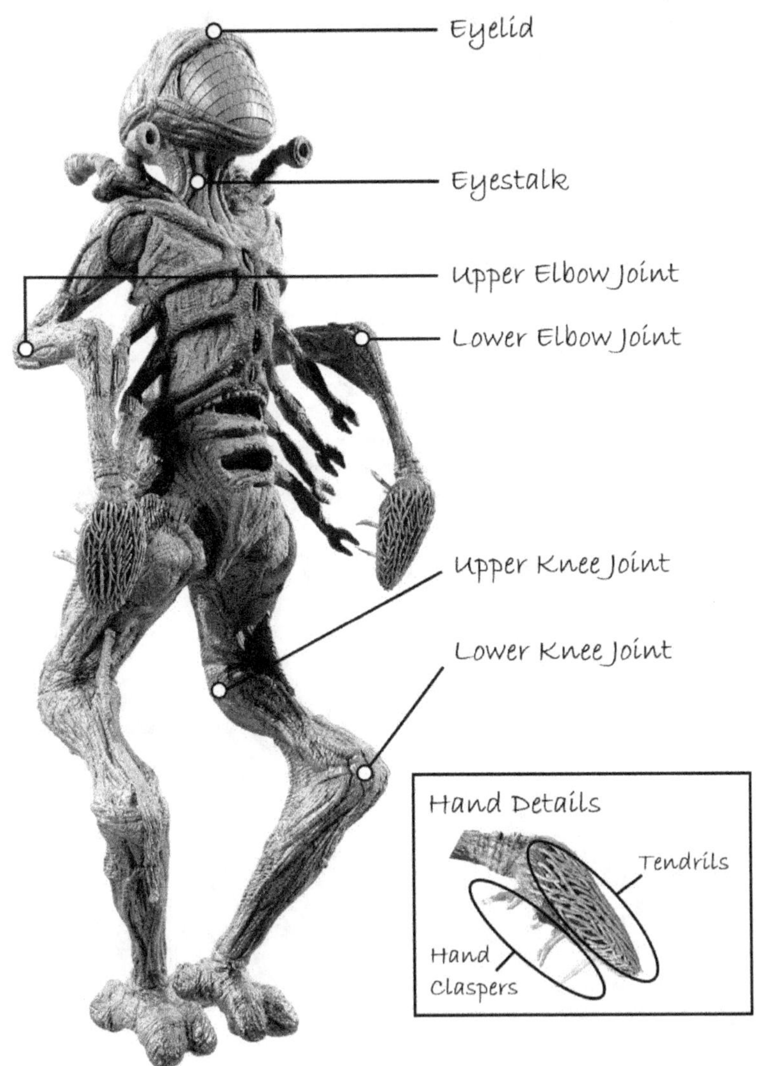

PART 1: KELVOO

ONE: WORSHIPPED

The crowd of jabbering, excited humans, dressed in blue jackets, swept me along the wide corridor and up the ramp onto the expansive stage in the high temple. Some of the humans beamed with happiness while others cried with joy. An altar constructed from a massive slab of gleaming white rock supported by sheets of glass stood at the center of the huge circular, domed chamber. The humans lifted me over their heads and slid me onto the altar.

From my prone position, I shifted to a crouch on my lower set of knees and elbows, but before I could stand, the anti-gravity components of the altar top powered up and the slab began to rise. The glass that had supported the slab on each side pivoted up on hinges, forming walls.

Is this intended to stop me from falling, or prevent me from escaping? I wondered.

As the altar approached the mid-point between the stage floor and the apex of the golden dome, it slowed enough for me to safely stand.

I paced back and forth to either side of the rising platform, peering over the glass at the humans fifty meters below. Brenna gave me a helpless look as our bot rose toward me. I commanded the bot to return to Brenna and remain with her. It descended accordingly.

The Kelvonists bolted from the stage, determined to witness the spectacle from the best vantage point. They left to join the throng that had gathered on the vast, manicured grounds outside, leaving Brenna standing alone with the bot hovering behind her.

Seven huge latches, each weighing thousands of kilograms, were situated along the edge of the dome that faced the temple grounds. As each latch snapped open, a deep metallic boom reverberated through the vast empty space. Massive hinges on the left and right screeched as the forward section of the dome rose and folded back, like a kloormari eyelid. That's when I realized the entire structure was intended to resemble a kloormar's eye dome.

As the edge of the golden dome separated from the stage floor, the roar of countless human voices poured in. When the edge rose higher, I saw a sea of humans clad in white robes with gold trim. As the dome rumbled open, the humans closest to the temple wall were the first to see me. Some dropped to their knees and bowed. Others stood and extended their grasping hands toward me. Some wept, some screamed, some danced and twirled in place, and some prostrated themselves and rolled back and forth on the ground. The humans' reaction formed a visible wave, radiating from the temple's base and rippling outward as I became visible to more of the horde.

Once the dome stopped retracting, the full extent of the scene was revealed. The throng extended as far as my eye could see. White robes covered the expansive grounds, the fields beyond, and the rolling hills in the distance. Based on the scene before me, I estimated that ten million or more humans had come to worship.

I tried to shout, which only confirmed that I couldn't be heard over the din, even with all eight of my vocal outlets bellowing at full volume.

A swarm of loudspeaker drones cast shadows over me as they blocked the mid-morning sunshine, before fanning out and stationing themselves over the crowd.

The high priest's amplified voice boomed forth from the sky.

"Kelvonists of Terra, I bring unto you, Kelvoo of Kuw'baal! Kelvoo, the supreme being who lights the way for us! Kelvoo, our inspiration. Kelvoo, our savior. Kelvoo, our teacher.

"Oh, great Kelvoo! We beseech thee in our time of need to heal our divisions, to right our wrongs, and to reveal unto us the one true path to the enlightenment of humanity."

The crowd exuded a joyous roar. Then the altar moved forward over the throng, rose high into the air, and then hovered. Music blared from the drones and the crowd burst into song. I was able to discern the words only because a choir's rendition was also playing from the loudspeakers.

> Oh Kelvoo, how our hearts do yearn
> for the glorious day of your return,
> when Terra sees a bright new morn
> and young and old shall be reborn.
>
> Oh Kelvoo, Kelvoo, glorious one; so innocent yet wise.
> Oh Kelvoo, Kelvoo, hear our praise and feel our love arise.
>
> Your wisdom shines bright as a star.
> Your words shall be spread, near and far.
> Our minds and souls will all ignite
> when you bring forth your guiding light.
>
> Oh Kelvoo, Kelvoo, glorious one; so innocent yet wise.
> Oh Kelvoo, Kelvoo, hear our praise and feel our love arise.
>
> Our lowly species shall be healed,
> when all the secrets are revealed.
> Peace and love shall come to be,
> when you fulfill your prophecy.

As the final strains of the hymn faded, the altar resumed its ascent. Two minutes later, I noticed that the altar top was higher than the mountains in the distance and the noise of the crowd had faded away, replaced by the sound of the wind rushing by.

The great white slab took on an arcing trajectory as it moved westward and began a gradual descent on its way to some unknown destination.

The outpouring of love and worship from the humans was so overwhelming that I couldn't analyze it in detail. In fact, only one thought percolated through my mind:

What a bunch of idiots!

TWO: A WELCOME ISOLATION

Eighteen years after my return to Kuw'baal from Terra, I gladly retreated into a life of isolation. I had reluctantly accepted the label of "hero" after my escape from the Terran civil war, and I served the Planetary Alliance in roles such as special envoy, goodwill ambassador, and mediator for a variety of projects and initiatives.

Having earned a doctorate in the study of human nature, I was sought out for my expertise and my observations of humans from an outsider's perspective. I was hosted, fêted, and celebrated on all the Alliance worlds and the thriving, human-colonized planets of Exile and Perdition.

One place I didn't go in those eighteen years was Terra. My human foster daughter, May, and her older sister, Brenna, weren't interested in Terra either. May called Terra "the forbidden planet" while her sister referred to Terra as "the planet whose name we do not speak." All three of us had lived on Terra and had been traumatized when the anti-immigrant Human Independence Movement and its political wing, the Humanity Party, were elected as a minority government and then staged a coup, plunging Terra into a bloody war.

Extraterrestrial citizens of Terra had been hunted down. The fortunate ones had been deported while those deemed to be enemies of humans were imprisoned, tortured, and executed. All three of us had been fortunate to escape, but we lost many friends and colleagues along the way, as recorded in my memoir, *Kelvoo's Terra*.

Even if we had wanted to return to the human home world due to some form of mental defect, we couldn't have, since Terra was declared off-limits to all outsiders. This was in accordance with the wishes of the Terrans, and with full support from the Planetary Alliance and its member species.

After our escape from Terra, the civil war raged on. I followed the events closely as refugees provided harrowing accounts. Within a year, the leader of the Humanity Party, Gloria Truscott, had been captured, tortured, and executed. She had served as the proverbial "useful idiot" for the Taylor family—who wielded the power and finances behind the Human Independence Movement. The Taylor Foundation blamed Truscott's mismanagement for the destruction of the Terran economy to divert attention from the purging of skilled extraterrestrials and intelligent humans, which had been the true cause of Terra's economic ruin.

As more humans suffered under the brutal Terran government, the ranks of the resistance swelled. The rebels were hopelessly outgunned, but they were resourceful, disciplined, and motivated, in contrast to the disorganized, hate-driven militias and gangs that were plagued by corrupt leadership and escalating infighting.

Eventually, the divisions between competing government militias and their internal bickering turned violent. Five years after the war began, the resistance declared victory, but they were also divided into various factions with differing ideas on how to reform Terran society. With further violence being unthinkable and Terra already in ruins, a planet-wide peace conference took place with the leaders of all significant resistance groups.

Before the conference ended, the delegations agreed that Terra had to find its own way forward without outside assistance or influence. Many of the leaders put forward the idea that humans were deeply defective and, until they could reform their entire way of thinking, they could only bring suffering to extraterrestrial species. As a result, the human home world entered a state of self-imposed exile. Citizens who wanted to leave had six months to do so, and about 500 million did, most of them settling on Perdition or the ironically named planet, Exile.

Apart from small embassies on Alliance planets, as well as Exile, Perdition, and Kuw'baal, the Terrans withdrew and made no effort to establish interplanetary communication. Even the humans in the embassies were secretive about developments on

Terra. Their role was to keep a low-key presence until Terra was ready to emerge from isolation.

A rumor originated from the Terran embassy on Kuw'baal that said the Terran humans had a fascination with my previous books, *Kelvoo's Testimonial* and *Kelvoo's Terra*. For some reason, they thought my stories could help them find a path toward a better society and perhaps help them reintegrate with intelligent species on other worlds. I was troubled by the notion that beings, human or otherwise, should take direction from me. I certainly hadn't written my books with such a purpose in mind. I chose not to react to the information since it was only a rumor. I was also confident that my writing had been precise and clear enough that it was unlikely to cause harm.

Over the years, as Terra went dark, news from the planet became vaguer and less frequent. The Planetary Alliance had accepted Terra's withdrawal, reasoning that the Terran humans needed time and space to sort themselves out. Personally, I was in full agreement.

Brenna and May were enjoying successful lives of their own. I had met the sisters on the vessel *Jezebel's Fury* when May was four and Brenna was ten. Eight other kloormari and I had been captured and enslaved by a criminal gang, not long after the human first contact expedition had left my home planet and word of our planet's location had been leaked. Brenna and May were aboard *Jezebel's Fury* because their father had taken them along "for an adventure" as he and the rest of the crew trafficked drugs, weapons, and other humans on an interplanetary crime spree. My kloormari teammates and I taught the illiterate sisters how to read—a task that provided a welcome respite from the brutality and degradation of our captivity.

When we learned of our captors' plan to execute us, my group fought back, taking control of *Jezebel's Fury* and enabling the capture of its crew by a Sarayan warship. To our horror, the Sarayans executed the crew, leaving May and Brenna orphaned. The girls ended up in my care and after several years, we emigrated to Terra, due in large part to the girls' desire to leave the cloudy confines of Kuw'baal and live on a developed planet among humans and many other species.

Raising the girls, especially in their teenage years, was more challenging than I could have imagined. When a kloormar gives birth, the child is fully independent and able to fend for itself. The child's education is the responsibility of the village, and there is no bond between parent and offspring. I had studied human behavior extensively, but nothing could have prepared me for the challenges of raising humans. Despite the struggles and conflicts, I developed a deep appreciation for parenting, and I loved the girls very much.

Brenna provided the greatest challenge. The lowest point came on Terra when she was eighteen years old. She had been lured away by a young man named Griffin Taylor, the scion of the wealthy family at the forefront of the burgeoning anti-immigrant Human Independence Movement. Brenna, and the fact that I had been raising her, were used as propaganda to whip up hatred against extraterrestrials, eventually leading to the coup and civil war. Once she was no longer useful, the movement cast Brenna aside. After our rescue and return to Kuw'baal, Brenna was deeply remorseful. Following a year of counselling and healing to address her guilt, she decided to repay her supposed debt to society by volunteering to teach basic reading skills to illiterate adults on the human-colonized planet, Exile.

Brenna went far beyond teaching people how to read. She established a charitable foundation to teach literacy and basic life skills to humans on Exile and the other "outlier" planet, Perdition. Brenna worked tirelessly and remained humble despite receiving numerous humanitarian awards and recognition throughout the Planetary Alliance. She had never been in a long-term relationship and had never parented a child.

Brenna's younger sister, May, lived in my home until she completed her basic education. Whenever possible, she accompanied me as I travelled to the Alliance worlds and the human outlier planets. We made sure to catch up with Brenna whenever we visited Exile or Perdition.

When she completed her basic education, May worked as my personal assistant on various assignments. On a trip to Saraya, she met a human male of a similar age. Tristan had moved from Perdition for a short-term contract at Perdition's embassy on Saraya. When Tristan's contract ended, he and May moved to Perdition where they teamed up with three other humans—a male and two females—to form a new family conglomerate. Between them the group produced ten children. May's kindness, good nature, and common sense made her an excellent mother.

"Pa" was the term of endearment that May, and later Brenna, called me after our return from Terra. For the girls, "Pa" didn't mean "papa" since, as a kloormar, I am neither male nor female. For the girls, "Pa" was short for "parent," though technically, I was the girls' legal guardian.

On one of my visits to Perdition, May asked, "Pa, are you disappointed that I've chosen marriage and children while Brenna is out there changing countless lives?"

"First off, May," I replied, "disappointment is a human construct. While I understand the concept, it doesn't resonate with me as a kloormar. More importantly, Brenna chose her present path because of some unfortunate choices she made in her teenage years. Those choices helped fuel the hatred that had tragic results not only for the extraterrestrials on Terra but also for countless humans and Brenna herself. She feels compelled to sacrifice a family life to help others, as a form of atonement for her past actions and their unintended consequences.

"On the other hand, May, your life has always been guided by kindness and common sense. You have no reason to feel remorse or to repay any debt to society. As such, you deserve to make the choices that make you happy. From everything I've seen, you have chosen your partners wisely, and your offspring are content, well adjusted, and have good prospects for happy, successful lives. Disappointment would not be a rational reaction to your life."

As May and Brenna got on with their lives, I immersed myself in my career. Focusing on the important work of the Planetary Alliance helped me move beyond the pain of my experiences on Terra, but as the years passed, I yearned for a simple life. I grew more nostalgic for the life I had before my species had any contact with species from other worlds, back when we had no knowledge of a universe beyond the clouds that shrouded my planet.

Since first contact, our society had become infused with technology, which made our lives more convenient and interesting but was not a requirement for our survival. In our earliest existence, we had no written language, no tools, and not even structures to live in. We were perfectly adapted to living on the ground of our planet, which had a climate with afternoon rain nearly every day and temperatures that only varied by a few degrees. Our only food, algel, grew abundantly along the shores of our rivers, streams, and narrow, salty lakes.

Over the millennia, we developed two sets of technology—houses and writing. Both were driven by our need for survival. Every few thousand years, our planet would experience an "upheaval" event, when the next planet out from our star would pass close to Kuw'baal. Ryla 6 is a rocky, icy planet about ten times more massive than Kuw'baal, but on rare occasions, it makes a close pass due to its orbit being tilted in relation to the other planets of the Ryla star system. Upheavals subject Kuw'baal to massive gravitational forces that result in quakes, volcanic eruptions, and immense rockslides. In our more primitive state, we had no knowledge of the cause of the upheavals.

Our oral history told of a mountaintop falling during an upheaval, with bouncing rocks raining down on a crowd, killing scores of kloormari and injuring hundreds more. As word of the incident spread, we developed shelters with sturdy roofs to protect us from falling objects.

An earlier upheaval led to our written language, for the purpose of instructing future kloormari on surviving upheaval events, but the advent of writing brought about far greater benefits.

Writing seemed to awaken new circuits in our brains, and our species started to write compulsively. We recorded everything about our lives and the surrounding environment. By the standards of humans and other Alliance species, our writing was extremely detailed, dull, and mundane, but to the kloormari, it was fascinating.

Since my youth, decades before first contact, I enjoyed the benefits of writing and shelter. Although I knew nothing about the existence of a greater universe, I was content.

Seventy years after first contact, after all I had learned, witnessed, and experienced on Terra and the Alliance planets, I longed to return to something resembling my primitive early days. I wasn't alone. Hundreds of thousands of my fellow kloormari felt the same way. They reduced their use of advanced technology, moved out of their prefabricated houses into traditional mud-brick huts, and in many cases, started writing down their daily observations using natural pigments and parchment. I should emphasize that these "back-to-basics" kloormari reduced but did not eliminate their reliance on technology. They still had their Infotab devices for communication. They justified the use of instant communication over great distances in the interest of gathering information to support their writing.

In the final few years of my work with the Planetary Alliance, I shifted my focus away from leadership and toward passing my thoughts and knowledge along to others who would take my place. I took on fewer speaking and policy-making roles so that the public spotlight wouldn't shine so brightly on me. Given my accidental yet prominent role in Alliance history, I did whatever I could to fade into obscurity. It never happened completely, of course, but eventually, I managed to escape from public life without leaving a void.

I was able to find an isolated island in a remote lake. I wanted a home where I could host Brenna and May and other visitors who were important to me, along with their friends or families. That ruled out the construction of a small hut with my own hands. Having earned an immense amount of SimCash over the years, and with nothing else to spend it on, I hired a construction crew to build a large mud-brick structure with its own micro-fusion power source and all the comforts that my visitors might require.

I also started to spend my days writing. In the beginning, I would take daily walks and forage for algel. When I returned home, I would record my observations using parchment and pigment. Though my activities were antiquated and the things I wrote about were mundane, I found pleasure in living as I had before first contact made my world so interesting yet so frenetic.

Brenna and May would board an interstellar transport and visit me once or twice each year. Sometimes, May would bring one or two of her spouses and some of her children. As odd as it was for a kloormar, I loved my extended family, and I enjoyed their visits. Between visits, we would communicate weekly via live vid, using our Infotab devices.

After several years avoiding information from outside my island, curiosity got the better of me, and I started using my Infotab to reacquaint myself with current events. I moved slowly with the rationale that, if first contact had gone as planned, my species would have moved along at a similar speed and been spared the culture shock and colonization that had caused so much damage.

I recorded my thoughts and sent my writing to various infosites. I did so without providing my contact information, so I would not be inundated with replies or questions.

As the years progressed, Brenna and May got older and wiser. May's children grew to adulthood, and some produced grandchildren. Humans say there is no greater tragedy than a parent outliving any of their children. As time marched forward, I came to appreciate that sentiment since, with my expected lifespan being just over 300 years, it seemed inevitable that Brenna and May would die long before me.

THREE: PREPARATION

As the years passed, I looked forward to the upcoming planetary upheaval with great anticipation. During their first contact mission, the human crew of the *Pacifica Spirit* took me and nine other kloormari aboard for a trip encompassing a survey of Ryla 6, a resupply stop, and a courtesy visit to Saraya. By then, the humans had taught us that the geological upheaval events in our history were caused when Ryla 6 passed close to Kuw'baal.

By surveying Ryla 6 and analyzing the data, the science team was able to predict the timing of each upheaval event for the following 2,001,876 years. We learned that the next upheaval would happen 70 years and 142 days from that date—well within my lifetime. Rather than dreading the coming upheaval, I was fascinated and excited, knowing that with the help of outside technology and with decades to prepare, there would be minimal loss of life, if any.

As the upheaval approached, the news on Kuw'baal was focused on the preparations. Most residents planned to leave for other planets during the expected thirty-five days of seismic activity. Some would stay with family, friends, or colleagues while others would live on vast orbiting temporary habitats called "arks," built in orbit around Kuw'baal, or provided by the government or relief agencies of other planets.

Maintenance of many homes and buildings was postponed since there was a significant chance that the upheaval would damage or demolish them. Property owners were prepared to fix structures where they could, or to rebuild, possibly in a new location if required. High-value structures were to be separated into modules and supported on hover platforms, which would lift them if the ground shook or shifted beyond specific tolerances.

My island home was expendable. I had it built from traditional mud bricks with the full knowledge that the upheaval could obliterate it. Unlike humans, who often attach great value and sentiment to structures and possessions, I wasn't bothered by the prospect of losing my house. All I needed was my Infotab for communication and a few other conveniences.

I emerged from isolation thirteen months pre-upheaval. I reunited with many of the kloormari that I had known decades before. I stayed in a house belonging to Kroz, in the village of my birth. As my kloormari friend and a fellow abductee from *Jezebel's Fury*, Kroz was a software and AI development expert, who had hacked into *Jezebel's* control systems to free us. Living on Terra at about the same time that I did, Kroz's work led to the development of an innovative spacecraft that was later used to rescue Brenna, May, and me from Terra. While I stayed in Kroz's home, Kroz was usually in orbit, coordinating the construction of some of the massive arks where evacuees would live during the upheaval.

Another of my old kloormari acquaintances was Keeto, who had extensive knowledge of Kuw'baal's geology. Keeto was part of an interplanetary team that had surveyed Kuw'baal to map the areas that would likely be the most affected by the upheaval. As Keeto and I discussed the survey, I learned about the areas where the planet's crust might sink or collapse into the underground water table, and other areas where material deep beneath the surface would be thrust upward, breaking through the crust.

Keeto was excited about Kuw'baal giving up its geological "secrets" as rock and mineral deposits would be revealed and exposed to the atmosphere for the first time since Kuw'baal was formed from its molten core and interstellar dust.

During my time in the village, I wrote extensively. My work included the following poem, inspired by Keeto's research.

> When planets fall into alignment,
>   tidal force will tear,
> to cause the quake and rockslide
> and lay the new ground bare.

We'll rise above the firmament,
to save us, one and all,
while witnessing the power
that makes the mountains fall.

The timeless bedrock guards its secrets,
locked away and sealed,
but when upheaval splits the mantle,
all shall be revealed.

I had no inkling of the unintended impact that my poem and much of my other writing would have.

Thirty-two days before the upheaval, I purchased a small orbital shuttle that had ferried beings between Kuw'baal and the arks during the height of construction. The shuttle would let me leave the ark for trips where I could enjoy close-up views of the upheaval by hovering near Kuw'baal's surface.

In the final days, I went back to my house and disconnected the fusion generator, placing it on a hoverlift that I programmed to rise if the shifting and shaking became too great.

Evacuation of the village took place over fourteen days. My turn came just two days before Ryla 6 would start to influence Kuw'baal. I was assigned space on the ark named *Platform 313*. Kroz had remotely programmed my shuttle with the coordinates and approach instructions.

On the final day, I took a stroll around my nearly deserted home village. I walked to the site where eight other kloormari and I had built small mud huts after our ordeal on *Jezebel's Fury*. It was the place where we had supported each other and begun the healing process. Most of the site had been built over with newer structures.

I walked over to the home where Brenna, May, and I had lived before we left for Terra and after we returned. It looked grubby and sported a fine layer of reddish dust due to lack of recent maintenance. This was true for most buildings due to the uncertainty of whether they would withstand the upheaval.

I made my way toward the landing pad that stood on pilings on the mineral plain. The only sound was the crunching and scraping of my feet on the downhill portion of the gravel path, bringing back memories of walking down the same path where I once said farewell to my human friend, Jasmit Linford, and to Brenna when she moved away to Exile.

Just before the path crossed the village stream, I turned right to follow the streambank to the algel falls. At the base of the falls, I assumed a meditative stance, closed the lid over my eye, and let the slurping and plopping of falling gelatinous algel lull me into a deep state of meditation. In my mind, I replayed the fateful day when I was meditating in the same place and was awakened by the sound of a probe arriving and ushering the kloormari into the post-contact era.

I woke myself and then climbed to the top of the falls. I used the stairs that had replaced the loose gravel that I had scrambled up over seventy years earlier. I stood at the vantage point where I had witnessed the humans' unmanned probe touching down across the plain, then broken into a run, joining my fellow villagers in our exuberance to see the strange visitor.

As I stood there, I gazed upon the gentle slope where the village's original homes were once perched, overlooking the stream below and the bright, white plain of crystalized mineral deposits beyond. While the residents and I still called the area the "village," it had grown into a sprawling city.

I scanned the hills that lined the far side of the plain. On the left, I saw a boulder that marked the location of a ramshackle encampment where my friend Samuel Buchanan had last lived and where the two of us would write and reminisce.

Farther along the hills lining the plain to the right of Sam's encampment was the city of Newton—the site of the first human settlement on my planet. Newton had started as a bustling frontier town when unregulated human colonization was in full swing, and corporate interests were harvesting Kuw'baal's resources and contaminating its environment with abandon. After I returned from captivity and the citizens of the Planetary Alliance read my account in *Kelvoo's Testimonial*, Terra was faced with expulsion from the Alliance unless the humans returned full control of Kuw'baal to the kloormari. The subsequent exodus turned Newton into a virtual ghost town, with a few kloormari maintaining the buildings in case they were ever needed in the future.

When I escaped from Terra and returned, I was astonished by the transformation of the village, the plain, and Newton. With vast numbers of humans and extraterrestrials fleeing the war, Kuw'baal had become a transit hub for refugees. The plain and the areas behind the village and Newton were dotted with temporary shelters for as far as my eye could see. As I stood by the top of the falls and surveyed the scene, Newton was a true city. Its residents were a mixture of kloormari, humans, and other species who were mostly descended from refugees who decided to settle on Kuw'baal.

Finally, adjacent to the falls were mountains, with a large ancient rockfall that spilled down onto the plain. Over the rockfall and the ridge that had birthed it was a bowl-shaped valley. It held a lake, which fed a stream that ran below the rockfall onto the plain. During the first contact mission, Sam and I hiked to the lake and viewed the vibrant colors of the vegetation and the exposed minerals in the surrounding rock face. Sam was in awe of the spectacular scenery. At that time, I had not been exposed to the human concept of beauty, so I had found Sam's response puzzling.

When I returned to Kuw'baal from *Jezebel's Fury*, I had developed a newfound appreciation for beauty, which was born out of the trauma of having seen and being subjected to the ugliness of evil people and evil deeds. When Sam selfishly took his own life, my friend K'tatmal and I carried his body up the rockfall and to the lake. In the tradition of my village, we buried Sam's corpse under the bed of a stream where it flowed from the lake, so the nutrients from Sam's body would nourish the natural environment. At that moment, I fully appreciated the beauty of the area that became known as "Sam's Lake."

For reasons detailed in *Kelvoo's Testimonial*, a piece of human classical music called "Pachelbel's Canon," resonated with Sam on a deep, personal level. When K'tatmal and I buried Sam, I used my unique kloormari ability to simulate any sound by "singing" Pachelbel's Canon and listening to it reverberate through the valley.

As I stood on the day of my departure for *Platform 313*, I took in the stillness and emptiness of the scene before me. For reasons I don't fully understand, I used all eight of my vocal outlets to recite Pachelbel's Canon once again.

As I "sang," reproducing the sound of the cello and violins, my recollections of the village, the plain, the human settlement, and the natural beauty came to the forefront of my mind. Using my perfect kloormari memory, I relived the moment I crawled from my host's reproductive pouch. I recalled running through the village as an infant. I remembered feeding on the wild algel, building homes, and writing my observations every day. I also recalled standing beside the same stream when the human lander appeared, and I was taken aboard the *Pacifica Spirit*. I remembered my return from my kidnapping, when seven years had passed on Kuw'baal, during which our village, environment, and culture was decimated. I remembered the cluster of huts where my fellow abductees worked through our trauma and helped one another heal. I also remembered doing my best to raise two human girls with all its challenges and rewards.

My mind turned to our escape from Terra and our return to the village, with refugees filling the surrounding area until they were resettled and Kuw'baal eventually transitioned to a "new normal."

As my song ended and the echoes faded from the surrounding hills, I was filled with nostalgia and a poignant appreciation for the place and the moment, knowing that when the ground shook and opened and crumbled, yet another set of profound changes would leave their mark on my beautiful world.

FOUR: MR. AMBASSADOR

At the appointed time, I boarded my shuttle and gave the command to perform the pre-programmed flight to *Platform 313*. My vessel provided an excellent all-around view with its forward quarter enclosed in transparent panels, and multiple monitors that displayed the scene from cameras aft of the vessel.

As the shuttle rose, I could see the entirety of the village, the plain, Newton, and Sam's Lake. I said a silent farewell just before the shuttle entered the clouds.

After several minutes, the clouds gave way to the vibrant blue sky above, which darkened to indigo and then deep black. Kuw'baal's star, Ryla, was to the stern, just as it was about to be obscured behind my planet.

The luxuriant blackness of space was punctuated by a myriad of stars. A line of orbiting arks showed themselves as a string of white shapes above me. The shapes on the string seemed to disappear on one end as the arks entered the shadow of Kuw'baal, blocking the light that the arks reflected from Ryla. Suddenly, the cause of the upheaval, Ryla 6, became visible from behind Kuw'baal. Relative to the size of my planet, Ryla 6 seemed only slightly bigger than Terra's moon, Luna, when viewed from the Terran surface. As the interloper neared my planet in the coming days, it would appear much, much larger.

The jet-black basalt cliffs and mountainsides of Ryla 6 stood in stark contrast to the gleaming white ice cap that covered the flatter areas and the mountaintops. Blue swirls indicated frozen lakes deep in the valleys. The serene beauty of Ryla 6 belied the enormity of its forces, which had caused terror and death among the kloormari when it passed by in preceding millennia.

The shuttle adjusted its trajectory to match the altitude, orbital velocity, and position of *Platform 313*. During the approach, I was close enough to see the shape of other arks that the shuttle passed. One of those vessels was the *Orion Provider*, an enormous former supply ship, shopping complex, and tourist destination that I had visited while on the *Pacifica Spirit* during its first contact mission. Kroz had told me that the *Orion* had been decommissioned and mothballed forty-two years ago but had been refitted and pressed back into service as an ark.

As the shuttle closed in on *Platform 313*, its scale became clear. Seventy years before, I had been in awe of the staggering size of the *Orion Provider*, but in comparison to *313*, I realized the *Orion* was one of the smallest arks in service. *Platform 313* must have been as large as my village. The ark was shaped like an elongated disk with edges that curved from its "top" surface to the bottom. Interior light glowed through tens of thousands of windows.

On final approach, my shuttle had to stop relative to the ark, and wait for clearance to land. Ahead of me were dozens of lineups with hundreds of small craft in each line, waiting to enter the cavernous landing bays and garages. It took forty-seven minutes before my shuttle started to move again. I used that time to meditate while keeping my eye open the whole time to soak in the majesty of my surroundings and to ponder the enormity of the evacuation effort and the coming upheaval.

The shuttle entered a landing bay crowded with other vessels of varying sizes. It took twenty-one minutes for the huge bay doors to close and air to enter. Kloormari attendants escorted the occupants into reception areas and then moved each vessel into its assigned parking spot in adjoining garages.

To non-kloormari, the reception areas must have seemed chaotic, but each kloormar had specific assignments and worked rapidly, in perfect coordination with the others. Many of my kloormari friends were waiting for me in reception, with Kroz, K'tatmal, Ksoomu, K'raftan, Keeto, Kleloma, K'aablart, Keesooni, and K'pai in attendance. They all warmly greeted me.

"What an amazing coincidence that all of us happened to be assigned to the same ark!" I exclaimed to Kroz.

"Are you attempting to relate a joke to me?" Kroz inquired. "The human concept of humor is something I have not grasped in all the years since first contact. Please do not attempt further jocularity with me."

I knew Kroz well enough that Kroz's reply was, in its own subtle way, an attempt at humor. "Of course, there is no coincidence," Kroz continued. "In my position as ark construction coordinator, I may have 'pulled a few strings', as the Terran expression goes. There is one additional string that I managed to pull," Kroz said, motioning toward a support pillar.

"Hey there, stranger!" Brenna exclaimed as she stepped out from behind the pillar.

I rushed toward Brenna, and she walked toward me as fast as she could manage. She was quite spry for a seventy-two-year-old human. I embraced her with my upper limbs and claspers, and I nestled her head under my eye dome while she hugged me tight. When we separated, I held her hands with my hand paddles, placing myself at arm's length so we could take a good look at each other. My kloormari friends were used to me displaying affection to humans, but they still appeared puzzled as they watched.

"I thought you had conferences to attend!" I said.

"No, Pa, I lied!" she replied, smiling. "I wanted to surprise you, so I cleared my calendar, and Kroz got me aboard. Here's someone else who'd like to say hi."

Brenna pulled out her Infotab, revealing the live vid feed from a call. I saw May in the center of the vid, surrounded by her large family, who all called out to greet me. May expressed her regret at having too many family obligations to visit me, but she assured me that she would stay in touch and follow news about the upheaval every day.

"Love you, Pa!" May called out, having to end the call due to intense traffic on the quantum entanglement network as millions of well-wishers were calling their friends and families on the arks.

Brenna had been on board for the past day, so after chatting with my kloormari friends, she showed me the nearest algel feeding station, the cafeteria for other species, gathering spaces, and my quarters, where there was just enough room for me to write on my Infotab or meditate. In other words, I was provided with everything that a kloormar required. My room was located on the rim of the ark, on the side that faced Kuw'baal. The outside wall of my accommodations was one large window, affording me a view of the clouded skies of my planet and, periodically, Ryla and Ryla 6, whenever they came within view.

Brenna's accommodations were next to mine. With a narrow bed, a desk, a small closet, and a washroom with just enough space for a human to stand, Brenna's room was about three times the size of mine. Brenna found her accommodation to be cramped, but she appreciated the need to conserve space in vessels used to house millions of displaced beings.

I had a restorative meditation that night, bathed in the light reflected from my home, alternating with near blackness when *313* passed into Kuw'baal's shadow.

The next day, the ark was a hive of excitement. All sorts of beings were striking up conversations with one another. The anticipation of the upheaval, due to start the next day, produced a collegial environment infused with an excited buzz. Brenna and I were in the gathering area closest to our accommodations. Those who were able to tell me apart from other kloormari were excited to meet me or to be reacquainted with me. Many were delighted to meet Brenna and peppered her with questions about her history as my foster daughter.

During the ark's "daylight" hours, an average of about 2,000 beings would be present in the gathering area for my sector of the ark. When we weren't having animated conversations, we stared at huge display panels that provided vid feeds from the planet's surface or from control centers where monitoring equipment was in use.

At about midday, Brenna was chatting with a group of humans and a Sarayan. They decided to have a meal in the cafeteria. When they left, a short, unassuming human picked his way through the crowd.

"Kelvoo?" the man asked in a timid, tremulous voice.

"Yes, I'm Kelvoo," I replied, extending a hand paddle for him to shake.

The man didn't shake my hand though. The only thing being shaken was his body as he trembled and cast his eyes downward. *Not another sycophant!* I thought as I prepared to be fawned over with unbridled praise.

"Are you alright?" I asked.

"F-f-forgive my nervousness," he said. "I-I promised myself to keep my composure when I met you, b-but I don't seem to be doing a great job!"

"Sir, please relax. I promise not to bite!" I said, hoping my words would be taken as a humorous attempt to encourage conversation. "There's no need to look away," I continued. "I may not be the prettiest sight to the human eye, but it will be easier to talk with you if we make eye contact."

My statement flustered the man even more. "Oh, dear! I'm so sorry! Oh, no! I didn't mean to offend you! Please, Kelvoo! Please forgive me!"

"It is I who should ask for your forgiveness," I replied. "I was trying to be witty, but after all these years, I still struggle to understand humor."

The man hesitantly looked up at me. "I-I just wanted to introduce myself. I'm with the Terran embassy on Kuw'baal, I-I mean *Platform 313*. Well, at least during upheaval."

"How wonderful to meet you," I said. "I know that representatives from Terra like to keep a low profile, so I'm delighted that you're making an exception for me. What is your line of work at the embassy?"

"Er, I'm the ambassador," he said.

"You're Mark Muller?" I replied with genuine surprise.

"At your service, Kelvoo," he said, bowing.

"I hope, Ambassador, that you're not offended that I didn't recognize you. I knew your name from the news, but for some reason, I've never seen an image of you."

"Well, as you said, Kelvoo, we like to keep a low profile at the embassy. We forbid images of us from being recorded and shared. It's a matter of humility, recognition that we are not worthy to associate with higher beings." Muller shifted his feet, looking awkward as he continued. "My . . . my superiors on Terra asked me to reach out to you, but I'm uncomfortable doing so, given the terrible way that my people treated you when you lived on my planet."

"My misadventures on Terra occurred decades ago, Ambassador. It's my understanding that the people responsible for the coup were either killed in the war or captured and, later, dealt with by rebel tribunals, sometimes harshly."

"Yes they were, Kelvoo, though I can't claim any firsthand experience given that I was a child at the time. Still, I hope that Gloria Truscott met an end that was satisfactory to you."

"No, Mr. Muller, I can't say it was satisfactory at all," I said, eliciting a look of horror from him. "Yes, Truscott was an early leader of the Human Independence Movement. And yes, she led the so-called Humanity Party and its persecution of the extraterrestrials on Terra—and indeed, she instigated the coup and the war. Nevertheless, a slow, painful torture and death, broadcast live across your planet, was not an ethical or civilized punishment for her crimes."

"Kelvoo, please, allow me to explain," Muller said, verging on panic. "Those were terrible times! Much has changed! In fact, everything has changed since then!"

"So I've heard," I said. "Please correct me if I'm wrong, but I understand that Terran society has become peaceful and harmonious, though with almost no news from Terra, my information is based on rumor and speculation."

"Forgive me, Kelvoo, for assuming that you would be pleased by Truscott's fate. After the incomparable suffering you endured on Terra—"

"I would hardly call my suffering incomparable, Ambassador," I replied. "There are likely millions of beings who endured far worse torture than I did."

"Oh, dear! I'm so sorry, Kelvoo. I'm really messing this up!" Muller averted his eyes again. "The problem is that I'm assigning human traits to you. I've read so much of your work that I should have known that, unlike humans, your life has been based on kindness and reason."

"With all due respect, Ambassador, I know a great many humans who embrace kindness and reason."

"Kelvoo, I'm in awe of your wisdom. I know you don't like humans fawning over you, but there's so much you could teach us."

"Teach whom?"

"The people of Terra."

"What would I teach them?"

"How to live! How to love! How to be the best beings we can be!"

"Ambassador, I'm utterly unqualified to teach anyone anything of the sort. Even if I had the hubris to advise humans how to live, bitter experience tells me that my efforts would only make things worse."

"Kelvoo, you are, of course, correct. Please forgive me for the intrusion. I think I've failed to make a good first impression. I don't suppose there's any chance of us meeting again. There's something I'd like to discuss with you in a more private setting."

"In an official capacity?"

"No, no! Well, yes. Well, maybe. I don't really know at the moment."

"That would be fine either way, Ambassador," I said, causing his face to light up with delight, "but in the interest of transparency, I'll have to notify my contacts in the Planetary Alliance. I must also advise you that I have no power to make decisions for any level of government or other beings, and I won't divulge any sensitive information. In other words, I may be of little value to you."

"Kelvoo, just the opportunity to converse with you has been the greatest thrill of my life! Your value can't be overstated!"

"Why, Mr. Ambassador, surely you aren't fawning over me?" I asked, triggering further embarrassment on his part.

Muller wanted to schedule a meeting with me the following day. I had to explain that I would be extremely busy meeting with people and observing the upheaval's effects. After some awkward apologies, we agreed to meet seven days later. Muller wanted us to meet onboard in the embassy's temporary office on the opposite side of the ark. Given my past experiences with Terran humans, I stipulated that I would only consent to meet in a public area. We agreed to meet in the nearby cafeteria at 19:00, seven days hence.

As the ambassador and I parted ways, Brenna returned from lunch with her new friends. "Who was that?" she inquired.

"A rather irritating man," I replied.

I used my Infotab to send a text-only message to my contacts at the Planetary Alliance. I knew better than to attempt a vid or even audio message, given the extreme amount of interstellar communication traffic. In my message, I described my meeting with Muller. I also suggested that I continue to communicate with him as an individual, rather than a representative of the Alliance.

Over two hours later, I received a notification that my queued message had finally been sent, and I didn't receive a reply until 01:07 the following day. The message had the usual characteristics of bureaucratic posterior-covering caution:

Kelvoo, the Planetary Alliance Interplanetary Outreach Committee (PAIOC) leaves it to your discretion to decide whether to pursue further contact with the Terran ambassador to Kuw'baal. If you proceed, please do so with the understanding that you will be communicating with him on a being-to-being basis.

You are not to act as a representative of the Planetary Alliance, the PAIOC, or any affiliated organization. Do not make any promises or guarantees on behalf of the Alliance or affiliated organizations, and do not divulge classified or sensitive information that you may have obtained during your work with us.

A few minutes later, I received a more personal message from a Sarayan PAIOC delegate that I had worked closely with and befriended a long time ago.

Congratulations on the contact from the Terran ambassador! With the Terrans keeping themselves so isolated, it will be fascinating to learn more about them. Just between us, please dish the dirt on everything the two of you talk about!

```
    Also, I hope the upheaval goes well and doesn't cause
too much damage to your world.
    -- Alduvia  :->>
```

Alduvia had a far more casual demeanor than many Sarayans, who could seem cold and officious at times. She also had a way with words, especially when it came to using Terran expressions like "dish the dirt." I was puzzled by the characters that appeared after her signature. I wondered whether they were communication artifacts caused by glitches in the overburdened quantum entanglement network or whether she was trying to send a clandestine signal. It took me a few minutes to understand that the symbols were an attempt to simulate the facial expression of a Sarayan showing happiness, in the way that some Terrans used emoticons.

I had a momentary feeling of despair at the deteriorating state of literacy across the Alliance.

FIVE: UPHEAVAL

It's hard to describe the range of experiences and emotions that impacted me and all the other beings on the arks during the thirty-five days of upheaval. For the first three days, Brenna and I joined thousands of others in the nearby gathering area on *Platform 313*. Camera drones were stationed above much of the planet's surface. When something visually "interesting" happened on the planet, it would be shown on one of the giant vid panels. Some beings would use their Infotabs to receive live or recent vid feeds from the parts of Kuw'baal that were of personal interest to them.

At first, the upheaval events were minor quakes, often visible as clouds of dust rising from the surface, or loose rocks and gravel sliding down mountainsides. These disturbances took place in waves as parts of Kuw'baal rotated to face toward or away from Ryla 6.

The proximity of Ryla 6 also affected the trajectory of the arks. As they orbited toward the side of Kuw'baal that faced Ryla 6, they were pulled farther away from Kuw'baal. After passing Ryla 6, the gravity well of Kuw'baal pulled them into a tighter, faster orbit, much closer to the planet's surface. At times, it appeared as though *Platform 313* would skim through the top layer of Kuw'baal's clouds, though we always remained in orbit at an altitude of at least 200 kilometers.

The planet's surface wasn't always deserted. Scientists and engineers would visit areas on hover platforms, just above the ground. When the quakes subsided and the tidal forces were weak, some beings would step onto the surface to install, adjust, or retrieve monitoring equipment. My village and the surrounding area were visited and monitored frequently due to the historic significance of the place as the site of my species' first contact with outsiders.

On upheaval day five, we saw a hoverlift land a short distance downstream from the algel falls, close to the place where the walkway to the landing pad crossed over the village stream. A hover platform descended, a male human stepped off with a case of equipment, and the platform departed with its remaining crew. We assumed that they were intending to return a few minutes later to pick-up their coworker.

A moderate quake struck the area, but the man was able to maintain his footing. A wider shot on a different monitor showed that the quake dislodged a large mass of algel from the bank of the stream above the falls. The algel flowed to the top of the falls and jammed there, acting as a dam, and causing a buildup of water and algel. I, along with many others in the gathering space, saw the potential danger and made urgent calls or entered messages on our Infotabs. I received an automated reply from the monitoring center AI:

```
Situation understood. Attempting to contact individual
and crew. Return of hover platform and rescue requested.
```

No doubt the monitoring center was attempting to identify the man so he could be called on his Infotab and advised to run to higher ground. The hover platform crew was likely being called to return immediately.

Seconds later, we all watched in horror as the dam gave way. The gelatinous mass slurped and plopped over the falls, followed by a rush of water. Sections of the rocky cliff also fell away, deepening the channel and allowing additional water and algel to rush down. Many of the humans and a few Bandorians who were watching with me, instinctively shouted for the man to run, as though he could hear them.

The unidentified human was bent over, working on a seismic probe, which he had just removed from its case. We watched him pull his Infotab out of a pouch on his belt and look at the screen, indicating that he was receiving a call. He snapped his head around to look behind him, only to see the massive flood barreling toward him. He started to run, then turned back to pick up the valuable seismic monitoring unit. Instead of heading up the hill toward the village, the panicked human sprinted directly downstream, trying to outrun the slimy wave. The camera drone that was monitoring the area followed him.

The advancing semi-liquid fanned out over the flat plain, causing it to slow down and become far shallower. We were all relieved once we realized the man's life was no longer in danger. By the time it caught up to him, the slippery slurry was only knee deep. Nonetheless, the heaviness of the algel tripped him and he fell onto his buttocks, making a mighty splash and a wave in the surface of the algel. I heard a few muffled snorts from the humans around me. The man lost his grip on the seismic unit, which was swept away in the algel. He remained in a sitting position as the flow propelled him along the plain. He rolled onto his hands and knees and tried to stand, but a transparent, goopy layer of algel clung to him, weighing him down. As he tried to stand, his knees trembled and then collapsed under him, making him fall back into the slime face-first. He rolled so he was facing up, then wiped the gel off his face. From there, he flipped, flopped, and flailed, his antics being broadcast by the drone as it followed his awkward journey.

I heard a peculiar sound from Brenna, then I noticed that she had her hands clamped over her mouth and her body was shaking. "Are you quite alright?" I asked.

"I'm sorry!" Brenna exclaimed after making a couple of squeaking sounds. "I shouldn't be laughing at the poor fellow. He's lucky to be alive, but—"

As Brenna descended into silent paroxysms, I noticed that the other humans in attendance were laughing too. Soon, they couldn't restrain themselves, and Brenna joined their howls of amusement. Shortly after that, the hover platform and crew returned. A crew member laid on the platform's deck and reached down to grasp the man's hands, but they were covered in slime, so the crew member kept losing his grip.

Eventually, the leading edge of the advancing slurry became shallow enough that the man's unintended journey came to a stop, and the platform could position itself just a few centimeters above the plain's surface. The human was too exhausted to stand, but his crewmates were able to slide him onto the platform.

As the platform ascended, the humans in the audience around me applauded and cheered, but the kloormari and other non-humans were perplexed. Despite having known humans for over seventy years, I was just as confused. "Why would humans find that man's predicament so amusing?" I asked.

"There's no way to explain it," Brenna replied. "We were all so stressed when we thought he was in danger. I think our laughter was triggered by the relief we felt when we knew he was safe. By the end, it was just like something out of a slapstick comedy sketch." She chuckled.

"Indeed," I replied, "I've never grasped the concept of slapstick comedy. How is it amusing to see another being falling over, flailing about, or struggling ineffectually? For that matter, why are humans so entertained by pratfalls, blunders, food fights—" There was no point continuing my questions as Brenna had found my thoughts equally amusing, slipping into another fit of laughter.

I withheld any further inquiries for the day.

Fifteen days into the upheaval, I received clearance to visit Kuw'baal in my shuttle, as long as it remained twenty meters or more above the surface and stayed clear of mountainsides and areas where pools of magma had been mapped. Brenna was eager to accompany me.

We began at the mineral plain. When we descended below the cloud deck, the terrain appeared misty and reddish due to a layer of fine dust in the atmosphere. The plain was now a lake, covered with opaque, turquoise water, tinted by dissolved minerals and suspended particles. Near the center of the lake, more water was bubbling up from deep under the crust, squeezed by the shifting tectonic plates. Beside the village, the stream had disappeared, consumed by the lake. Water lapped at the bottom of the hill, threatening the lowest buildings.

The water was nearly at the top of the pilings supporting the landing pad that served the village and Newton. A section of the elevated walkway between the pad and the village had collapsed, likely weakened by the bursting of the algel dam and then undermined by waves from the rising lake. The algel falls had also been changed forever. With the top section collapsed, the falls now consisted of two cataracts as the water fell and algel slurped from the top, onto a section of broken rocks and then down into the lake.

As I guided the shuttle up the hill toward the center of the village, we saw sections of the community center along with other vital buildings, rising into the air atop their hover platforms, signaling the first rumblings of a new quake. Seconds later, the ground shook and a fissure opened directly under a hovering administrative building.

Dust rose from the trembling ground, and some of it settled onto the shuttle's windows. The shuttle automatically increased its altitude to avoid the dust, and its AI voice warned that the flight may need to be terminated if visibility diminished any further. A moment later, a gentle rain spattered on the windows, smearing the dust into rivulets of red mud, which were soon rinsed away as the showers became a short, torrential cloudburst that cleansed the air and the windows.

With the quake over, the elevated buildings settled back into place, except for the administrative building, which moved away from the new fissure in the crust and descended to a different area of flat ground.

Up to that point in the trip, Brenna hadn't said much. She seemed content to observe the upheaval in silence. "Pa," Brenna said as the shuttle was turning to leave the village, "do you think we could take a closer look at our old house?"

I commanded the shuttle to descend and fly to the house where Brenna, her sister, and I had lived before our fateful trip to Terra and after our subsequent escape. We saw our former home intact, but precariously close to the top of a landslide, which held the wreckage of other houses at its base.

"As a kloormar, you don't miss our old house, do you, Pa?" Brenna asked.

"No, that's a human emotional construct. With my kloormari memory, I can recall every moment, whether it occurred yesterday or the day I crawled from my host's pouch. I don't have a connection to objects because I don't need them to remember events. Perhaps humans use the sight of objects as a memory aid. I wonder, Brenna, does the sight of our house make you feel more connected to your past and those you were with at that time? Do you feel that the destruction of this building would further erode your memory of the events that happened here?"

Brenna paused to think about what I had said, "No, I don't think so, Pa. It's more like the feeling that a part of my past would be closing. It would almost be like I'm closer to the end of my life."

I instructed the shuttle to slowly circle our previous home, rotating to keep it in front of us.

"I know you think you aren't attached to buildings or other things," Brenna said, "but when you wrote about our experiences on Terra, you described leaving our home at the university. You wrote about May saying 'goodbye house,' and you admitted that you silently repeated her words."

"You're correct, Brenna. I suppose that I did associate that home with a sense of security. When we left, May and I also lost our freedom and safety. I also must admit that seeing the changes to the algel falls just now was rather poignant, since it symbolizes how everything is shifting on this planet. Change can certainly be good, but it does introduce anxiety about the uncertainty that lies ahead. I suppose I do resist associating my feelings with places and things, because it challenges my kloormari instincts for logic and reason.

"Brenna, how much do you remember about our home on Terra?" I asked, mainly out of curiosity. I wanted to know how accurately Brenna remembered places and events from her youth.

"I'm afraid that's one place I don't want to remember." She sighed. "I'm sure the house was destroyed when the military swept through the university, but I would never want to see that house again! I did a terrible thing there, and I still feel ashamed." Brenna's voice cracked with emotion.

"Brenna, those were terrible times for all of Terra. There was so much turmoil and disinformation. You were still reeling from your father's death, which you hadn't fully processed. As a teenager, you were struggling to understand and define yourself. You left us because people who appeared to understand and sympathize with you lured you away. The same thing could have happened to anyone in your situation."

"I know, Pa. I also know that if you had been a *human* foster parent, you would never have forgiven me."

"I doubt that, Brenna. I'm sure that anyone else would have known the wonderful person that you are inside. Besides, like I told you at the time, there was nothing to forgive."

"Thanks, Pa," Brenna said, looking relieved. "Could we go back to *313* now?"

I commanded the shuttle to return to our temporary home, and it started ascending into orbit.

"Pa?" Brenna said on the return trip.

"Yes, sweetie?"

"Thanks for letting me come along in the shuttle. I love you."

"I love you too, Brenna. I always have and I always will."

My conversation with my foster daughter filled me with joy.

Over the remaining twenty days on *Platform 313*, Brenna and I made five additional sorties to the planet. We passed by volcanoes and rivers of lava, we saw mountains that had been reduced to hills and we witnessed lakes that had dried up and new lakes that had been formed.

We visited the park known as Sam's Lake and looked with wonder at how the landscape was even more beautiful than before. Parts of the mountainous bowl that surrounded the lake had shaken loose and tumbled into the water. The incident had made the lake slightly smaller, but it also revealed bands of minerals that had never been exposed to the elements. The yellows and blues in the exposed rock face were even brighter and more colorful than before.

We also made two visits to my island home. There was a valley at the foot of the lake that contained a brook, which provided the only drainage. I wondered whether a landslide might block the entrance to the brook, making the lake rise, covering my island, and inundating my home. Instead, the valley floor had collapsed below the foot of the lake, making the brook deeper and forming another small lake farther down on the valley floor. The depth of my lake had dropped by ten meters and my island had doubled in size. The house itself sustained minimal superficial damage and would remain inhabitable.

Overall, the great upheaval was an exciting time. I knew that my world would survive, and the parts that needed rebuilding would be restored better than before. I felt immensely grateful and awed by the power of the Planetary Alliance and its capacity to bring the resources and natural kindness of its many species and worlds together for the greater good of beings.

As a side note, vid recordings of the hapless human who was knocked over by the algel wave made their way across the Planetary Alliance. Billions of humans found the spectacle uproariously funny, making the man an instant celebrity far and wide—at least for a short time. Humans are indeed an odd lot.

A great many interesting things happened in conjunction with the upheaval itself. Great exchanges of ideas and new friendships formed aboard the lifesaving arks orbiting my planet. These events included ongoing contact between Ambassador Muller and me and, for a while, a deepening of our mutual respect and trust.

SIX: A GIFT FROM TERRA

Seven days after our first meeting, I met again with Terran Ambassador Mark Muller in the cafeteria. Immediately after our initial meeting, I had notified my Planetary Alliance contacts and then updated Brenna.

I was taken aback by her reaction. "Why would you want to meet with *him*, of all people?"

"Is there something you know about Mr. Muller that I should be aware of?" I inquired.

"I don't know the slightest thing about him. That's exactly the point! We don't even know what's been happening on Terra. We *do* know that nothing good ever comes from Terran humans!"

"That's what you used to say about outlier humans, Brenna."

"OK, fair point. But you need to be *careful*. With all the secrecy around Terra, we don't know what we're dealing with."

"Alright, Brenna. Why don't you accompany me when I meet with him?"

"No, I'm not comfortable with that. How about if I sit close to you and watch for any trouble?"

"That should be fine," I said, "but the meeting is supposed to be private, so don't be so close that you can listen in. If things don't look right, perhaps you can walk over and introduce yourself."

When we arrived at the cafeteria, I saw Muller waiting for me at a table. I pointed him out to Brenna, who went ahead of me and took a seat three tables away and behind him.

I waited for a minute, then entered the cafeteria and greeted the ambassador. He stood and clasped my extended hand paddle, shaking it firmly with both hands. He asked me to make myself comfortable. Since my anatomy is not conducive to sitting in a chair, I took up a kneeling position at the opposite side of the table.

The ambassador started by making small talk, asking me about my reactions to the upheaval and expounding on the recent geographical events that he found interesting.

"I must say, Ambassador Muller, you seem to be considerably more relaxed than you were during our first meeting," I said.

"Thank you, Kelvoo," he replied, "and please, call me Mark."

"I shall. Thank you, Mark."

"I apologize again for my previous awkwardness," he said. "I was just a bit overwhelmed to meet you. Since then I have been telling myself that it is simply your extraordinary circumstances and history that differentiate you from any other kloormar. I know from reading your works that you dislike receiving praise and excessive admiration, so I'm just trying to be relaxed and focus on nothing more than getting to know you."

"I'm glad to hear that, Mark," I replied. "So, are you saying our conversation today has nothing to do with official embassy business?"

"No, Kelvoo, that's not an assurance I can give in good conscience. As ambassador, one of my roles is to learn as much as possible about other species, cultures, and beings. Whenever we talk, I'm likely to find out something new about you. It may turn out that I learn something that could be useful at some point as Terra expands its contacts and starts reaching out to other worlds. With that in mind, I will understand completely if you are reluctant to speak about some subjects."

"I doubt that will be a problem, Mark," I replied.

We continued to chat amiably about innocuous subjects while Brenna observed us intently. When she started shifting in her seat, I assumed she was getting uncomfortable and possibly bored, so I shortened my statements and replies in the hope that Mark would soon conclude our meeting.

"I should let you get on with your day," he said, "but first, there's one small matter that my government would like to address with you."

"By all means," I replied.

He stood and gave a nod to a smartly dressed human female who was standing close to a wall. Beside the woman was a cube-shaped transport container, each side of it measuring just under one meter. The container was lying on a hovercart. The woman started toward our table, the hovercart following close behind. She left the container at the table and then walked away.

As the woman left, I saw Brenna spring out of her seat and march toward us with steely determination.

"What's going on here?" she said from behind Mark, startling him.

I was shocked by her interruption. "Please forgive the intrusion, Mark," I said, feeling abashed. "I would like to introduce my foster daughter, Brenna."

Mark's mouth hung open for a few seconds. "Brenna? Brenna Murphy? Oh, my goodness, won't you please join us?"

Brenna pulled a chair over from another table and sat between Mark and me. "I'm sorry," he said. "Allow me to introduce myself. I'm Mark Muller, Terran ambassador to Kuw'baal."

"I know *exactly* who you are," Brenna replied.

"Mr. Ambassador," I said, "I apologize for Ms. Murphy's outburst. I wasn't expecting her to treat you in this manner."

Brenna glared at me. "Let's just say I don't exactly trust Terran humans," she said, turning to Mark.

"I understand completely," he replied, looking down at the table. "The way that you and Kelvoo . . . I mean, your 'Pa' . . . That's what you call Kelvoo, right?"

"What I call my foster parent in private is none of your business!"

"Forgive me, Ms. Murphy. I was going to say, the way that you and . . . *Kelvoo* . . . were treated when you lived on Terra was beyond terrifying. It's to my eternal shame and to the shame of all Terran humans that we let our society descend into such a brutish, vile state. Given what you, Kelvoo, and your sister endured, it's completely understandable that you would have no trust in my people whatsoever. I do not seek your trust or Kelvoo's trust, nor do I expect it."

He took a deep breath before continuing. "My people have isolated themselves for the last fifty years because we don't even trust ourselves not to make a mess of things. We have been engaged in self-reflection and soul searching. It's only now that we are considering the idea of emerging into the view of other civilizations. That's why my government has asked me to contact Kelvoo."

"Why Kelvoo?" Brenna demanded. "Why wouldn't you just contact the Planetary Alliance?"

"I'm sure we will," he replied, looking up and reestablishing eye contact with her. "We're starting with Kelvoo because we see Kelvoo as a symbol of all the wrong we did to the extraterrestrial species on Terra. We admire Kelvoo and we follow Kelvoo's writings. I have read Kelvoo's original testimonial and Kelvoo's account of your time on Terra. I have also read hundreds of documents written by Kelvoo, including stories, reports, and general observations."

Mark's assurances seemed to placate Brenna to some extent, but I felt I had to interject. "Mr. Ambassador . . . *Mark* . . . I don't wish to serve as any kind of symbol or source of truth to the people of Terra. I also don't think my writing is worth—"

"I know," Mark said. "You're a humble being and I respect that. I just wanted to explain to Ms. Murphy the reason why I reached out to you specifically."

"OK," Brenna said in a much calmer manner. "Let's dispense with the 'Ms. Murphy' stuff. Please call me 'Brenna'. I'm sorry for my outburst, but I was alarmed when I saw this box being brought over. What's in it?"

"It's a gift."

"Well, if you know so much about Kelvoo, you'd know that money or valuables aren't going to get you anything."

"Brenna, please!" I interjected, becoming annoyed by her rudeness.

"It's nothing of the sort, Brenna," Mark insisted. "Well, I suppose it has some historical value, and it could be a collector's item, but it's a simple present. My people hope that Kelvoo will like it, but I think that you might appreciate it even more."

"I suppose there's no harm in taking a look," Brenna conceded.

Mark tapped a latch on top of the container, causing its lid to open and fold back. The contents rose from the box and hovered just above it.

"A bot?" Brenna asked.

"It's a Luxor P-1 domestic service bot," I said. "We had the use of one of these when we moved to Terra."

The bot's surface was shiny as though it had recently been cleaned and polished, but its outer shell also had deep scratches, gouges, and abrasions.

"Servitor bot, what is your designation?" Mark said, addressing the device.

"My designation is 'Pollybot,'" it replied.

Brenna and I were shocked but also skeptical. Could it possibly be the servitor bot that was provided with our home on Terra so long ago? I decided to conduct a test. "Pollybot, what is my designation?"

"I compute your designation to be 'Kelvoo,' with ninety-three percent probability."

"What about me, Pollybot? What's my designation?" Brenna asked.

"Uncertain. Voice analysis indicates your designation as 'Brenna' with sixty-seven percent probability. However, visual appearance provides only thirty-five percent certainty. Last contact with Brenna occurred fifty-four years and three hundred and fifty-two days ago. Has Brenna's appearance changed significantly during timespan indicated?"

"Oh, great!" Brenna exclaimed, rolling her eyes. "Even bots think I've turned into an old hag!"

Mark maintained a calm, professional demeanor, but I knew enough about human facial expressions to detect that he was suppressing a smile.

I decided to test the bot some more. "Pollybot, on the first day that we moved into our home on Terra, I said to you, 'Please provide hot dogs for May and fettuccine Alfredo and a green salad for Brenna.' Please recite the first sentence that you spoke in response to me."

"The first sentence of this unit's reply was, 'Please specify number of hot dogs, style of hot dogs, grain composition and style of buns, and preferred condiments.'"

While my story in *Kelvoo's Terra* recounted the past conversation about our first in-home meal on Terra, the exact wording had never been recorded. The bot's precise recitation convinced me of its veracity.

Brenna and I were astounded. "Where did you find Pollybot?" I asked.

"In the wreckage of the university," Mark replied, "only twelve years ago. It had sustained some serious damage, as you can see, but its processors and memory were intact. The bot was powered down, but we believe it had been functioning for about twenty years after you fled the university. If your Pollybot had been sentient, I'd say it must have been rather clever to find power sources for recharging all that time, not to mention managing to remain incognito for so long.

"A woman who worked as a scavenger and scrap dealer found your bot. She reviewed its settings before she powered it back up, and she noticed that it was set to 'avoid' mode. It's a good thing she switched off that setting before powering up, or your Pollybot would have taken off again."

"Yes," I replied, "my friend, the chancellor of the university, switched the bot into avoid mode. So, what happened after the scavenger powered the bot up again?"

"When she reviewed its memories, it didn't take long for her to realize that this unit was, in fact, your 'Pollybot!' When my government saw what the woman had, we purchased the bot and put it into secure storage while we debated what to do. Our original plan was to place it in a museum, until someone suggested that the bot should remain in storage so that someday, if we ever contacted you, we could reunite you with your lost property."

"You should be aware that this bot was not ours but was owned by the university," I pointed out.

"Sadly, Kelvoo, the university was reduced to rubble. The site was abandoned and remains that way to this day. If Chancellor

Linford were alive today, I'm sure he would be pleased to turn the bot over to you."

"I have no doubt about that, Mark. I accept this gift with immense gratitude."

"There are two more pieces of property that I would like to return. One is for you and the other is for your other foster daughter, May," Mark said. "Pollybot, please return the items you've been holding for safekeeping."

A small tray opened in Pollybot's side. It held two locator capsules, each the size and shape of a grain of rice. One of the capsules had been implanted in my arm and the other in May's arm when she was eleven years old. The locators were standard issue on Terra and were intended to keep beings safe. Ironically, once the coup started, it was very dangerous for May and me to be locatable. That was when we had our locators surgically removed. Chancellor Linford gave the locators to Pollybot and put it into avoid mode. That way, if the soldiers had tried to track our locators, Pollybot would lead them on a wild goose chase.

My reaction to seeing the locator capsules surprised me. Although they were inanimate objects, the sight of them brought my memories of our desperate flight to the forefront of my mind, along with the fear and sadness of those times.

Brenna looked uncomfortable and distant, and Mark seemed to pick up on her emotions. "How are you doing, Brenna?" he asked.

"Just thinking about those terrible times," she replied. "By then, I already had my locator removed, but I did it so Kelvoo couldn't find me. That was when I had run away from home. I took my unresolved issues around the death of my biological father and turned against Kelvoo. The people I ran to were involved in planning the coup. In the end, they were just using me to further their cause. That entire episode was the biggest mistake of my life."

Mark nodded in understanding. "I know."

"Of course you do! You've read Kelvoo's books, so you already know the whole sad story."

"The same things could have happened to anyone in the situation you were in, Brenna, and you went through hell as a result." Mark seemed to know how to reassure Brenna. "The important thing was that you learned from your experience. You grew as a person, and you did a great deal of good for a great many people. When I look at you, I see someone who is kind, smart, and compassionate, someone who has achieved greatness."

Brenna chuckled and shook her head. "Boy, you sure have a way with words! But don't start thinking that I trust you!" she added, her smile indicating that she was making a joke while still maintaining a degree of suspicion.

With the ice between Mark and Brenna starting to crack, the ambassador stood. "I'm sure you'd like some time to get reacquainted with Pollybot," he said. "If it's not too much trouble, could we get together again next week, same time, same place? Brenna, you're welcome to come too if you wish."

We agreed to our next meeting and then Mark left the table.

"Well, that was interesting," I remarked.

"I can't believe Pollybot is back!" Brenna said.

"Do you have any thoughts about what we're going to do with an outdated servitor bot?" I asked.

"Not a clue, but it's a good conversation starter!"

"Shall we go to the gathering area and watch the vid feeds from the surface?"

"Sure thing, Pa, but first, let's see if we can call May."

I followed Brenna to her quarters as Pollybot followed close behind.

It took only two tries to contact May on the entanglement network. She was concerned that Brenna was calling with bad news, since we usually contacted May when it was daytime or early evening at May's location. Our call came at night for May as she was getting ready for bed.

"No May, nobody has died and there's no emergency. There's just someone here who'd like to meet you," Brenna said. She turned her Infotab to reveal the bot hovering beside her. We were surprised when May recognized it immediately.

"Pollybot!" she exclaimed. "No way! That's not possible!"

"Why don't you ask Pollybot a question to verify?" Brenna suggested.

May thought for a moment. "I have a better idea!"

She clapped her hands twice, then pushed her palms toward her Infotab twice in an action known as the "pat-a-cake" maneuver. Then she recited a rhyme I had never heard before.

> Pollybot, Pollybot, turn around.
> Pollybot, Pollybot, touch the ground.
> Pollybot spin and Pollybot flip.
> Pollybot rise and Pollybot dip.

Pollybot followed the commands even before May had finished reciting each action, indicating that Pollybot was already familiar with the routine. To our astonishment, Pollybot recited the next verse and May performed the actions.

> May Murphy, May Murphy, hands in the sky.
> May Murphy, May Murphy, close one eye.
> May Murphy turn and May Murphy hop.
> May take a bow and May Murphy stop.

As Pollybot spoke, May's face was a picture of unrestrained glee. Pollybot spoke with the correct cadence but was incapable of being expressive. Instead, the words came out in a near monotone. That didn't matter to May; she laughed with delight and struggled, between giggles, to get the final words out. For the last verse, May and Pollybot alternated their lines.

> Pollybot, Pollybot, shake and twirl.
> May Murphy, May Murphy, silly girl.
> Pollybot, Pollybot, is it true?
> May Murphy, May Murphy, I love you.

Brenna's mouth hung open. I wasn't sure what to make of the display. "Where did *that* come from?" Brenna asked.

"I made it up when I was eleven," May said. "I taught it to Pollybot. For some reason, it's stuck with me, and I remember every word and every action like it was yesterday!"

"Why haven't I ever heard that rhyme or seen that routine before?" I asked.

"I think I was kind of embarrassed at the time. I probably thought it was a bit babyish for an eleven-year-old. Anyway, I used to play with Pollybot and teach it after I got home from school and before you got home from work. I used to read a lot in my spare time, but I also liked to goof off every so often. Games like that were fun, just between Pollybot and me!"

Even though May was sixty-six years old, seeing the joy on her face made her seem like an innocent child again.

***

In the remainder of our time on *Platform 313*, Mark and I met on several occasions. Our meetings were mostly relaxed, collegial, and interesting. Sometimes Brenna would join us, and other times we met one on one. We dispensed with the requirement that we meet in public spaces, so we met in private lounge areas or in the embassy's small office.

Mark asked many questions about my life and experiences but never delved into subjects that were confidential. In turn, I learned more about Terra. Mark assured me that Terra had become a wonderful world of peace and harmony, though I tempered his rosy imagery with the knowledge that he would be biased and lacking in understanding of other worlds, species, and cultures.

As the upheavals diminished and we anticipated our return to Kuw'baal in fourteen days, Mark asked me whether I would be interested in visiting Terra as his special guest. From the time we first met, I had been wondering whether he might have been intending to ask such a question.

I politely declined, and Mark dropped the matter—at least for the remainder of that meeting. In our subsequent meeting, he asked me why I didn't want to visit Terra.

"Because I'm done with Terra," I replied. "Nothing good came from my previous time there. When I escaped, I resolved to keep myself distant from human society at large. I think it was the correct decision since humans—and for that matter, I—have been doing fine since then."

"But, Kelvoo, we think the time has come for us to reach out and contact other civilizations. We've been a peaceful planet for a full generation. Don't you think we're ready?"

"That's not for me to decide, Mark. Terra has been so isolated that nobody on the outside can verify that it's a peaceful world. If Terra would like more outside contact, the correct procedure would be to contact the Planetary Alliance Interplanetary Outreach Committee. I'm sure they would be pleased to send a delegation to visit and evaluate the risks and benefits of closer relations. If you wish, I can contact the PAIOC on your behalf."

"No!" Mark blurted, then seemed to realize he had overreacted. "Sorry about that, Kelvoo. It's just that *you* are the individual that my government trusts the most. You're the one they know best."

"Mark, please! They don't know me at all, unless you're saying there are high-level officials who knew me when I lived on Terra. I'm sure they would be quite elderly by now."

"Kelvoo, everyone on Terra knows you through your writings. They know you from *Kelvoo's Testimonial* and *Kelvoo's Terra* and many of the things you have written since then. Children learn about you in school from an early age. Scholars study you and analyze your teachings—"

"My 'teachings?'"

"OK, bad choice of words. I'm just saying that you've had a profound influence on my world, and that's why you're the perfect choice to visit us and begin the process of reintegration."

"I'm sorry, Mark. Even if I had remotely considered coming to Terra, the words you just said would convince me to stay away. You're quite correct that my existence has had a profound influence on Terra. When I wrote *Kelvoo's Testimonial*, I couldn't have imagined that it would lead the Planetary Alliance to demand sweeping reforms on Terra. Then, years later, my move to Terra was the catalyst for the rebellion against the reforms, leading to the coup and civil war that ripped your planet apart!

"Now you're telling me that the Terran humans learn about me from childhood? You're telling me that scholars study me? Mark, given my history with Terra, I'm terrified by what you are saying!"

"No, no, no, Kelvoo! It isn't like that. Oh no, I've completely messed this up! I'm so sorry!"

"That's alright, Mark. I'm truly flattered by your government's interest in me, but they're just going to have to find another way."

When the meeting ended, I updated my Planetary Alliance contacts on our interaction. They were troubled by my revelations and asked me to keep them informed and to terminate contact when and if I saw fit.

Mark and I met two more times. Brenna was present for both meetings. In the first of those meetings, it didn't take long for Mark to broach the subject of a visit. He offered me various monetary incentives, but he did so half-heartedly, no doubt knowing I had no need for money. He asked Brenna whether the Terran government could persuade her to influence me, but his suggestions only served to annoy her and increase her suspicion. "Surely, you aren't trying to bribe us!" she exclaimed.

When our meeting ended, Mark left in a very disappointed state.

Three days later, he sent me a message, apologizing for trying to lure Brenna and me with "inappropriate incentives." He asked me for one final meeting, so we wouldn't end our contact on a sour note, and he promised not to ask me again to travel to Terra. Brenna was reluctant, but considering Mark's apology, we agreed to the meeting. To accommodate his wish for privacy, but also to address our concern for security, we stipulated that the meeting would take place in one of the private lounges that had glass walls, so the public could see inside.

When the meeting started, it didn't take long for Mark to stray from his promise.

"Again, Kelvoo," he began, "I apologize for asking you to do something you're not comfortable with. I just want you to understand the pressure I'm under. I have had no greater honor than to meet with you. Doing so has been fascinating and has also been a great privilege, but as far as my superiors are concerned, my only mission is to convince you to visit Terra. Those above me aren't going to take no for an answer. If I fail, my career as a diplomat is as good as finished. Kelvoo, I'm *begging* you to reconsider. Terra *needs* you to visit. We need your wisdom, and our citizens need to see you.

"My tour as ambassador to Kuw'baal will end in twenty-one days," he continued. "If I return to Terra empty-handed, I don't know what will happen to me. If you won't come to Terra for the Terran government or for our people, please do it for me. I'd like to think that we've become friends, so I'm asking you, as a friend, to please grant me this small favor."

I could tell that Brenna was becoming annoyed. I paused to let Mark know that I was putting thought into the words that followed. "I regret that my refusal puts you in a bad position, Mark. When you say you don't know what will happen to you, are you saying that you'll be in danger? If so, I'm sure you could request asylum and remain on Kuw'baal or relocate to a safe planet or space platform."

"No, Kelvoo." He sighed. "I'm steadfastly loyal to Terra, and I will return there, no matter what happens to me. I just thought we were friends, that's all. When I approached you, I was intimidated by your stature among my people. It took a lot just for me to approach you. Talking to you was terrifying, but I did it. Then I spent hours with you in meetings, getting to know you. As a gesture of goodwill, my people reunited you with your Pollybot. Did that gesture mean nothing?"

"If you would like us to return the bot—"

I stopped, seeing the look of panic on Brenna's face, as if I were suggesting that we give up a member of our family.

"No, Kelvoo!" Mark said. "Please keep your 'Pollybot.' We want you to enjoy its presence as much as possible."

"Are we done?" Brenna asked, her voice stern.

"Are we, Kelvoo?" Mark said. "Is there truly nothing I can say or do to make you change your mind?"

"There's nothing that will make me change my mind," I said in a strong, firm voice.

"Fine!" Ambassador Mark Muller said as he shot out of his chair and then strode to the glass door.

"We're all going to regret this," he muttered as he stormed out of the room without so much as a backward glance.

SEVEN: HOME SWEET HOME

The mass migration back to the planet commenced once Ryla 6 had passed Kuw'baal and no longer presented a danger. It took ten days to empty the arks and return the displaced beings to the surface. The arks would remain in orbit indefinitely and would be repurposed as interstellar transit hubs, visitor accommodations, factories, or scientific research platforms. Some would become orbital cities for those who preferred to live in space.

Since I had my own shuttle, Brenna and I, with Pollybot in tow, were able to leave on the second "resettlement" day. When we touched down outside my house, we walked around my island, which had grown due to the permanent drop in the depth of the lake. I slid the fusion generator off its hoverlift, reconnected it, and powered up my home's internal systems.

The house was in surprisingly good condition, with just a few significant cracks in the outer walls and some cosmetic damage in the form of hundreds of hairline fractures. I had some equipment and material left over from the original construction, so I pulled those items out of the house's workshop area. I could have hired a crew to perform the repairs, but there would have been a long wait due to the need for workers and construction bots to repair and rebuild structures across my world. Brenna said she wanted a chance to do some "hands-on" work as she had in her twenties as a relief worker. She also hoped that sharing some hard labor would help us to bond on a different level.

We started by boarding the hoverlift and moving to a grove of k'k'mos plants. We used an energy beam cutter to harvest the plants' long, spiky leaves, then we used other tools to pull the stringy fibers out of the leaves. Pollybot followed the hoverlift to the grove and floated close by. Brenna took it upon herself to show the bot how to separate the fibers. I hadn't thought it would be possible for an old domestic service bot to perform such tasks, but Brenna proved to be an excellent instructor, perhaps because of her experience teaching human adults to read.

The fibers were tough and hard to tear out, so our progress was slow. Brenna was perspiring and breathing heavily, and I was concerned for her wellbeing.

"Are you alright, Brenna?" I asked. "We can take a break if you wish."

"So, you don't think I'm up to the task?" she asked, smiling.

"Would it offend you if my concern is due to your age? Seventy-two years is an advanced age for humans. It's only natural that your capacity for physical activity would be reduced substantially."

"Well, it's a good thing I had a round of rejuve treatment, isn't it, Pa?"

"When did you do that?"

"When I was sixty-four. I've always kept active and in shape, but I could tell I was starting to slow down, so I thought I'd give the treatment a try. It arrested the aging process and it's supposed to be good for about ten years, so I figure I've still got a couple of good years in me."

I was surprised and concerned about Brenna's decision to receive a treatment that was still quite new and had documented side effects. I didn't want to question her judgement since doing so had resulted in angry reactions when she was in her youth. I reminded myself that Brenna had grown immensely since those troubled times and was a confident, successful person.

"Have you experienced any side effects?" I asked.

"You worded that very diplomatically," she replied, smiling. "The only effects have been more energy and strength. My research suggested that negative results usually come from repeated treatments. Rejuve will slow aging in tissues that grow or repair themselves, like muscles and tendons, but parts like bones and teeth will wear down at a normal pace, so the side effects can be extremely painful after more than a couple of treatments. I thought about getting another treatment in a few years, but I've decided against it. Rejuve has been helpful to keep me active in my charitable work, but I think I'll retire in a couple of years and enjoy life more. I might even visit you a bit more often if it's not too much trouble."

"That would be wonderful!" I assured her.

When we had collected enough fiber, we returned to the house and picked kobo plants. We instructed Pollybot to put the plants into a press and collect the juice in buckets. The afternoon rain started earlier than usual, so we set the hoverlift to remain above the ground. The three of us placed the buckets under the lift, so the rainwater wouldn't dilute the kobo juice, then we retreated into the house.

By the time the rain tapered off, so did the remaining daylight. Brenna and I were exhausted. Our loyal bot connected itself to a power port in the wall as Brenna opened an instant meal from my storage bin marked "Guest Supplies (human)." After consuming her dinner of protein noodles in "mystery sauce," Brenna said goodnight and retired to the guest suite.

I carried my portable algel incubator and dispenser vat outside in the fading light and rode the hoverlift about 200 meters to a stream that fed into the lake at the foot of a waterfall. I scooped up some fresh algel that grew there and placed it into my feeding pouch, then I added algel to the vat until it was full. When I returned to the house and placed the vat in the kitchen, I moved to the main living area and assumed my meditative stance. I looked out across the lake, closed the lid over my eye dome, and slipped into a deep state of rest. I contemplated the remarkable events of recent weeks, along with my gratitude for all the wonderful experiences and beings in my life.

We had a late start the next day and were quite sore as we transported clay from a section of the lakebed that was previously underwater. The bot assisted us as we mixed the k'k'mos fibers with the clay and kobo juice to make the construction material known as ksada. Brenna blended the ingredients in a mixer. When a bucket of ksada was ready, Pollybot would take it to the house, placing the buckets at regular intervals along each wall. My job was to fill or cover the cracks in the walls. For larger fissures, I used a portable ksada pump to force the material through a nozzle, deep into the cracks. For superficial fractures, I applied a skim coat of ksada using a trowel to cover the imperfections.

We worked on the repairs for three more days. As we neared the end, we only had to finish the skim coating. Brenna and I decided to try teaching Pollybot how to perform the task. We were amazed by how quickly and accurately Pollybot was able to finish the work, likely due to the micron-level precision of its extendable gripper appendage, which it used to wield the trowel. By the end of the last day, Pollybot was so caked in mud that it resembled a floating clod of dirt more than a domestic servitor bot.

I felt a great deal of satisfaction when the work was complete. Brenna was correct when she suggested that shared labor could strengthen the bond between us. I hadn't seen her for more than a few days at a time after she left Kuw'baal and set out on her own, so her extended visit during the upheaval and her contribution to repairing my home taught me more about her and gave me a new appreciation for her intelligence and skills. Given her age, Brenna's stamina was also impressive.

The day after the repairs were completed, my Infotab chimed. I was pleased to receive a call from Kroz, who had a few days off due to the resettlement efforts winding down and most of the ark workers being demobilized.

"I am going back to our village," Kroz said, "but I was wondering whether I could stop by for a short visit. I am curious about the post-upheaval state of your home and any of the repairs that you might have made."

"I would welcome a visit from you, old friend," I replied. "Brenna hasn't returned to Perdition yet, so I'm sure she would be pleased to see you again."

Brenna and I were outside with Pollybot hovering close by when Kroz's car touched down. "I am pleased to see both of you," Kroz said. "Where did you get that bot? It looks exactly like a Luxor P-1 domestic service bot, but that model hasn't been in production for over fifty years! In fact, the last time I saw one was in your home on Terra."

"Yes," Brenna replied. "Do you recall the designation we gave it?"

"Of course, Brenna. Your bot was designated as 'Pollybot.' Have you forgotten that we kloormari have perfect memories, rendering us incapable of forgetting—"

Brenna's mischievous smile made the proverbial penny drop for Kroz. "Ah, yes," Kroz said, "you are attempting humor. I have never understood the concept of humor, especially by humans, so I hope you are not offended by my lack of any expected response. I recommend that you not direct any further attempts at humor toward me."

Brenna laughed, apparently delighted at Kroz's response. "Kroz, I'd like you to meet Pollybot!"

"So, you have given this antique bot the same designation as the bot you had on Terra?"

"No," I said, "this is the one and only original Pollybot!"

"But . . . how?" Kroz replied, perplexed.

Kroz was enthralled as I related the story of my meetings with the Terran ambassador and how Pollybot was returned to us.

Kroz looked Pollybot up and down and explained that current servitor bot technology was about five generations more advanced than Pollybot. Kroz thought it would be an interesting project to upgrade Pollybot's processors with the latest artificial intelligence technology.

"Would that change Pollybot's personality?" Brenna asked.

"Oh yes, Brenna, especially since this bot doesn't possess any personality now. If we upgrade the bot, you or Kelvoo could select new personality traits. This bot would appear to 'think' for itself. It could offer informed advice, anticipate the need for actions, and perform those actions autonomously."

Brenna didn't seem to be impressed. "That's alright, Kroz," she said. "I think we like Pollybot the way it is."

"Why?" Kroz inquired.

"I can't explain it . . . but I like how Pollybot is simple and unsophisticated. I guess I'd say I like its homespun charm."

"What do you think, Kelvoo?" Kroz asked.

"Whatever Brenna wants is fine with me," I replied, leaving Kroz more nonplussed than before.

I showed Kroz around my property, explaining the minor repairs we had made. In turn, Kroz described many of the unique challenges and successes of the ark project and the evacuation and return of the inhabitants of Kuw'baal.

When it was time for Kroz to leave, we said farewell outside the house. "Goodbye," Brenna called out as Kroz's car crested a hill.

"Speaking of goodbyes," she said, "I suppose I should be on my way soon. My charity work is in the hands of some good people, but they're going to start wondering what I'm up to if I don't return shortly."

"When do you want to leave?"

"I can't say that I *want* to leave, Pa. I've loved spending the last couple of months with you, but duty calls. How about three days from now?"

"I've truly loved having you with me, Brenna, but I understand the importance of your commitments. I look forward to spending the next three days with you."

We walked back into the house with Pollybot trailing us. Brenna opened a packaged dinner, and I filled a bowl with algel from my dispenser. Brenna ate her dinner while I absorbed mine.

"You know, Brenna," I said, "as much as I appreciate the Terrans returning Pollybot, I don't have much further use for it. Since you were excited to see it again, I'd like you to take Pollybot with you when you go home."

"Thanks, Pa, but I wasn't half as excited about it as May. She was beside herself! Since May didn't get to enjoy any time with you, would you object if I gave Pollybot to her?"

"I think that's a great idea!"

The next day, I asked Brenna whether her literacy organization could benefit from a slightly used orbital shuttle. "Since my car survived the upheaval intact, and I'm not planning any trips into orbit, I'd like to see my shuttle used for a worthy cause," I said.

Brenna enthusiastically accepted my offer. That day, she called her foundation's procurement coordinator to arrange for the shuttle to be picked up from Newton, put into an interstellar freighter, and shipped to her foundation's headquarters on Exile.

The day before her planned departure from Kuw'baal, I used my Infotab to transfer ownership of the shuttle to Brenna's foundation. The transfer had "pending" status until the shuttle could be delivered to the vehicle transfer office in Newton. Once there, an official would validate the transfer.

For the shuttle to fly to Newton, my Infotab had to be inside the vessel to unlock its controls. Brenna asked to borrow my Infotab so she could command the shuttle to go to Newton. "Would you like me to accompany you?" I asked.

"No thanks, Pa," she said. "I'd like a little bit of alone time so I can think and make plans for my return to the office."

I handed my Infotab to Brenna, then watched her enter the shuttle while Pollybot hovered beside me. "See you in a couple of hours," Brenna said.

When I went back inside, I saw that Brenna had inadvertently left her own Infotab on the counter in the kitchen. It never failed to amaze me that humans could lose track of personal items. I knew that Brenna couldn't complete the transfer without providing the pending record from her Infotab. I picked up her Infotab to call mine, but she had locked her device, so it was unusable without a scan of her biometrics. I could only wait until Brenna realized her mistake and returned to retrieve her Infotab.

Twelve minutes later, Pollybot received a signal from the exterior sensors. "Incoming shuttle. Incoming shuttle," it advised.

Thirty seconds later, Brenna rushed into the house. "Sorry, sorry! I'm an idiot!" she declared in a singsong voice.

"Incoming shuttle. Incoming shuttle," Pollybot said again.

"That's odd," I remarked.

"Well, Pollybot's pretty old," Brenna said.

Brenna took her Infotab from the counter. "I don't know why I'm so clueless," she said. "I probably have too much on my mind with me heading back to work tomorrow." She closed her eyes and spoke aloud to herself. "OK, do I have everything I need? Am I missing anything?"

Without warning, an armed human burst into the house, followed by ten more.

Brenna dropped both Infotabs, and we clung to each other in terror as the humans poured in, brandishing weapons. They were wearing black armored clothing and helmets, their faces covered by dark goggles and black fabric. We dropped to the floor and huddled beside the kitchen counter as the invaders started shouting at us incomprehensibly. Above the din, Pollybot said, "Danger! Stop your action!" at a high volume, continuously repeating its warning.

The invaders surrounded us with weapons pointed at us. "What the hell is *she* doing here?" One of them shouted.

"Just grab 'em both! Let's go, let's go, let's go!" their apparent leader shouted.

Everything happened so quickly, there was no time to formulate an escape. The sight of armed humans attacking us, the shouting, and Pollybot's alarming words blended into such a blur that it felt as if I were watching from afar as Brenna and I were dragged from my home.

"Grab those Infotabs!" an invader shouted to those who were still in the house.

I heard a voice coming from an invader's comm unit. "Abort and hold! The female has returned!"

"Too goddamn late!" the intruder replied. "Operation underway. You should've told us sixty seconds ago!"

Pollybot followed close behind. "Danger! Stop your action!" it repeated.

The invaders carried us to their shuttle, which was fifty meters from the house, and hustled us into the side hatch. As the hatch closed, the shuttle rose into the air. Pollybot pushed its way inside just before the hatch clunked shut.

Our abductors shoved us to the shuttle's aft section where two benches faced each other. Brenna and I were placed on a bench with an armed human on either side of us. Uncomfortable on seating designed for humans, I had to lean forward, so that the bench's backrest didn't impede one of my breathing inlets. Three more armed humans sat on the bench across from us. One of them passed our confiscated Infotabs to a fourth unarmed human who was already seated on the same bench.

Pollybot hovered between the benches, still issuing its warning. One of the raiders pointed his sidearm at Pollybot. "Shut that damn thing up!" he shouted.

"Pollybot, silence yourself!" Brenna said between gasps of terror.

As the shuttle rose and accelerated, the unarmed human across from us removed his goggles and face covering.

"Kelvoo, I'm so sorry it had to come to this," Ambassador Mark Muller said.

EIGHT: NOT AN ABDUCTION

"Should I take it, Mr. Ambassador, that this is your final 'invitation' for me to visit Terra?" I said after the initial shock of recognizing him wore off.

"I had no choice," he replied, "but please accept my assurances that it's for the best and that no harm will come to you."

"You bastard!" Brenna shouted. "You use a bunch of armed thugs to barge into Kelvoo's house, you terrorize us, you kidnap us, and we're supposed to accept your assurances?" She leaned in close and jabbed her index finger at his face. "I knew you were a liar right from the start!"

Brenna got too close for the liking of one of our abductors who shoved her back into her seat. Brenna's shoulder struck the backrest first. She winced in pain and reached up to rub her injury.

"You morons!" Muller shouted. "You were specifically instructed not to hurt Kelvoo. That goes for Kelvoo's family members too! Do you want to get paid or not?"

He reached over, presumably to pat Brenna's knee in a reassuring manner, but the moment he touched Brenna, her knuckles came down hard on the back of his hand, making him cry out in pain.

"I'm sorry, Brenna," he said rubbing his hand. "We thought you had left Kelvoo's house. We weren't supposed to take you too, but with what you witnessed, we couldn't exactly leave you there!"

"How would you know whether or not I was there?"

"I can't reveal that at this time, but don't worry. Kelvoo isn't the only one who's revered on Terra. You are also loved by all the people. We would never hurt anyone close to Kelvoo. We don't want to hurt anyone at all!"

"If we are truly valued," I said, "why would you abduct us?"

"Kelvoo, it's the last thing we wanted to do. Soon you'll see that this is not an abduction. The citizens of Terra *need* your help."

"And what happens when that help has been provided? What happens if I prove to be of no use?"

"You will be returned to Kuw'baal immediately. It may feel like it now, but this is *not* a kidnapping. Soon, you'll realize why we're doing this. Once the truth has been revealed, you'll understand. We'll earn your trust and then you'll be free to go wherever you please. I promise."

"So, what's this 'great truth?'" Brenna asked.

"It's not mine to tell, Brenna. All will be revealed after we land."

"I told you we couldn't trust him," Brenna exclaimed, turning to me.

A chime sounded, and a yellow indicator light flashed above us. "We're going to jump soon," the ambassador said.

"How is that possible?" I asked. "This vessel couldn't be fast enough to be at a Ryla jump point yet."

"I'm afraid we don't have the luxury of using a jump point. This isn't exactly an authorized flight, so we could be subject to inspection if we approached the jump point. We're going to make a stealth jump from clear space, but don't worry. We'll materialize in a nice, safe jump point in the Sol system."

I realized the vessel was equipped with advanced technology. Looking through the porthole in the hatch, I noticed how fast we had cleared the cloud cover on Kuw'baal and entered the blackness of space. The vessel must have accelerated rapidly, but an advanced dampening field had made the acceleration almost imperceptible. More than five decades in the past, Kroz had helped develop such dampening fields for small craft. Another indication of advanced tech was the jump itself. The freezing of motion and sound lasted less than two seconds as we jumped across many light years of distance.

"Alright, you can both relax now," Muller said to Brenna and me. He looked around at the raiders. "That goes for all of you. You might as well take off your headgear now."

My anxiety spiked, and Brenna seemed to be on the verge of panic when the raiders' faces were revealed. One of the humans had a very dark complexion and black hair with tight curls. Another had blue eyes and reddish-blonde hair.

"Outliers?" I said, astonished. "Terra is doing business with the Brotherhood?"

"As I said, Kelvoo, the people of Terra are pacifists," Muller replied. "It would go against everything we believe if we forced you to do anything against your will."

"So, you hired a criminal organization to *indirectly* force me to do your bidding? Is that what you're saying?"

"I'm so sorry, Kelvoo, but you must understand that it was a necessary evil since you gave us no other choice."

Brenna shook her head, "You're insane!"

"I have to agree with Brenna," I said. "You say the humans on Terra love and revere me, but your actions indicate the opposite. Be assured that I will make my feelings known on Terra, assuming I'm given the opportunity to express myself."

"You *will* have that opportunity, Kelvoo. If you tell the Terrans that they've done you wrong and you despise them, they'll listen and they'll believe you. If my people endure your wrath, it's because we *deserve* it."

"Have all of you gone mad?" I asked.

"I can say no more, Kelvoo. I have already said too much. All will become clear soon enough."

Brenna and I spent the rest of the trip in silence. She looked distraught, so I draped an arm over her shoulders. She held my hand paddle and rested her head on my shoulder. I extended my eyestalk and wrapped it over her, nestling her head under my eye dome.

A long time ago, I would have been overwhelmed with anxiety. But now, I just felt a crushing weariness. Yet again, humans were preventing me from living in peace, but at the same time, I felt so much love for my human foster daughter, and I would have done anything to protect her from whatever awaited us.

As we approached Terra, I considered my feelings toward the human species. I thought about my suspicion and fear of humans in general and how sharply those feelings differed from my love for the individual humans who had enriched my life.

We all felt a slight bump as the vessel pierced the upper limits of the Terran atmosphere, and I saw the blackness turn to indigo and blue as we descended. I had no clear perception of speed due to the vessel's inertial buffering. Suddenly, it became apparent that we had almost slowed to a stop as we entered an enclosed space. There was a slight clunk as the vessel settled down onto a hard floor.

"Kelvoo, Brenna," the ambassador said, "to you, this moment might not feel like a cause for celebration, but I would be remiss if I didn't say, 'Welcome to Terra.' For all of Terra, this is the greatest day in our history as a planet."

"You clearly have a penchant for hyperbole," I replied.

As the hatch opened, the raiders shuffled forward in their seats. Some looked as though they were preparing to stand.

"You will all remain seated until our guests and I are well clear of the shuttle!" the ambassador shouted.

The hatch folded open, and Muller stood. He extended a hand toward us, but Brenna slapped it away. "We're quite capable of standing without your assistance," she said.

The ambassador stepped through the hatch and motioned for us to follow him. We walked down the ramp with Pollybot close behind, realizing that we were inside a hangar. The floor, walls, and ceiling were covered in pristine white stone, resembling the marble walls of a centuries-old palace. The hangar must have been 300 meters in length, with the vessel about 70 meters from the huge exterior doors that had shut behind us. Close to the vessel's hatch was a small pallet stacked with gold ingots and various silvery metals.

The ambassador led us toward the far end of the hangar. Our footsteps echoed from every surface. Once we had walked about fifty paces, he turned back to the vessel. "Alright, you jackals!" he shouted. "Take your payment, then remove your foul carcasses from this peaceful planet!"

The raiders pushed past one another to exit the vessel. They laughed, whooped, and shouted, raising a jumbled, echoing din as each one grabbed an ingot or two and shoved them into the vessel. We watched for the two minutes it took for the outliers to run back and forth until the stack of metal disappeared. When the hatch closed, the huge doors at the end of the hangar slid open. The vessel rose and turned toward the opening. The moment there was just enough room to clear the doors, the vessel shot forward and turned skyward, then roared away the instant it had cleared the hangar.

We walked to the far end of the hangar where two plain white doors with long golden handles were inset into the wall. I walked on Muller's right side, Brenna on his left. Pollybot trailed behind us.

The ambassador stopped a few paces before we reached the door.

"Now what?" Brenna asked as she crossed her arms, looking furious.

Both white doors swung open, revealing a tall human male. He had a slightly dark complexion. His long black beard hung in contrast to his clean white robe with gold trim. On his head was a hat with a tall, pointed panel at the front and back, resembling a bishop's miter, which I had seen in old illustrations.

The man stepped forward and extended his arms as if to embrace me. His hands were wrinkled and bony, shaking slightly.

The man stopped short, apparently giving the ambassador his cue.

"Your Supreme Excellency," the ambassador said, in a clear, crisp voice. "I present to you, Kelvoo."

As soon as the ambassador introduced me, he turned and moved to the wall where he stood, watching.

"His excellency" removed his miter, cradling it under his right arm. Then he dropped to one knee, placed the miter on the floor, and bowed, touching his forehead to the floor. His arms were extended straight toward me, both palms pressed to the floor.

"Oh, Kelvoo!" he said. "Oh, glorious one! Oh, innocent one! Oh, wise one! Oh, beloved one!"

"Oh, stop it!" I replied.

NINE: NOT A RELIGION

The human did as I said, ending his pitiful display of praise. He lifted his head to look directly at me while still kneeling. Then his face broke into an impish grin. "Of course, Kelvoo!" he exclaimed.

He stood up and brushed off his robe, even though the hangar floor was so clean, there wasn't a trace of dust on him. He picked up his miter and tossed it to the ambassador who, startled, fumbled it before managing to regain his grip.

The man in the robe extended his hand to me. "I am Kozoltoo. I arranged for you to come here, so I am the one human that you can blame for your unscheduled . . . diversion."

Kozoltoo kept his hand extended as he stepped toward me. I was hesitant to reciprocate, but I decided to put on a display of confidence. I grasped his hand firmly, to the point that I saw him grimace, then I shook it.

"Kelvoo," he said, "please excuse my excessive groveling a moment ago. Based on your autobiographical accounts, I suspected that you would find it distasteful, but I didn't want to incur your wrath if I treated you with less respect than you expected."

"Why would you pay any heed to my wrath, Kozoltoo? Didn't you think that abducting my foster daughter and me would be cause enough for anger?"

"Yes, I knew you would be upset, but I also know that you're a reasonable being who would understand that your prior refusals left us no choice but to bring you here. Everything will be explained soon."

Kozoltoo stepped sideways to stand in front of Brenna. She stood stiffly with her arms crossed, fuming with anger. "Brenna!" he exclaimed, smiling. He extended his arms as if to embrace her, but she scooted back, maintaining an icy silence. Kozoltoo's smile remained unchanged. "Ah, Brenna, you are just as I pictured you—fierce and strong!" He shook his head in admiration. "I'm sure you know that you're an unexpected addition to this visit, but—"

"If you didn't want me here, why the hell did you grab me too?"

"We weren't expecting you to be at Kelvoo's residence when our people came to 'escort' Kelvoo to Terra. Nonetheless, your presence is a welcome gift. You are loved and admired across Terra. During your stay, you'll be treated as an honored guest."

"More like an honored *prisoner*!" Brenna spat.

Kozoltoo's smile didn't waver. "Follow me," he said, turning toward the doors.

"And if we refuse?" I asked.

"Then remain here. You may do as you please. You can explore this place and wander anywhere you wish because you are *not* prisoners! I would advise you, however, not to leave these buildings—especially you, Kelvoo. You're the only kloormar on Terra, and the people have been told you're coming soon. If you don't wish to be mobbed by adoring humans, and possibly injured in the process, my advice is to follow me, so all your questions can be answered."

Given our desire to know what was happening, we followed Kozoltoo. On our way out of the hangar, Kozoltoo stopped to thank the ambassador for his "brilliant work". Mark Muller bowed low before walking away.

We walked down a short, plain hallway and then entered a vast, semicircular room. Twenty-four humans stood at attention, forming a corridor with twelve on each side. The men and women were wearing blue trousers and jackets over white shirts. The lapels and cuffs on their jackets had gold embroidery that matched the pattern of zigzags, interspersed with circles, that were featured on Kozoltoo's robe.

"Kelvoo, Brenna, allow me to introduce my most trusted staff," Kozoltoo announced. His people bowed.

"No! Our guests have no wish for formal greetings!" Kozoltoo announced, causing his staff to snap back to attention.

"Please return to your stations," he said. "I'm sure Kelvoo and Brenna will grace each of you with a personal greeting at an appropriate time."

"Don't count on it," Brenna said. Her reaction troubled me, making me wonder whether she would cause unnecessary trouble.

Kozoltoo's staff went to their workstations, which were scattered around the room.

Kozoltoo turned back to Brenna and me. "I hope you'll grant me the honor of allowing me to provide a short tour of this place."

Brenna crossed her arms again and stood rooted in place. "Come on Brenna," I urged. "Let's just get the 'lay of the land,' so to speak."

Brenna reluctantly followed as Kozoltoo led us to the outer wall of windows. That's when I realized we were at a high elevation, relative to the ground below. The building was perched on a supporting structure at least 500 meters tall. Sol's brilliant light flooded through the windows, which were curved from top to bottom, so we could see sky above and the ground below. Looking straight down, I saw the edge of a body of water that seemed to serve as a decorative moat around the base of the support structure.

"Please take a moment to relax and enjoy the view," Kozoltoo suggested.

The scene before us was a stunning blend of nature and human engineering. Far to the right was forested land with rolling hills that cradled the blue waters of a lake. A river flowed from the lake, going past us and disappearing from view on our left. A few buildings made up a village on the opposite bank, directly across the river from us. Farmland stretched back from the flatter parts of the river valley, extending into low hills. Starting at the midpoint of our view, the farms gave way to open meadows and then manicured parks with curving paths, fountains, and flowering plants.

Down below to our left was a gleaming white building with a golden geodesic dome on one side. Paths and vast green lawns radiated out from the building. I was impressed by the way the structure stood out, yet somehow blended in with its surroundings. I had many questions, but I decided to keep quiet and observe as much as I could.

Kozoltoo led us along the edge of the building toward the side that faced the golden dome. A wall interrupted the curve of the windows, so we walked around it, realizing it delineated a private area. "Brenna," Kozoltoo said, "these will be your quarters. I hope you'll find them suitable."

He opened a door, revealing a luxurious suite of rooms with the same panoramic view we had been taking in. A female human in a dark blue uniform was supervising several servitor bots, which were cleaning all surfaces and arranging pillows on a huge bed. All sorts of human food and beverages were visible in glass cabinets, and meal preparation equipment was on hand.

"Maria!" Kozoltoo called out. The woman was startled, though not nearly as much as when she turned around and saw Brenna and me in the doorway. She started to bow, but then stopped when Kozoltoo raised a hand. "Please say hello to our guests," he said.

"I am deeply honored to serve you," Maria said. "Brenna, I shall be your personal attendant in the roles of assistant, guide, concierge, and whatever else you may desire. You will find clothing and footwear of all sizes and styles in the closets, but if you lack anything, we will move mountains to bring it in for you. If you need any services, I will be here in the room or waiting outside if you require privacy. We had little notice of your blessed arrival, but the bots should have your room fully prepared shortly."

Brenna didn't reply or even acknowledge Maria's existence, which made me uncomfortable. "Thank you, Maria," I said.

The next room along the outer rim was enclosed by glass walls. A large desk and plush chair faced us with the windows behind them. The room also held a boardroom table and presentation equipment. "This is my office," Kozoltoo said as we walked past.

The room after Kozoltoo's office had solid walls. "Kelvoo, this is the space we have set aside as your accommodations." He opened the door, revealing a small, empty space with some shelves and a desk. A combination algel incubator and dispenser were placed on the desktop. There was also a servitor station where Pollybot could enter sleep mode and charge its energy supply. "It took considerable effort to get a functioning algel vat here," Kozoltoo said, "let alone a starter supply of fresh algel. There was also quite a debate regarding appropriate accommodation for you. Many of my associates thought a palace should be built for you, given your importance, but those of us who follow your writings thought you would consider such luxury to be unnecessary and wasteful."

"These accommodations would be perfectly adequate if I had any intention of remaining here," I said. "Seeing as I have no such intention, I must insist on our immediate release and return to Kuw'baal."

"I'm so sorry, Kelvoo. Terran humans aren't spacefaring people. The few interplanetary vessels we have are for transporting our diplomats between Terra, Kuw'baal, and Planetary Alliance headquarters. No such vessel is here on Terra at this moment. With that in mind, let's meet in my office, so I can explain why we brought you here." Kozoltoo turned to Brenna. "I see that Maria is stationed outside your suite," he said, "which means it's ready for you to move in. Won't you please make yourself comfortable while Kelvoo and I step into my office?"

"Hell no!" Brenna replied. "I'm not letting Kelvoo out of my sight!"

"As you wish, Brenna. In that case, won't you please join us?" Kozoltoo held the door to his office open.

Brenna entered first, followed by Kozoltoo and me. Our ever-present Pollybot entered last. "Please Brenna, take a chair. Kelvoo, please assume a comfortable position."

I knelt on my lower knee joints, placing my eye dome at Kozoltoo's eye level when he was seated.

"So, Kelvoo, you must have no end of questions for me!" he said.

I decided to be unpredictable in case it flustered Kozoltoo and led to more information being revealed, so I didn't start by asking why I was there.

"I'm curious about your name," I began. "It doesn't sound like any Terran names I've heard. I'm also hearing you pronounce the K with a slight click, as if you're emulating kloormari speech. What is the origin of your name?"

"What an interesting question," he said. "My parents named me Terrance, and my family name is Chang. Kozoltoo is the name assigned to me when I ascended to my current position. As I'm sure you've figured out, Kozoltoo means 'keeper of the light.'"

I was incredulous. "Keeper of the light? The closest human pronounceable equivalent would be 'K'tshol'tyoo.' A kloormar would pronounce it as," I vocalized the kloormari sounds that made up the phrase. "Of course, you wouldn't have heard part of what I just said since some of it is pronounced at a higher frequency than human hearing can detect."

"I do hope that our unintentional abuse of your language hasn't offended you, Kelvoo," Kozoltoo replied, "but this perfectly illustrates why we need your help. You see, Kelvoo, we've been isolated for so long, and we know so little about other worlds and cultures. We think the time has come to reach out to the stars and find our place among greater cultures. There's so much you can teach us!"

"This is ridiculous! I can't just sit here and listen to this!" Brenna said. She stood, walked to the windows, and stared at the scenery. Sol was low and was casting an orange glow across the sky and the land.

"What am I supposed to teach you?" I asked Kozoltoo. "How to pronounce kloormari phrases?"

"No, nothing like that! I'm sure you've already realized that you are revered by everyone here on Terra."

"Yes, though it's undeserved."

"So, it wouldn't surprise you to know that every Terran studies your teachings from an early age?"

"'Teachings' is a rather odd word for you to use. Ambassador Muller used the same term in one of our earlier conversations, though he treated it as if it were a slip of the tongue. The point is, the only 'teachings' I've created are the course materials from my time as a professor almost sixty years ago and perhaps procedural manuals from my work with the Planetary Alliance. I don't see why that material would be useful to the citizens of Terra."

"Kelvoo, what I'm going to say may seem implausible, but I ask that you hear me out with an open mind." He paused, seeming to gather his thoughts, then he continued in a low, earnest voice.

"There are lessons to be learned from *all* your writing, your speeches, your interviews, and your academic records. We have been compiling and researching all the records we can get our hands on, and we've concluded that an unrealized power lies within you. Whether you believe it or not, *we* believe that you've been predestined to guide humanity to a new level of peace, knowledge, and enlightenment. That's why we brought you here."

I was troubled by Kozoltoo's words. I wanted to end the conversation, along with any notion that I had any kind of superpowers, but I held off speaking my mind, so I could gather further information.

"Kozoltoo," I said as calmly as possible, "you've been referring to 'we.' I take it that you're an official in some sort of organization. Based on Ambassador Muller addressing you as 'Supreme Excellency,' I would imagine that you're a high-ranking—"

"You see, Kelvoo?" Kozoltoo exclaimed, cutting me off. "This is what I'm talking about! You used your power to determine the existence of our organization! Your supernatural insight told you that I'm its leader!"

"How delusional can you be?" I asked. "Any fool could have come to the same conclusion! Your beliefs are flawed, but you hold them to be absolute truths! You're so convinced you're right that you draw conclusions from the flimsiest coincidences, to confirm your beliefs."

"Again, Kelvoo, don't you see? You say our beliefs are flawed; therefore, you must be correct! Terra needs you, so we can learn to discern truth from error. In doing so, we can correct ourselves and follow the one true path!"

"Allow me to back up a bit," I said. "Let's return to your use of 'we.' What organization do you lead?"

"We are the Kelvonist Society."

"Surely, that name isn't derived from mine!" I replied, flabbergasted. Kozoltoo just smiled.

"How many followers do you have?"

"The entire human population of Terra."

"I highly doubt that!" I exclaimed. "Since Ambassador Muller brought me to you, should I assume that this 'Kelvonist Society' is supported by the government?"

"We *are* the government! Well, at least we're the spiritual arm of the Terran government. Nothing happens without our approval. By passing all important decisions through the filter of your teachings, you have been indirectly safeguarding our people from our own foolish human tendencies!"

Brenna, who was still standing by the windows with her back to us, reached her breaking point. "This is effing nuts!" she cried. "I'm going to my room!"

She stormed out of Kozoltoo's office, and I watched through the glass wall as Maria opened the door to Brenna's suite and let her in.

"So, where were we?" Kozoltoo asked.

"I was about to ask you about your doctrine."

"I'm sorry, Kelvoo. I'm not familiar with that term."

"The tenets of your beliefs. Your manifesto. The core text that the Kelvonist Society follows."

"You must be referring to this." Kozoltoo pulled a huge book from under his desk. It had been decades since I had seen an actual bound paper book. It reminded me of my meetings with the Sagacity Club when I taught at the Interplanetary University on the Mediterranean Sea after I immigrated to Terra. The club met in an old-style library with shelves full of priceless ancient books.

Kozoltoo slid the book across the desk to me. The title was engraved into the thick, white cover: *The Book of Kelvoo.*

The full realization of what I was dealing with appalled me. "So, this is a religion!"

"Oh, no, Kelvoo! It's absolutely nothing of the sort! Please don't think that!"

"You can deny it all you want," I replied, "but I know a religion when I see one. Your Kelvonist Society is a religion, and you're its high priest! In fact, I'm going to refer to you as the high priest from this point forward."

"No, Kelvoo! Please! We would *never* form a religion. Your teachings have exposed the evil of such superstitions! When we study *Kelvoo's Testimonial*, we see how the evil Reverend Hol tried to convert you and your disciples, and—"

"Disciples?"

"I'm sorry, teammates! We were horrified to read about how your team was labeled as abominations because you're a genderless species that reproduce as a group. We were disgusted when the so-called holy man called for your execution. But worst of all, we were devastated when—" His voice caught in his throat. "When one of Reverend Hol's followers murdered your precious Baby Sam. Oh, Kelvoo! Oh, poor, poor Baby Sam!" he said as his voice took on a wailing tone. He bowed his head, and his shoulders shook, but when he looked up again, his eyes were still clear and dry.

"And then, in your next great work, *Kelvoo's Terra*," he continued, "you reported the formation of a new religion around the vile prime minister and coup leader, Gloria Truscott, who proclaimed herself 'God-appointed adjudicator of the faith.' The Truscovite religion was formed while you were in prison where you were abused and tortured—" His voice caught once more, and he buried his face in his hands and shook his head. "Oh, Kelvoo! How you suffered to save us all!"

"No Mr. High Priest!" I said, "I did *not* suffer for you, I did *not* suffer for humanity, and I did *not* suffer for Terra. I suffered because extraterrestrials like me were blamed for the changes happening in Terran society. We were blamed by manipulative people who fed the fear and ignorance of their followers in the interest of power and wealth. In other words, Mr. High Priest, I suffered for *nothing*!"

"How tragic, Kelvoo, for you to feel that way, but I have glorious news! For, you see, it's through your sacrifice that peace has come to Terra. Your wonderful teachings have shown us the way. By following your path, we have embraced peace and banished hate. We have rejected violence and welcomed love. And finally, we have accepted truth and abandoned the falsehoods and superstition of religion. This is core to our existence."

"And yet, Mr. High Priest—"

"Please, Kelvoo. Please don't call me that!"

"And yet, sir, your Kelvonists praise and worship me. In what way is that not religion?"

"Kelvonism is a *philosophy* and nothing more. It's not a religion because religions are based on non-existent, imaginary deities, but here you are in front of me. I can reach out and touch you!" He reached over the desk and grasped my hand paddle. "Religions are also based on leaders who have died and, therefore, can't refute the interpretation of their teachings. Yet here you are, not only alive but also engaging in dialogue with me, teaching me, correcting the Kelvonist interpretation of your word."

"In that case, sir, if my definition of a religion doesn't match yours, perhaps there's a better term for Kelvonism. There's a word that defines the worship of living beings. That word is 'cult.' I put it to you that Kelvonism is a cult, built around me, and I want nothing to do with it! I demand that you release Brenna and me and return us to Kuw'baal."

Kozoltoo appeared to be utterly defeated. He stared at me for a full minute before replying.

"Very well, Kelvoo. I have failed to convey the importance of your presence and the pivotal role you would have had in the advancement of humanity on Terra. Nonetheless, your wisdom and your wishes shall prevail.

"If I could, I would return you and Brenna to Kuw'baal immediately, but as I mentioned, our planet lacks interstellar transport capabilities. We can recall a diplomatic shuttle from Planetary Alliance headquarters, but that will take time. The earliest we can transport you would be tomorrow evening. You and Brenna will be treated as honored guests tonight, and in the meantime, I hope you can forgive our stupidity."

"Thank you, Kozoltoo," I said, dropping the "high priest" label. "If you return us home tomorrow evening, there will be nothing to forgive. I can see that you're upset by my lack of enthusiasm for your cause, so I hope you'll forgive *me* for my reaction and for dashing your hopes. I would guess that your people's reverence toward me is due to your planet's long isolation, the trauma caused by war, and a need to unify around a central theme, which for some reason, is me.

"I hope the people of Terra will come to understand that every being has flaws, and I'm no exception. It's only my past circumstances that make me *appear* to be extraordinary. The people of this planet do not need to follow a religion or doctrine or however you would categorize Kelvonism. History shows that such movements get commandeered by individuals with their own interpretations, each declaring their version to be the absolute truth. This inevitably leads to conflict, violence, and suffering."

"I hear what you're saying, Kelvoo; I really do," Kozoltoo assured me. "But you'll never convince me that you're an ordinary being. Your teachings—I mean, writings—speak for themselves. Nevertheless, if you wish to leave us, and if you command that we dismantle our great movement, we shall abide by your wishes."

"I command nobody," I replied.

"You must understand, however," he continued, "it will be incredibly difficult, if not impossible, to dismantle what has been built over the last few decades. Can you imagine the damage to our society if I told the people that Kelvonism is false, and all their studies and practices had no purpose?"

"It's a terrible problem, Kozoltoo, but perhaps I can help with the process. Maybe I can speak with the people of Terra via vids and interviews and introduce them to reality over time. But I won't do so here on Terra. My physical presence isn't required. I can reach out to the Planetary Alliance, and perhaps we can all find a way to transition away from Kelvonism while achieving the goal of reintegrating Terra back into the interplanetary community."

With Kozoltoo looking despondent, our conversation shifted to a more conciliatory tone. We chatted about our past, our loved ones, and our hopes for the future. On some level, I took a liking to Kozoltoo, and I pitied him for his misguided expectations. Long after darkness had fallen, I explained that I needed to enter a meditative state since my internal clock was still attuned to the time on Kuw'baal.

"Goodnight Kelvoo," Kozoltoo said, "but before you retire, I have something for you." He retrieved two Infotabs from under his desk. "I believe these belong to you and Brenna. My apologies for our 'retrieval team' taking them from you. I hope they are still functional, though you'll find that you can't use them for communications. Unfortunately, Terra's comm networks use older technology, and we are not connected to the quantum entanglement network for interplanetary communications."

I put my device in its holster, which had dangled from my hip, empty, since Brenna and I were taken.

"If I may ask a favor, could you please authorize your Infotab to accept a document from me?" Kozoltoo inquired.

I complied with his request. "What did you send me?" I asked.

"A copy of the *Book of Kelvoo*. I hope you'll read it, if not for inspiration, then simply out of curiosity about how we've interpreted your writings, even though we may have been terribly misguided."

I was moved by Kozoltoo's sincerity, feeling sympathy for him. "I'd be pleased to read it," I said.

I reached across the desk, grasped one of his hands in both of my hand paddles, and bid him goodnight.

TEN: OTHER KELVOO

I stayed in my room only long enough to ingest a serving of algel, before making my way to Brenna's quarters with Pollybot in tow. Maria was on guard outside Brenna's door. I explained that I had to return Brenna's Infotab. Then I knocked on the door and announced my presence. Brenna opened the door, dressed in a nightgown and slippers, looking relieved to see me.

After she apologized for leaving the meeting, I told her that I understood how frustrating it must have been for her to hear Kozoltoo's nonsense. While Pollybot hovered close by, I recounted the remainder of the meeting and I assured Brenna that, in my assessment, we were in no physical danger. She was glad to know we would be returning to Kuw'baal the following evening. We both had been anxious about how our personal and professional acquaintances would react when they learned of our disappearance. We hoped we would return home before anyone realized we were missing—especially May and her extended family.

After we talked for a while, Brenna became sleepy. She asked me to stay the night in an adjoining room so we could both feel safer, then she retired to her luxurious bed.

Before starting my meditation, I read the *Book of Kelvoo*. The book was substantial and would have taken an average human more than forty-eight hours to read, but I was able to read and retain its contents in forty-three minutes.

The book began with a word-for-word copy of my original book, *Kelvoo's Testimonial*, chronicling my encounters with humans from first contact through my abduction, rescue, and return to Kuw'baal, concluding with the initial aftermath of first contact on my species and the suicide of my human friend and mentor, Samuel Buchanan.

The next section included a selection of notes I had kept over the next several years as my fellow abductees and I supported one another while we recovered and moved on from our traumatic experiences. This was followed by a summary of my doctoral thesis regarding my studies into human nature. I had created the summary as part of my teaching material, just prior to moving to Terra.

The next major section was a verbatim copy of my second memoir, *Kelvoo's Terra*, which told the story of my move to Terra with Brenna and May, my tenure as a professor at the Interplanetary University, the rise of the Human Independence Movement and its persecution of extraterrestrials on Terra, the subsequent coup, and my capture and eventual escape from Terra with my foster daughters.

The book concluded with a collection of documents that I wrote during my career in the Planetary Alliance—memos, procedural manuals, policy papers, analyses, and so forth. There was nothing special about the documents as they were all part of the public record across the Alliance.

In all, the sacred book of the Kelvonists was nothing more than accounts of past events and observations. The only additional content was on the final page. It advised readers to consult with their assigned Kelvonist instructor for the correct interpretation of my writings. The text also suggested regular attendance at a guidance center to "receive the supreme teachings of Kelvoo in their full context and truth."

Following the same pattern as most of the religious texts from human history, the *Book of Kelvoo* was little more than a curated collection of stories, letters, and documents, vague and open to interpretation.

Based on my conversation with Kozoltoo, and given the contents of the *Book of Kelvoo*, it seemed that Terra had united around the highly organized Kelvonist Society and its interpretations, which, to my relief, seemed to focus on peace and harmony, likely due to the trauma of past warfare.

When I finished reading, I assumed my meditative stance by the windows along the outer wall of Brenna's suite. My meditation that night was anything but restful. Seeing humans once again falling victim to superstition was tragic enough, but having such a thing happen *in my name* was unbearable. When my writings dealt with superstition or supernatural forces, they revealed my deeply negative viewpoint, often backed up with specific examples. None of that mattered. Here was a religion, founded on written words that opposed religion, but these ever-ingenious humans had engineered a simple workaround—the denial that their beliefs constituted a religion.

In all my dealings with humanity, this was the ultimate example of irony.

My meditation ended when Sol cleared the horizon and shone directly onto my eyelid. As I woke, the first sight that greeted me was the building with the golden dome, bathed in Sol's orange light. Having read the *Book of Kelvoo*, I realized the edifice was a Kelvonist "guidance center," though I would classify it as a place of worship or a temple. I saw several dozen humans, dressed in white, making their way along paths toward the lawns in front of the temple.

At Brenna's insistence, I had kept the door to her bedroom open, so we could watch over each other. Forty-two minutes after Sol rose in the east, Brenna stirred and groaned in response to a soft knock at the entrance to the suite. I opened the door to find Maria in her uniform.

"Good morning," she said.

"Do you ever sleep?" I asked.

"No," was her puzzling reply. "I've been asked to invite both of you to have breakfast with His Supreme Excellency at his residence. Fresh algel will be provided to you, and several choices of food will be available for Ms. Murphy. Please meet me here in one hour."

When I returned to Brenna, she was sitting up in bed. "How the hell am I supposed to make myself presentable in an hour?" she asked, having overheard the conversation.

At the appointed time, we met up with Maria and followed her to a vast balcony the size of a sports field. We boarded a waiting car, which descended over the edge of the balcony toward a complex of gleaming white structures to the rear of the temple below.

"Which of these buildings is Kozoltoo's residence?" I asked Maria.

"Why, all of them," she replied with a friendly smile.

We landed in a grassy courtyard and were led into a dining hall with a table that must have been three meters wide and twenty meters long. Thirty ornate chairs were placed on each side of the table and two were located at the head of the table with extra space between them. Humans in their now-familiar blue uniforms were standing behind fifty-nine of the chairs. As Maria walked toward an empty chair, Kozoltoo emerged. "Kelvoo, Brenna, please join us for breakfast as our most honored guests!" he announced.

Pollybot hovered just inside the large glass doors while Kozoltoo guided Brenna to a chair at the head of the table. He asked me to place myself between the chairs where an algel dispenser and a golden scoop and bowl were placed on the table. I assumed my usual kneeling position while Kozoltoo took the chair next to me. I surmised he was putting me in a symbolic position of power while he sat as my "right hand man."

Kozoltoo motioned to his staff. Each person took their seat in almost perfect unison.

Then he addressed the group, though his words were undoubtedly for my benefit. "As I said in our meeting this morning, Kelvoo made it abundantly clear that your praise, obedience, and fawning is neither desired nor welcome. Thank you for your restraint.

"As you also know, Kelvoo and Brenna have made it clear that they wish to return to Kuw'baal, and I have arranged for that to happen this evening."

I saw a subtle shift in the staff's facial expressions, indicating sadness.

"Having said that . . ." Kozoltoo continued, "our guests are free to change their minds anytime between now and then. Let us show them our utmost respect and love in the hope that they'll extend their visit."

Kozoltoo stood and applauded, every staffer following suit.

When the group took their seats, bots with hovercarts entered the hall. They made short work of unloading the carts, which were heaped with breakfast items that humans would likely describe as "sumptuous."

Throughout the display of hospitality, Brenna remained stone-faced and silent as she tolerated the proceedings and looked forward to our departure. She must have been famished, though, since she didn't hesitate to help herself to a large assortment of food and beverages. Kozoltoo made typical human small talk, asking us whether our accommodations were adequate, whether we were sufficiently rested, and so on. At the same time, the other diners spoke softly with one another, filling the hall with the sound of conversation and the light clanking of cutlery and porcelain.

Kozoltoo clapped three times, and the assembly fell silent. He invited each member of his staff to stand and introduce themselves.

"My name is Sylvia. I hope you'll extend your visit."

"I'm Omar. You are loved throughout Terra."

"I'm called Reinhart. Welcome Kelvoo and Brenna."

"My name is Monique. Your presence honors us beyond words."

The introductions continued up one side of the table and down the other. Each person spoke politely and clearly, nodding to me when they were done. Out of respect, I nodded back, using my eye dome to do so. The absence of praise was a welcome change.

By the time the dishes were being cleared, Brenna was more engaged, and her stern demeanor had softened.

When Kozoltoo stood, so did his staff. Brenna and I followed his lead. "All of you, please remain here," he said to his staff. "I'll spend a moment with our guests and then I will return to meet with all of you. In the meantime, Kelvoo, if you and Brenna would accompany me, there's someone who would like to greet you."

Kozoltoo led us to a glass wall and doors on the side of the dining hall opposite to where we entered. The doors led to a courtyard with curving paths, manicured gardens, and a few statues. A lone figure in a robe stood in the farthest corner. A pergola, adorned with flowering vines, covered the courtyard. Sol shone through in dappled patches, and the air was filled with the fragrance of blossoms. I had never understood the appeal of floral scents, but I saw Brenna close her eyes and inhale deeply through her nose. She seemed to become more relaxed as she savored the intense aroma.

"Kozoltoo," I said, "when you addressed your staff, you said you were hopeful that we would change our minds and stay longer. When we ended our conversation last night, you seemed to understand that we had no intention of staying. Has something changed?"

"Well, for one thing," Kozoltoo said, "I stayed up late and studied your teachings in the context of our conversation and your wonderful visit—"

"When you say 'teachings,' I think you mean random written documents, and when you say 'visit,' I think you mean abduction," I interjected.

"Well, I'm sorry you still see it that way, Kelvoo, but as I was saying, your . . . *documents* convinced me that you're destined to remain here for a while. I take it you had a chance to browse through the *Book of Kelvoo*?"

"I did not 'browse' through it; I read it in its entirety."

Kozoltoo smiled. "Then surely you understand now why we see you as a divine being!"

"Not in the slightest."

Kozolotoo's smile did not change. "Well, I'm counting on you to 'come around' in the next few hours, but for now, there's somebody I'd like both of you to meet."

He motioned to the robed person across the courtyard, who strode toward us.

"Kelvoo, I'm pleased to reintroduce you to Kelvoo!" Kozoltoo announced.

The man before me was in his sixties. His slightly curly hair and facial stubble were speckled with grey. I could tell right away that he was the son of Sam Buchanan, my teacher and friend from human first contact. Sam's son was born on Kuw'baal while I was a captive on *Jezebel's Fury*. Since Sam assumed that I had perished, he and his partner, Lynda Paige, named their son Kelvoo Buchanan-Paige in my honor.

"Please, call me Kelly," my namesake said as he shook my hand paddle.

"I'll let the three of you get reacquainted," Kozoltoo said as he returned to the dining hall.

Kelly's presence brought many of my memories to the forefront, along with the deep feelings that they invoked. I recalled the moment when Sam told me about his son. "We named him in memory of my hero," Sam had said. The gratitude I felt at that moment was tinged with guilt as I felt I had done nothing to deserve such an honor.

The first time I saw Kelly in person was seven years after Sam's horrific suicide. By that time, Kelly was in his early teens. Brenna, May, and I had just moved to Terra where the university hosted a reception for me immediately after they announced my employment. Many of my human friends from first contact were in attendance, including Lynda Paige, who had served as chief navigator on the *Pacifica Spirit*. Lynda brought her son to the reception so he could meet the being after whom he was named. When Lynda introduced me to her son, he was shy, clearly feeling awkward as he expressed disdain for his late father's alcoholism. I reassured him that his father had been intelligent, kind, and a great friend of mine despite his personal flaws, which eventually culminated in his death.

The last time I had seen Kelly was during my rescue from prison in a Human Independence Movement "devotion center". As the Terran civil war raged, I was captured and taken to the devotion center's medical clinic where I was held while recuperating from near-fatal injuries. As soon as I was well enough, I was thrown into a prison where I was interrogated and tortured on a regular basis.

A group of resistance commandos blasted a hole in the prison's outer wall, rescuing me and dozens of other political prisoners. One of the commandos guided me into the forest as guards fired at us. As he helped me into a freight pod to take me to safety, he removed his mask and revealed that he was Kelly. He was still a teenager. I admired his courage, but I was saddened that someone so young had been thrust into the brutal insanity of a needless war.

My reverie was interrupted when Kelly turned to Brenna. "I don't imagine you'd remember me from the party at the university," he said as he shook her hand.

"I do, actually!" she replied. "Kelvoo's first contact friends were in a group, and they all wanted to meet May and me. They'd read about us in Kelvoo's first book, but they hadn't met us in person. I remember seeing Kelvoo talking with you. He told me who you were a couple of days later."

"I remember you well," Kelly replied. "You were wearing a beautiful white dress with a low back. When you got out on the dance floor, all the guys and a few girls wanted to dance with you."

"Mercifully, I don't remember any of that," Brenna said, chuckling for the first time since we had been taken from my home. "I had been downing glasses of wine all night," she continued, "so by then I was out of it! I puked my guts out when I got home, and I suffered for the entire day after that!"

Kelly laughed and then turned to me. "I'll give you one guess as to why His Supreme Excellency brought me here to see you," he said.

"Could it be that you're here to talk sense into me?"

"It could very well be, Kelvoo. Why don't the three of us have a chat in the gazebo?" He motioned for us to follow him into the garden.

We ambled along the path with Pollybot close behind. On the way, we passed a gleaming white stone statue of a kloormar that was about double my size. "What do you think?" Kelly asked, motioning to the statue.

"I think that's me," I said. "Apart from the scale, it's so accurate that I'd say it was based on an actual scan of my body. They probably got the data a long time ago from a security scan as I passed through a spaceport. I also think it's a travesty!"

"A travesty?"

"Yes. It's idolatry, plain and simple. I'm sorry if that offends you, Kelly, but I utterly reject the notion that I should be worshipped. Nothing good can come of it!"

Without responding, Kelly continued to the next statue along the path. "Do either of you recognize this one?"

The statue depicted a young woman with a slender build, smooth skin, and long hair flowing down her bare back.

"It looks like statues from ancient Terra that I've seen in museums," Brenna replied. "It looks like a goddess of beauty that would have been worshipped in an old civilization. If I remember my ancient history lessons accurately, it looks like something from ancient Greece or maybe the Roman Empire."

"No, Brenna. That's supposed to be you!"

"What the hell?" Brenna blurted, aghast. "I look nothing like that!"

"I'm afraid you can blame me for that," Kelly said. "You see, after the war ended and the Kelvonist Society was emerging, they commissioned a statue of you. The problem was, there were no accessible images of you, and no artists had ever laid eyes on you. They knew I'd seen you at the university because it was mentioned in *Kelvoo's Terra*. So, they brought me in to work with a sculptor. I protested that I had only seen you for a few minutes, many years in the past, but that was good enough for them."

"So, this is how you remembered me? I'm not sure whether I should feel complimented or horrified," Brenna said, laughing.

"Please keep in mind that I was thirteen years old at the time. I thought you were one of the most beautiful creatures I'd ever seen, but I was way too shy and awkward to even consider approaching you. So, I'm sorry if you don't like the way you're depicted, but look on the bright side . . ."

"The bright side?"

"I didn't see what you looked like the next morning."

Brenna and Kelly laughed, lightening the mood considerably and providing me with some relief from my anxiety.

"So, why the hell would they create a statue of me in the first place?" Brenna asked. "Ambassador Muller and Kozoltoo said I'm loved and revered on Terra. How's that even possible? If they've read Kelvoo's stories, they'll know I abandoned Kelvoo and May when I was suckered in by some evil people."

"Because they also know that your conscience paid a heavy price. The people of Terra know you took ownership of your mistakes, that Kelvoo forgave you unconditionally, and that you've spent the rest of your life engaging in charitable work. On Terra you set the example of taking personal responsibility for mistakes, and you symbolize redemption, humility, and atonement."

"That makes me extremely uncomfortable," Brenna replied.

"Which is exactly the kind of humility that your admirers would expect," Kelly countered.

When we arrived outside the gazebo, we saw the third statue.

"Alright, that's definitely May when she was a kid," Brenna said, "but that sure is an odd pose!"

May's likeness was positioned in what I would call a heroic stance. Her feet were rooted on the simulated ground and were spread apart so they were directly below each shoulder. Her hands were balled into fists, and planted on her hips, with her elbows sticking out. Her head was tilted up and to her right as her eyes looked skyward while her mouth and jaw were firmly set. The only thing missing was a billowing cape, sculpted onto her shoulders.

I agreed that May's likeness was a close resemblance, even though I had never seen her in such a stance. "What do Terrans admire about May?" I asked.

"She represents honesty, virtue, and strength of character," Kelly said.

"If she were standing here, seeing this and hearing us, she'd probably be laughing her head off!" Brenna said as we entered the gazebo.

Kelly took a seat on a bench that ran along the gazebo wall. He looked up at Brenna and patted the space beside him. Brenna sat beside Kelly, and I squatted across from them. "So, you're going to talk sense into us now," I said. "Is that right?"

"Before we do anything, there's one matter we need to take care of," he replied. Kelly pulled out his Infotab and entered text onto the screen. He showed the text to Brenna and me, shielding the screen with the palm of his hand, presumably to hide it from prying eyes.

```
I need to see your bot up close. Please.
```

Pollybot had been hovering just outside the gazebo.

"Pollybot, come to me," Brenna commanded.

As Pollybot approached, Kelly reached inside the left sleeve of his robe and pulled out a small disk-shaped object. When Pollybot stopped in front of Brenna, Kelly touched it with the object.

Brenna and I watched in horror as a buzz came from the object and a snap emanated from Pollybot, which shut down instantly and fell. Kelly caught Pollybot before it hit the ground, then set it on the floor where it lay on its side, inert and unresponsive.

"You goddamn bastard!" Brenna cried, leaping to her feet. "You killed Pollybot!"

ELEVEN: ALTAR EGO

Brenna's face was a mask of fury, and her fists were clenched with anger. Before she could scream with rage, Kelly grabbed her wrist. "Wait," he said in an urgent whisper. "Your bot is fine, but it's been spying on you. I'm about to fix that!"

"I think I might know what he's talking about," I said. "On our way to Terra, I was wondering how Ambassador Muller and his hired abductors knew when I'd be at home alone. I've also wondered about the ambassador's eagerness to bestow the 'gift' of Pollybot on us. Now the pieces are fitting together. Pollybot must have been part of a back-up plan to use if I turned down Ambassador Muller's invitation!"

I turned to Kelly. "This bot has been transmitting our coordinates, hasn't it?"

"Your coordinates, your movements, your conversations, all of it!" Kelly said. "It's been transmitting live vid and audio from the moment you were reunited with it. When you were orbiting Kuw'baal on *Platform 313*, it was transmitting to the Terran embassy office.

"How long have you known about this?" I asked.

"Not long. I was given the details yesterday when Kozoltoo asked me to speak with you."

"So, the day we were taken, the person monitoring the bot's transmission would have known that Brenna had left for Newton. When they noticed Brenna's early return to my home, it must have been too late to abort the mission to extract us," I concluded.

Brenna hardly seemed to notice the conversation as she sat back down. "Oh, Pollybot!" she said as she stroked the inert bot's outer shell. I pitied Brenna, even though I had never understood the human trait of assigning emotions to objects.

"Don't worry. Your 'Pollybot' will be alright," Kelly assured her. He pulled a multi-gadget wand from under the same sleeve where he had kept the bot deactivator, then he ran it over Pollybot, causing a hatch on the bot's side to open.

"I'm replacing a sub-processor," Kelly said as he removed a module from Pollybot. "This one's been tampered with."

"Oh! So, you're some kind of quantum control genius, are you?" Brenna said.

"Hell no! I just happen to surround myself with some exceptionally smart people," Kelly replied.

"Before I reactivate your bot, I need you to understand that the information I'm about to share puts me at enormous risk, but it's obvious that you find Kelvonism as ridiculous as I do, so I'm going to take a chance by telling you that there are those of us who find the whole thing dangerously ignorant. I'm trusting you to keep that to yourselves."

"You can trust us," Brenna said, "at least for now."

"It's comforting to know that the *entire* population of Terra hasn't lost its mind," I added.

Kelly put his index finger over a switch on the inside surface of Pollybot's access hatch. "I'm going to reactivate your bot now," he explained. "I don't think its transmissions are being monitored here on Terra, but to be safe, the replacement module no longer contains the code that was added to spy on you. Now that the Kelvonist Society has you where they want you, they don't need to keep monitoring you."

Kelly tapped the switch, and Pollybot hummed back to life and hovered in front of us. "Luxor P1 Servitor Bot initializing," it said in a basic electronic voice that lacked intonation. A few seconds later, it indicated that it was loading its modules. "Ready," Pollybot said in its familiar friendly voice.

I asked the bot to identify itself, Brenna, and me. "My assigned designation is 'Pollybot'. The female human is Brenna. You are Kelvoo."

"We can speak freely," Kelly said, looking relieved.

"Look, Kelly," Brenna said, "I don't know what's going on here. Kozoltoo introduced you, and the Kelvonists supposedly trust you, but now you're saying you're against them. You also seem to know a hell of a lot about their plan to bring us here. Whose side are you on?"

"We don't have a lot of time," Kelly replied, "so let me give you the story as briefly as I can.

"I'm a high-ranking member of the Kelvonist Society. They've made me wealthy and famous, but like you, Kelvoo, I don't want the attention."

He paused, looking back at the path. "The society was created about twenty years after the war ended. When Kelvonism started, it was called the Peace Movement, and it was nothing more than a viewpoint shared by a large portion of the humans who survived the war. We believed our species had flaws that had caused suffering to other beings, and we thought it would be best to reduce that suffering by isolating ourselves until we got our proverbial house in order.

"Kelvoo, as the most famous extraterrestrial on Terra at the start of the war, your struggles symbolized the negative impact of humanity on others. The Peace Movement admired your species' embrace of logic and learning. When we read *Kelvoo's Testimonial*, we suffered along with you when you learned about the dark side of humanity and experienced the terrible consequences. Your books gave us an outsider's view of ourselves, which provided us with insight and self-awareness.

"Please don't misunderstand me, Kelvoo; it's not as though we thought you were some kind of god back then. You were simply an important historical figure whom we admired. Sure, some people wanted to elevate you to 'supreme being' status, but their zealotry was kept in check by most of the people who had survived the war, especially those of us who experienced the brutality of combat. Sadly, not many of us were left alive, and a sizable number of those people moved to other worlds before Terra became fully isolated.

"As you know, I was an underage soldier in the rebellion. My fellow warriors were considerably older and most of them have passed. As our influence diminished, along with our numbers, younger factions in the Peace Movement started promoting the idea that you were something more than a normal member of your species. I don't know why, but the movement exploded. Soon, it was renamed the Kelvonist Society, and Terrance Chang—Kozoltoo—seized control. Frankly, the movement has lost its original meaning and intent, and the whole thing's out of control now."

"Excuse me, Kelly," I said, "but what's your role in the society?"

"I'm what they call a founding member or a legacy follower. Anyone who ever had even the slightest contact with you is held in reverence. I'm the last founding member. Anyone else on Terra who saw you in person had left a long time ago or has died. Also, bearing the name 'Kelvoo' has elevated me to an almost mystical level."

"Would I be correct in assuming that 'Kelvoo' has become a popular name on Terra?"

"No! Your name is held in such reverence that naming a baby after you would be akin to blasphemy! They make an exception for me because my parents were your friends, and you wrote about being honored that I was named after you."

"You told us earlier that the Kelvonist Society has made you wealthy," I said. "How did that happen?"

"Once the society was formed, I was provided with housing and a generous regular income. I've also been granted exclusive access to business and investment opportunities, and I've made full use of them."

"And what have you had to do in exchange?"

"Nothing. Not a damned thing! Out of courtesy, I make a few speeches and spout a few platitudes. All I do is demonstrate my success and serve as a trophy for mainstream Kelvonism."

"What do you mean by 'mainstream' Kelvonism? Are there other varieties?"

"Yes, Kelvoo. Telling you this would be frowned upon, but there's a splinter group—the Reformed Kelvonists. They're a much smaller organization and, officially at least, they've been ignored. I don't know how much longer that'll last because they pose a potential threat to the mainstream group's monopoly on your so-called 'teachings.'"

"So, this is how it starts, isn't it?" Brenna asked. "This is how religious movements start splitting, with each side thinking it represents the one and only truth!"

"That's right," Kelly said. "I know it, those Terrans who fought alongside me knew it, and anyone who hasn't spent decades in isolation here on Terra knows it. But the concept has been lost on everyone else, given how ignorant of the past most Terrans are. I know where this is likely headed and I don't want to end up on the wrong side of history. That's why I'm not going to play along with Kozoltoo's plan. Instead, I'm going to try to help you."

"Kelly," I said, "I appreciate everything you're telling us, and I'm grateful for your willingness to help, but I'm afraid it's all for naught. You see, Kozoltoo has agreed to return us to Kuw'baal tonight."

"Are you sure about that, Kelvoo?"

"Do you know otherwise?"

"I don't know what's going to happen. You see, Kozoltoo is certain that you'll change your mind. If I'm not able to do it, he's sure the next event will convince you."

"What event are you talking about?" Brenna asked, an apprehensive look on her face.

"Have you noticed the amount of traffic overhead?" he replied.

"Yes, I've noticed it growing in intensity," I said, "but I'm unfamiliar with traffic patterns in this area. Are we seeing an abnormal level of activity?"

I certainly had been aware of vehicles passing above us, with the volume of traffic increasing steadily. From the top of my eye dome, I could see cars through the gaps between the vines and flowers covering the pergola. When our meeting started, the shadows from lower-flying vehicles would occasionally make the light flicker, but now, Sol's light kept flashing as hundreds of vehicles passed over, with traffic flowing at multiple altitudes.

"They're all heading to the big event!" Kelly said.

"Would that event happen to be at the temple?" Brenna asked.

"Temple?" Kelly replied, frowning in confusion.

"I believe Brenna is referring to the guidance center," I said.

"Oh, yes. I suppose you could refer to it as a temple," Kelly replied. "Anyhow, Kelvoo, next on the agenda today is for Kozoltoo's staff to take you to the 'temple' and present you to your loyal followers. All those cars above are trying to land anywhere they can, so people can get as close as possible to the guidance center, just to catch a glimpse of you. They'll be shutting down the airspace shortly before your appearance, so the Autonav system in each vehicle will prevent entry into the area."

"This is bad, Pa!" Brenna said. "I don't like where this is going!"

"What's the purpose of my appearance?" I asked.

"It's intended to be the first step in the fulfillment of your prophecy."

"What prophecy?"

"The one that ends with: 'the timeless bedrock guards its secrets, locked away and sealed, but when upheaval splits the mantle, all shall be revealed.'"

I could hardly believe what I was hearing. "But, Kelly, that's just a verse from a poem I wrote about the upheaval event on Kuw'baal. I was referring to new geological features that would be exposed due to the tidal forces from Ryla 6."

"I know, but that's not how the Kelvonists see it. They believe the upheaval was a cosmic event of great supernatural significance. They've been planning for your return for a long time. When Ambassador Muller sent your poem to the Kelvonist Society, they saw it as a sign that the time of your return was at hand. When they read the final line, 'all shall be revealed,' they believe you're destined to reveal the true path that humans must follow to achieve your level of 'perfection.'"

"In that case, the human home world has gone mad," I said.

Kelly nodded.

"So, what happens if I refuse to address the crowd or what if I tell them that Kelvonism is foolish, and I command them to stop?"

"I don't know, but I'm guessing that Kozoltoo has planned for that possibility."

"So, what do *you* suggest?" Brenna asked, looking at Kelly.

"As far as I can tell, you have two choices. The first option is to play along. Just tell them I've convinced you to stay longer, see where all of this goes, and try to escape from the stupidity. I'm sure your friends on Kuw'baal and the Planetary Alliance will realize you're missing and then they'll investigate. At some point the momentous news of your arrival on Terra is bound to leak out, and your return will be demanded. Your other choice is to refuse to cooperate and see what happens."

"I'm *not* going to play along, Kelly. Enough damage has already been done in my name. Experience has taught me that the situation will only worsen if I cooperate."

"I knew that's what you'd say," Kelly replied. "I also know you're right."

"I'm guessing that you don't expect us to be leaving tonight, do you, Kelly?"

"You need to understand, Kelvoo; Kozoltoo believes the Kelvonist interpretation of your writing. He believes in the prophecy that foretold your presence here. He thinks you'll remain on Terra long enough to reveal the true path, whatever that's supposed to be. My impression is that he's so certain you'll be convinced to stay that he hasn't made any arrangements for your departure. I guess we're going to have to wait and see what happens."

At that moment, we heard the crunch of footsteps on the path from the dining hall to the gazebo. Then Maria called us. "It's time! We need you to come back inside."

"We're on our way," Kelly shouted back. Then he turned to us. "Ready?"

"No," I replied.

"Hell no!" Brenna said.

The three of us stood and walked back into the hall anyway.

When we entered, we found Kozoltoo's staff lined up to the left and right of the doors. They snapped to attention as we entered. Kozoltoo was waiting at the end of the lines.

"So," he said, smiling at me, "was your namesake able to convince you to extend your visit?"

"He made many great and passionate arguments for the Kelvonist Society," I replied.

"So, you'll stay a while longer?"

"No," I replied, "we will not."

Kozoltoo bowed his head. "Very well," he said. "We have a few more people for you to meet before you leave us. Well, I'd better make that a few *million* more people." He looked at me with a mischievous smile. "James will lead the way," he said, motioning to the member of his staff closest to him. "Maria, close the airspace, and divert all incoming traffic." Maria pulled an Infotab from her jacket and entered some commands into it.

"No!" I replied. "Enough of this. I refuse to comply with your request."

"Take Kelvoo and fulfill the prophecy!" Kozoltoo shouted.

The blue jackets swarmed toward me from both sides. "As your leader, I command you to stop and to disregard the orders issued by Kozoltoo!" I shouted.

My command was ignored as members of Kozoltoo's staff seized me.

"What the hell is going on?" Brenna shouted. "Release Kelvoo now!"

Kelly grasped Brenna by her shoulders. "Just let it happen, Brenna," he said. "It'll be alright."

"My staff respects you completely," Kozoltoo said to me. "We have anticipated the possibility that you would resist, but your own prophecy must be fulfilled. Then you'll see why this action is necessary, and that's when you'll decide to grace us with your presence and your leadership. If the event that's about to unfold doesn't convince you, you'll be returned to your home world as promised, but I know that you'll decide to stay. It has been foretold. It is your destiny!"

Kozoltoo turned to his entire staff. "Take our wise, glorious, and beloved guest to fulfill the prophecy!"

Kozoltoo's staff propelled me down a ramp at the end of the hall and into a subterranean tunnel that ran toward the temple. Pollybot followed the crowd. "Danger! Stop your action!" it repeated.

I heard an exclamation of pain from Kelly. Through the back of my eye dome, I saw him grasp his shin as Brenna broke free and chased after the mob. "Pa! Pa!" she shouted. "Let me through, you bastards!" Despite her shoving and punching, she couldn't break through the cordon that surrounded me.

The crowd of jabbering, excited humans, dressed in blue jackets, swept me along the wide corridor and up the ramp onto the expansive stage in the high temple. Some of the humans beamed with happiness while others cried with joy. An altar constructed from a massive slab of gleaming white rock supported by sheets of glass stood at the center of the huge circular, domed chamber. The humans lifted me over their heads and slid me onto the altar.

That was when I was presented, on the flying altar, to the millions of insane, raving worshippers. Kozoltoo introduced me, and the crowd sang its absurd hymn, praising me. Then the altar rose above the clouds and swept me far away.

TWELVE: AN INCONVENIENT RESCUE

After twenty minutes of high-altitude flight, I started to wonder whether the altar had a destination. *Perhaps it has malfunctioned and will keep moving until long after I've died from exposure or malnourishment,* I thought. The airflow buffeted me, making me uncomfortable, so I crouched below the glass barrier that ran along the altar's leading edge.

Moments later, I detected a white triangular craft high above and on the same trajectory as the altar. Thirty minutes later, when the altar had descended to a few hundred meters above ground, three buses approached and flew parallel to me as the white craft turned away.

When my altitude decreased to about one hundred meters, the buses pulled ahead of me, turned to the south, and landed in a forest. The altar followed, and I saw a clearing with a few low buildings on an expansive lawn. Humans in robes were walking along a path from the buses to a building. Brenna was being escorted by the group, and Pollybot followed.

The altar hovered beside the buses, about thirty centimeters above the lawn. The glass walls folded outward, forming clear ramps down to the grass on each side of the altar.

Kozoltoo emerged from double doors on the building at the end of the path. He extended his arms to me as I walked toward him. "Kelvoo!" he exclaimed with a broad smile. "Welcome! Welcome!"

As I entered, Kozoltoo's staff greeted me with cheers and applause. Unlike our previous meeting, they did not line up or snap to attention. They just stood in place, smiling, and clapping and looking at ease, evoking a calm, casual atmosphere. Brenna looked concerned as she made her way to my side, then she smiled with relief as she held one of my arms and Pollybot hovered on the opposite side of me.

"Welcome to Keeto Retreat," Kozoltoo said. "Each of our retreats are named for a kloormar that you mentioned in your writings."

"What is the purpose of these places?" I asked.

"Our retreats are for Kelvonist staff and supporters to escape the pressures of life and reconnect with ourselves through study and meditation. Of course, since our human brains aren't as sophisticated as yours, and we only have one brain apiece, we can't achieve the same type or depth of meditation as a kloormar. Nevertheless, we do our best here to rejuvenate and refocus. Now, let's move to the conversation zone and talk about where we go from here."

Kozoltoo motioned the crowd to move farther into the building. The structure was a spacious, single-level building with a flat roof. Floor-to-ceiling glass lined the outer walls, and circular skylights provided light for indoor trees and shrubs. The floor sloped gently between areas that were defined by groupings of furniture and equipment instead of walls. Through the windows I saw palm trees with fronds that rustled in the breeze next to ponds and flowering bushes. I appreciated how relaxing the surroundings would be for humans and kloormari alike.

The conversation zone was a circular section of floor that was lower than the surrounding area. The circle was delineated by steps that led down on all sides. The treads were covered with soft floor coverings, making them suitable as seats, forming a small amphitheater.

Brenna and Pollybot stayed by my side as Kozoltoo guided me to the center of the area. His staff sat on the stairs, around us.

"Ah, Kelvoo!" Kozoltoo exclaimed with a joyous smile, "Now that you have witnessed and felt the love from the citizens of Terra, we can all move forward as you fulfill your wonderful prophecy and lead us into a new era! There are plans to be made and there is so much to do! Yes, yes! We shall all work together to serve you! No expense is too great, and no effort is too much! The time has come for you to lead us! Please, great one, we beseech you to tell us your vision and share your plan with all of us."

My frustration reemerged. With everything I had gone through, I thought I would have had more emotional control, but I was at a breaking point as I stepped forward to address the crowd.

"My vision and my plan call for Brenna Murphy and me to return to Kuw'baal," I began. "As for all of you and your Kelvonist Society, my vision and plan command you to stop this foolishness and to start thinking rationally! Don't you understand? I don't wish to be your leader, your advisor, your guide, or your inspiration! Your worship of me has been a total waste of your time! Give it up! I denounce Kelvonism and the insanity on which it's based! For the sake of your planet, your future, and every one of you, just stop!"

My words had a shattering effect. The joy that had been bubbling out of the Kelvonists fell flat, followed by several gasps and a few muffled sobs. At that moment, I realized my frustration had pushed me too far. Nonetheless, the damage was done, and I knew that if I backtracked, the longer-term situation would be far worse. I stood still and let the awkward silence linger.

"Why do you persist in testing us?" Kozoltoo demanded, sounding as angry and frustrated as I was. "What will it take, Kelvoo? What do you need from us to convince you? What have we done wrong? How have we offended you?"

"Tell us!" a staff member exclaimed.

"What if Kelvoo's right?" another shouted.

"No! Kelvoo is *not* right!" Kozoltoo yelled.

By then, several members of Kozoltoo's staff were crying. Some ran from the room, sobbing, while others stormed out. At first the severity of their reactions surprised me, but then I realized I was threatening the very foundations of their beliefs, which had been central to their lives and identities. About half the crowd remained as the conversation zone became a verbal warzone with newly formed factions engaged in heated debate.

"It's not possible!"

"We were arrogant and blind!"

"No! It's just a test! Have faith!"

"Kelvoo! How could you betray us?"

"I believe in you, Kelvoo! There must be an explanation!"

The shouting continued for several minutes until a female staffer ran into the room, screaming. "No! No! It's . . . Oh no! I can't . . ." She pointed through a set of doors as tears streamed down her cheeks.

As a group, we followed the young woman. In a panicked state, she led us through rooms and corridors to another large open space at the far end of the building. Up ahead, the ceiling was raised for a set of stairs that curved up to a rooftop patio. When we reached the perimeter of the stairs, we saw a pair of legs dangling in the stairwell. When we got closer, we were horrified to see a lifeless body, hanging under one side of the stairs. Nearby, several ceremonial robes were visible in an open closet. A belt from a robe was fastened around the victim's neck while the other end of the belt was tied to a baluster below the stairway's handrail.

A staff member was on the stairs, trying to untie the belt, but the weight of the body had tightened the knot, making the task extremely difficult.

"Pollybot! Cut the belt!" Brenna shouted.

"Please specify the belt to be cut," the bot replied.

"The one around the man's neck!"

"Please specify which man—"

"Goddamn it! Just cut him down!" Brenna screamed.

"Pollybot," I interjected, "sever the belt that is restraining the human male I am pointing toward, so he will fall to the floor."

Pollybot rose. A flap opened on its side, and an armature emerged with a small rotating blade attachment. When the belt was cut and the man fell, three Kelvonists grabbed his legs, but the momentum of the man's mass caused him to flip upside down. His head struck the white floor tiles with a sickening crack.

His body laid there, face up. It was obvious the man was dead, his bulging, bloodshot, lifeless eyes staring blindly at the skylight above the stairwell. If his heart had still been beating, blood would have flowed from his scalp where it was split open. Instead, there was just a small smear of blood, which was almost black, indicating the absence of oxygen due to asphyxiation. The man's throat had been crushed. Livid contusions surrounded his neck and spread up into his face.

The horror of the scene was too much for many of the Kelvonists. A few of them cried or screamed. One vomited, and others ran away. Brenna covered her mouth, closed her eyes, and leaned against a wall, slumping to the floor. I've heard that humans who are familiar with violent death and destruction learn to cope with the emotional trauma over time. That was the case for me during the Terran civil war, but this was different. Half a century had passed since my escape from Terra, but the scene before me brought the memories to the forefront, and the terror and revulsion returned with a merciless vengeance.

I sat on the floor next to Brenna and I pulled my knees up to my chest. My respiration spiked, my vision narrowed and darkened, and my limbs tingled as the noises around me faded into muffled, indecipherable sounds.

As I regained my senses, I realized Brenna was holding my shoulders, and I sensed Kozoltoo leaning over me. "Look at what you've done!" he exclaimed, droplets of spittle hitting my eye. "Poor Peter. He couldn't take it anymore after you dashed his hopes! You've done it to all of us. Your prophecy was false. Your teachings were lies and they've ruined our planet. You've destroyed our people and our civilization. It's all your fault! How could you mislead us? Tell me why, you damned alien!"

I was in no condition to respond. I couldn't make sense of the horror as the emotional mayhem unfolded before me. My senses tuned out most of the information that was flooding them, but through the large skylight above the stairwell, I observed a white triangular craft, high above. As Kozoltoo berated me, his head intermittently blocked my view of the skylight, but I glimpsed the craft three times as it stood out against the clear blue Terran sky. I could tell that the craft was the same type that had followed high above me when the altar brought me there.

My trance was broken when a staff member named Bjorn pulled Kozoltoo away from me. "Stop it!" he shouted. "Maybe we were all mistaken about the role that Kelvoo was supposed to play. Maybe Kelvoo's writings were just random documents that we interpreted as prophecy. That doesn't diminish Kelvoo's accomplishments or the example of Kelvoo's life! Maybe we got things wrong. That doesn't mean we can't learn while Kelvoo is still in our presence!"

Bjorn's statements drew me back to reality, though I had to tilt my eye dome, so the dead human was obscured from my view.

Bjorn's words seemed to steady the other Kelvonists. Their grief over Peter's death remained, but those who had been angry calmed down. As they gathered around me, Kozoltoo's anger drained from his face, and he knelt beside me. "I'm sorry, Kelvoo," he said with a downcast look. "I'm sorry for everything."

"What's that?" someone shouted. Through the glass wall, we watched as a white triangular craft touched down on the lawn. Two more similar craft landed farther along the side of the building. I heared two additional craft, landing on the opposite side of the building.

Humans carrying large sticks, poured out of the vessels. Unlike the Kelvonist Society members, they were dressed in everyday Terran garb. They surrounded the building and used their sticks to shatter the glass walls and charge inside.

"Danger! Stop your action!" Pollybot said, repeating the warning over and over again.

The confused, terrified group huddled together as scores of invaders surrounded us.

"Pollybot, stop," Brenna commanded in a shaky voice, silencing the bot's repeating message.

Some of the invaders recoiled when they saw the body of the suicide victim. I realized that, despite their attack, the Terrans had experienced relative peace and were not used to seeing death and gore. *That's why they're using sticks*, I thought. *This planet has no "real" weapons of war!*

An invader stepped forward. "You will release Kelvoo immediately!" she demanded.

Kozoltoo stood and placed himself between her and me. "We shall do no such thing!"

Some of the invaders at the front of the group raised their sticks with the clear intent of striking Kozoltoo.

"Stop!" I shouted, making the attackers freeze and everyone near me clutch their ears. "What do you want with me?" I asked, lowering my voice.

"We're here to rescue you," the woman replied. "We know you were taken against your will by these misguided fools and forced into posing as their god. We're going to save you," she said.

"Through violence?" I asked. "As much as I would like to return to my home, why should I trust a mob of stick-wielding humans?"

"Kelvoo, please! It's obvious these evil people have brainwashed you! Please understand that they kidnapped you. Also, remember your past and the horrors you've experienced at the hands of zealots."

"A moment ago, you called these Kelvonists misguided fools," I replied, "and now you're calling them evil. Let's calm down for a moment. I agree they're misguided and, much to their distress, I think they're starting to realize it, but they are not evil!"

"Then how do they explain *that*?" an attacker shouted, pointing to Peter's body.

"It isn't what it looks like," Kozoltoo said, using a well-worn human cliché.

"It's exactly what it looks like!" the attacker shouted. "Save Kelvoo!"

The attackers roared as their sticks came down on heads or were thrust forward to bludgeon the Kelvonists. I recoiled, grasping Brenna with my upper limbs and all my claspers, wrapping my torso around her to protect her amid the screaming and shouting and the crack of sticks striking human bodies.

Two attackers pulled my torso while others pulled Brenna in the opposite direction, tearing her from my grasp. I was held down, but Brenna had remarkable strength, surprising the attackers who hadn't expected a human of her age to wriggle free. She was stumbling back toward me when she was struck in the shoulder that had been injured during our initial abduction. Brenna fell to the floor.

I struggled against my new captors, but I was held fast, then dragged away from Brenna as she curled up and groaned in pain. My fear turned into impotent rage, as I reached toward Brenna while demanding my release. Pollybot's alarm added to the turmoil as the bot followed me. "Pollybot, stay with Brenna! Protect her!" I shouted. Pollybot returned to hover beside Brenna.

I was hustled through a broken section of the glass wall and shoved into one of the triangular craft where my upper and lower limbs were quickly shackled. Through the hatch, I saw attackers retreating toward their vessels, some being pursued by the few Kelvonists who weren't injured. A few attackers were limping or trying to crawl toward the vessels, injured by Kelvonists who had fought back. It became clear that they would be left behind. My mind was consumed with worry about Brenna, and I felt desperately alone, crowded into the windowless vessel.

"How do you expect to get away with this?" I shouted to the attacker closest to me.

"We've disabled their vessels," he replied.

"Well, I'm sure they're calling the authorities."

"Not for a while. We've set up signal-jamming transmitters in the forest. It'll take hours before they find 'em all."

As the hatch closed, the group's leader jumped in. "Please accept my apologies for the inconvenience," she said as the craft lifted off.

"Inconvenience?" I said. "I would hardly characterize a violent attack and abduction as an inconvenience. Especially since you've separated me from Brenna!"

"Brenna?" she replied, "I heard you calling a woman Brenna, but surely you don't mean your foster daughter Brenna Murphy, do you?"

"What other Brenna could you possibly think I mean?"

"Oh, Kelvoo, I'm so sorry! Did they snatch Brenna from Kuw'baal as well? If we had known, we would have rescued her too!" She paused for a moment, then touched my shoulder. "Well, don't worry. I'm sure they won't harm her. At least they're not going to force her to be some kind of god!"

"So, my heroic rescuer," I said with forced calm, "do you have a name?"

"How rude of me! I'm Tenisha Herzog" she replied as the vessel lifted off the ground. We're going to take great care of you."

"And who, exactly, are 'we?'" I asked.

"We're the opposite of those terrible Kelvonists," she replied as she removed my restraints. "We're the *Reformed* Kelvonists!" she announced as the vessel sped toward the setting sun.

This is the strangest rescue mission I've ever encountered, I thought, losing any hope I had that Brenna and I would be returned to a sane planet any time soon.

THIRTEEN: SPLINTER

We landed well after dark. "Where are we, Tenisha Herzog?" I asked as the vessel touched down.

"Please, just call me Tenisha."

"Alright. Where are we, Tenisha?"

"On the Australian continent."

"Could you be more specific?"

"No," she replied with a smile that contradicted the tension in her voice.

We exited the vessel into a large indoor space that reminded me of the hangar at Kozoltoo's headquarters, except this hangar was a fraction of the size. We moved through a short corridor into a large room with solid outer walls that were about two meters high and topped with windows that sloped up to a flat roof. The building appeared to be partly underground with some sand blown up against a few of the sloping windows overhead.

The interior was dim with most of the light coming from the wan glow of display panels that were scattered about, where a few humans were at work. As I entered, a human looked up and saw me. "Hey, that must be Kelvoo!" he said, nudging his comrade next to him. "Hello Kelvoo!" he called to me, waving.

Others joined in.

"Hi, Kelvoo!"

"Welcome!"

"Nice to see you!"

As the people greeted me, I was struck by their nonchalant manner and casual attire. It was a refreshing change from the adoration of the "mainstream" Kelvonists, but any relief I might have felt was negated by my worries about Brenna.

Tenisha led me to an area with soft flooring. She tapped her Infotab, causing a circle of light to illuminate the area from above.

Then she took a seat and invited me to join her, so I knelt across from her.

"First, Kelvoo, let me apologize again for what must have been a traumatic experience. We hadn't planned for things to be as violent as they turned out, and I have no idea why one of Kozoltoo's people was dead, but we can talk about that later."

"If you hadn't planned for violence, your decision to bring clubs seems rather puzzling," I retorted.

"Well, I suppose we hoped they wouldn't resist if we had weapons. That expectation seems a bit silly now, given their fanaticism. Our overriding concern is for your safety. You were in the hands of zealots who have whipped most Terrans into a frenzy of worship for you. I don't know whether it has crossed your mind, but a whole religion has been built around you."

"Yes, Tenisha," I replied. "I was aware of that from my first meeting with Kozoltoo. In fact, I've referred to His Supreme Excellency as the high priest."

"That is certainly an appropriate title! Please be assured that we have no priests, no robes, and no guidance centers."

"Don't you mean temples?"

"Once again, you've come up with a far more accurate term! Temples are exactly what those places should be called!" Tenisha said with a trace of a smile.

"So, what are your plans for me, Tenisha?"

"Our only plan was your rescue. There is no grand plan going forward, except that you'll be staying here tonight."

No plan going forward? What kind of amateur operation is this? I wondered as I considered some of the more practical implications.

"Will you be able to provide me with algel?" I asked. "I'm growing hungry and will need sustenance at some point."

"We're working on it. Our board of directors will be meeting first thing in the morning. We'll have to figure out how to feed you and how to retrieve the injured members who were left behind. Also, of course, we need to find a way to reunite you with Brenna."

"You forgot to include returning us to Kuw'baal."

"Yes. That's going to be difficult since the Kelvonists' friends in government have the only access to interstellar transport and communications."

"So, now that you have me, what are your expectations? I assume you want *something* from me." I did my best not to let my frustration color my tone.

"Well, of course, since you're here, we do hope you'll share your wisdom with us. You've experienced so much, you've been deeply involved in human history, and you understand the terrible cost of human conflict. When we broke away from the Kelvonist Society and created the Reformed Kelvonist Movement, it caused a terrible schism, but it had to be done. You've seen firsthand how ludicrous the traditionalists have become! We need your guidance to help us heal the rift and reunify. And we need your judgement to help us determine which side is correct and which has erred on a variety of subjects."

Tenisha's words gave me an all-too-familiar sinking feeling. "Are you sure you're that different from the Kelvonist Society?" I asked. "Both sides seem to think I'm qualified to advise humanity, and frankly, you're both wrong. To me, that puts both of you in the same category!"

"But, Kelvoo, as I've explained, the Kelvonist Society has become a religion and elevated you to a god. They bow down to you and worship you, which goes directly against your teachings!"

"I have never produced teachings that apply to present-day Terran humans!"

"Sorry, Kelvoo. What I meant was, they go against your . . . outlook on life. Anyway, don't worry; we aren't going to try to force you or cajole you or insist on your help. Your wellbeing is all we care about."

Tenisha suggested that I might be exhausted and in need of rest. She was right about that. She showed me to a room where I could meditate in peace.

"Goodnight, Kelvoo. It's wonderful to have you with us. Please try to get some rest," she said as she closed the door behind her. I didn't hear the hum and click of a locking mechanism, which came as a surprise.

Rest did not come easily as I wondered how long it would be until I saw Brenna again or my home world for that matter. With the future in doubt, I thought it was important to start recording relevant events. I decided to start writing my story on my Infotab, beginning with some background information about my years of relative isolation on Kuw'baal, and picking up around the upheaval event to which Terran humans ascribed so much significance.

Later that night, I tried to meditate, but the traumatic experiences of that day, my worries about Brenna, and my growing hunger impaired my mental recuperation.

I emerged from the room several hours later, wondering why no guards had been posted outside. As I walked toward the main work area, the building was buzzing with staff, working under the high, sloping windows that revealed full daylight under a cloudless sky.

Framed pictures and holographic images lined the outer walls. I hadn't noticed them the previous night since the main interior lighting had been switched off. I was featured in all the images. They showed major events in my life, and the order in which they had occurred. There were images taken by the first contact mission to my planet, pictures from the media when I returned to Kuw'baal after my rescue from *Jezebel's Fury*, my official staff image from the Interplanetary University, pictures from my speech after my escape from Terra, and many others. There were even a few artistic renderings depicting scenes that had no visual record, such as events from *Jezebel's Fury* and during my captivity on Terra during the civil war. Some images invoked horrific memories while others made me nostalgic.

An interior window provided a view into a boardroom off to the side, where I saw Tenisha meeting with nine other humans. A man at a desk was the first to notice me. "Good morning, Kelvoo!" he said, smiling. "Did you have a restful meditation?"

"Yes," I lied.

"Excellent! Would you please join a few of us?" he asked, showing me to an area where twenty-one others were seated.

I knelt beside a sofa. "Is there anything I can get for you?" the eager human asked.

"A large serving of algel would be very beneficial, thank you," I replied. "I'm rather hungry."

"Oh, I know, Kelvoo," he said with regret in his voice. "I can assure you they're working on it," he added, motioning to the boardroom.

One human in the group had a black eye, and two others had visible bruises on their limbs. Another had a bandaged hand. I recognized one of the injured people from the so-called rescuers who took me from the other Kelvonist group.

The group had many questions for me. Fortunately, none of them concerned my views on how humans should live. Mostly, they wanted me to share my experiences since my involuntary "visit" to Kozoltoo. They also wanted to know how it felt to be displayed to millions of traditional Kelvonists. They wondered about the dead human they had seen during the "rescue," and how Brenna ended up coming to Terra with me. They also expressed regret about leaving Brenna behind.

"Tenisha and the board are working on that too!" they assured me.

I decided to answer the questions honestly, feeling it was best to curry favor with my new "hosts" and confident that I had nothing to hide. Then, from the side of my eye dome, I saw Tenisha leave her meeting and stride toward me.

"Good morning, Kelvoo," she said. "Would you please come with me?"

I followed Tenisha to the boardroom, seeing that it was occupied by a dozen others. "There are lots of interesting developments," she said, closing the door behind her. She introduced each board member, including their names and titles.

The Reformed Kelvonist Movement was structured much like any other human non-profit. The diversity of individual humans had always fascinated me, but I was struck by how bland and bureaucratic the board members seemed to be. I had assumed that Tenisha was the organization's leader, but she turned out to be the chief operating officer, though I didn't know what the difference was. The chief executive was an elderly man whom Tenisha introduced as Xavier Livingston. He appeared quite frail, suggesting that Tenisha was the de facto leader.

I knelt at the table beside Tenisha.

"I want to start by telling you that news of your presence on Terra has made its way to the Planetary Alliance," she said. "It didn't take long for them to realize you were missing. They started an investigation and somehow a vid recording of your flight on the altar was sent to them. It's all very hush-hush so far, but they've been burning up the government's sole quantum entanglement link demanding your return. The government is making the absurd argument that they don't know anything about you being here, and they're saying the vid must have been faked. Still, they've promised to launch a full investigation and make every effort to find and return you."

"How would you know about 'hush-hush' government communications?" I asked.

"Contacts, Kelvoo. We have supporters in the governance and Kelvonism branches of government," Tenisha replied with a smile.

"More importantly," she continued, "I'm pleased to report that Brenna is well, apart from some bruises and a minor fracture in her left clavicle. I'm especially happy to say that arrangements have been made for you to meet with Brenna at a neutral location. We'll take you there tomorrow where representatives from the Kelvonist Society will meet with us to discuss ideas for resolving our respective situations. After the meeting, you'll return here with us.

"With regard to your nutritional needs, the Kelvonist Society dropped off some fridgepacks of fresh algel at the neutral location. They are en route and should arrive here at any time. We'll also be picking up an algel incubation vat at tomorrow's meeting, for your ongoing needs."

"Why would the Kelvonist Society want to help your group instead of demanding my return?" I asked, struggling to make sense of the bizarre situation.

"Our relationship with the Kelvonist Society is . . . complicated. Peaceful coexistence is core to the values of both groups, so negotiation is how we come up with solutions—or how we agree to disagree."

"Peaceful coexistence?" I asked, astonished. "Except for the times when you break into their facilities and club them senseless, I suppose!"

"I concede that was a step too far," Tenisha replied, "but so was their abduction of you and parading you in front of millions of zealots without your consent! We had an emergency meeting and decided that we had to rescue you by any means possible!

"Of course, the Kelvonist Society was outraged by our attack, but they're terrified that word will get out that your so-called visit came about by kidnapping. So far, their followers are certain that you *chose* to visit Terra to fulfill your supposed prophecy and usher in a new era of enlightenment. Kozoltoo's beliefs were absolute. He was certain beyond any doubt that you would be convinced by your millions of worshippers. Your refusal to play along has thrown them into disarray. There's even talk of deposing and replacing Kozoltoo!

"The Kelvonist Society has accepted our 'kind offer' to host you while they sort themselves out. We have agreed to set aside our differences and work with them. Please understand, Kelvoo, we're all in a precarious position. Kelvonism has become deeply ingrained in Terran culture. Ripping it away could have dire consequences!"

"Well, it seems to me," I said, "that the introduction of so-called Kelvonism has already produced dire consequences." I received bemused looks from everyone in the room.

"Excuse me, Kelvoo," the chief executive officer, Xavier Livingston said, "but I'd like to know why you seem to be offended that a planet full of humans would want to emulate you and ascribe to your values. Why do you suppose there's such an outpouring of love for you among the humans of Terra? Why would so much time and so many resources be spent studying your life and your words? Why would we build our children's education around your values?

"As for the traditional Kelvonists, why do you think they built guidance centers, monuments, and statues in your honor? As reformed Kelvonists, we disagree with their idolatry and their mindless worship of you, but there *must* be something profoundly special about you. How else can we explain all these things?"

"How indeed, Mr. Livingston?" I replied, speaking slowly, and enunciating each word with great clarity. "To know the answer would be to understand human nature. I've spent decades studying and trying to understand humans, but some things are simply inexplicable.

"I can't tell you with certainty why Terran humans view me the way they do. I suspect the reasons are as unique as each person. What I *can* do is examine human history and detect patterns.

"You humans seem to be obsessed with finding reasons for everything. You want a simple explanation for a complex universe, and you want a leader who will clear a path for you to follow.

"You may want to ask yourself why humans outside of Terra haven't elevated me to such an extent. One possibility is that they have not been subjected to your level of isolation. After the war, the humans of Terra chose isolation as an expression of shame for their past treatment of extraterrestrials. During that isolation, the Terrans have overcome their brutal past and, to their credit, formed a largely peaceful society. But that isolation has come at a cost.

"As humans turned inward and examined their shared trauma, perhaps they looked for a being who also suffered as a consequence of their war. As they wallowed in guilt for the supposed sins of humanity, perhaps they looked to a non-human to guide them into the future.

"So, then we need to ask, why me? During the war, I was kept in captivity and tortured for less time and with less severity than many of my fellow extraterrestrials, so what makes me special? I can only conclude that my writing provided references that humans rallied around. My initial autobiography unintentionally triggered the reforms known as the 'Correction' on Terra. We all know how the Human Independence Movement led the backlash against the Correction, resulting in the unspeakably horrific war.

"When I wrote about my time on this planet in *Kelvoo's Terra*, one of the unintended consequences seems to be that the Terran humans have incorporated it into a religion, or an overarching philosophy, that elevates me into an untenable position.

"Sometimes, I wonder whether I should have written *Kelvoo's Testimonial* or *Kelvoo's Terra* in the first place."

"Oh no, Kelvoo! Don't ever think such a thing!" Xavier replied with a mortified expression.

"I only have such thoughts in passing," I assured him. "Sometimes I use my imagination to picture history or, in this case, human history, as a river. The course of that river may have been accidentally diverted by my stories, but I can't control it. You and I and all humanity have simply been swept along in its inexorable current."

"Kelvoo, that's beautiful!" Tenisha said as she touched my shoulder. "You've got a unique ability to say things that are so profound! That's why you're so loved and why we look to you for guidance."

"Are you referring to my river comparison, Tenisha? I don't see it as especially eloquent. It's just a simple analogy. Perhaps some humans assign great depth and profundity to my words because that's what they're looking for or expecting."

All I received in response to my logic was a puzzled look.

"Whether you like it or not, Kelvoo," Xavier said with a deep sigh, "the citizens of this planet have a hunger for your leadership. This provides you with a unique opportunity to guide us. You may have been thrust into this role against your wishes, but think about the good you can do."

"No, Mr. Livingston. No good can come from my leadership."

"Why do you say that?"

"Just look at human history and the terrible consequences whenever humans have followed beliefs and leaders that they thought were infallible."

"You've given us much to consider, Kelvoo," Xavier said as a knock sounded on the boardroom door. A staff member opened the door and leaned part of the way into the room.

"Kelvoo's algel has arrived!" she announced.

"Wonderful!" Xavier replied. "I hope you don't mind if we take a break, Kelvoo. You've only been in this meeting for a short time, but the rest of us have been here for several hours."

"That's the best idea I've heard all day," I replied without exaggeration.

As we left the boardroom, the staffer opened a box and removed fridgepacks of chilled algel, setting them on a nearby table. I hurried over to the woman who handed me a pack. I tore it open and let the precious contents slurp into my feeding pouch. A wave of relief swept over me, making me realize I had been hungrier and weaker than I realized. Once I absorbed every drop of algel, I repeated the process with two more fridgepacks.

Just as I was consuming the last of my meal, Tenisha approached. "Would you like to walk with me outside and get some fresh air?"

"How do you know I won't try to escape?" I asked.

"We trust you," she said. "Besides, we're in the middle of a vast desert. Long before you reached other humans, you would starve to death. The nights here also get awfully cold at this time of year. Given your kloormari physiology, the cold would render you unconscious, and you would die from exposure. Plus, there's the fact that we're supervised by drones."

"Don't worry," I replied. "It was a rhetorical question. Even if I found other humans, I don't imagine they'd be willing or able to get Brenna and me off this planet."

We stepped outside after a short climb up a stairwell. Sol was baking the reddish sand and sparse, scrubby desert vegetation. I saw a few distant outcroppings of red rock, rounded by eons of weathering. Otherwise, the land was flat with wind-formed ripples and drifts of sand. Apart from the dazzling light, my surroundings reminded me of my distant home.

The top of the building rose out of the sand to a height of only a meter or two. The sloping windows surrounded a roof that was covered with sand and brush, making the structure blend into the vastness of the desert. Tenisha walked with me for a short distance along a dry streambed that meandered close to a corner of the building.

"Are we treating you alright?" Tenisha asked. "I hope this situation isn't too hard on you."

"Your group has been treating me with hospitality. I'm especially grateful for the algel. In terms of whether the situation is hard, how would you cope if you and a loved one were snatched from your home, forced into a spacecraft, transported across the galaxy to a planet you hoped you'd never see again, had demi-god status thrust upon you, been expected to lead billions into an enlightened state, separated from your loved one, then kidnapped again and taken to a clandestine location deep in a desert, where you have no idea what's going to happen next?"

Tenisha looked down, embarrassed. "I'm sorry, Kelvoo. All I can say is we're working toward some kind of resolution," she said. "At least you'll be reunited with Brenna tomorrow," she added, raising her head and smiling.

"Would you mind if I asked *you* a few questions?" I replied.

"Please, Kelvoo. Anything!"

"I'm curious about the schism between the traditional Kelvonists and your movement. Was it a gradual separation, or did a single event or issue become a tipping point?"

"Many of our differences revolved around your divinity. Kelvonism started evolving toward the belief that you possess supernatural capabilities, including the ability of prophecy. The Kelvonist Society searched your work for anything that could be twisted to support their beliefs. The majority of Terrans loved it! Engagement went through the roof, and donations, along with government support, went sky high, pushing the Kelvonist Society further from reason and closer to superstition."

"And was that the tipping point for the reformers?"

"No. That came from a debate about raising our children." She shifted her stance, looking uncomfortable. "In their effort to model the kloormari approach to child rearing, the traditionalists separate children from their biological parents at age four. The children are sent to communes where they're raised by a large community of adults who take turns providing their basic requirements for survival, as well as educating them and indoctrinating them in Kelvonist beliefs. Once they reach adulthood, they can meet their parents again if they wish."

"What? That's beyond outrageous!" I exclaimed. "That's not how humans are supposed to be raised!"

"That's what we thought," Tenisha replied. "We raise our children very differently. First of all, we think that four is too young. We wait until each child's fifth birthday. That day is marked with a great farewell celebration before the child is placed in a loving commune located close to the home of their birth. We do not separate the children from their parents. The parents visit the children every week to provide a familial anchor. We also don't *indoctrinate* these kids; we *educate* them. We include reformed Kelvonist philosophy among other subjects, to produce well-rounded, free-thinking individuals."

"I can't believe what you're saying," I replied, aghast. *Does she not see the irony?* I wondered.

"Yes!" Tenisha said. "I knew you'd think our way was better! You see, Kelvoo, this is how you can help us. Terra will listen to you. You can heal our divisions by guiding us to the correct interpretation of your teachings! Do you see now? Will you stay and help our people?"

I wanted to explain the obvious to Tenisha—that humans and kloormari are different species, with kloormari children being able to survive and fend for themselves from the moment of birth, making our family structures completely different. I was shocked that either branch of Kelvonism could treat human children in such an emotionally abusive way, all in the name of their absurd superstitions. I was unprepared to debate Tenisha at that moment, too busy trying to process my revulsion.

"I'd would like to go back inside now," I said.

"Of course, Kelvoo." She turned around and we walked back to the stairwell.

When I entered the building, Xavier called out to us. "Tenisha, Kelvoo, please join us again," he said, smiling. We headed back into the boardroom where the remaining board members had reassembled.

"Did you enjoy your walk?" Xavier asked. "Did you and Tenisha have an interesting conversation?"

"It was enlightening, to say the least," I replied.

"Good, good! I'm pleased to say I had a productive call with Kozoltoo during the break. They're still in shock and are trying to come to grips with how wrong they've been about you. We acknowledged their struggle and offered our apologies for invading their facility. We also told them that, given the monumental events of recent days, we're prepared to work with them to reconcile our differences and reunite to move Terra forward with a new, unified vision. So, you see, Kelvoo? Your mere presence itself has already advanced our planet, whether you were willing to intervene directly or not!"

"So, is my role on Terra finished?" I asked.

"Oh no, Kelvoo! Why, it's just beginning!"

"Are you saying that I won't be returned to Kuw'baal?"

"Oh, I'm sure you will, Kelvoo, but not anytime soon. Kozoltoo and I have agreed to this, and we've pledged to be open and honest with you. Your abduction by the Kelvonist Society has thrown our world into turmoil. Ordinary people are the problem. They're demanding to see you and hear from you. Your absence is drawing suspicion and leading to outrageous conspiracy theories. We have no choice but to keep you with us until the situation has stabilized. If you would just cooperate to some degree, you could greatly alleviate our problems."

"What about the Planetary Alliance, Mr. Livingston? Yesterday, you told me they suspect I'm here on Terra."

"A lot has happened since yesterday. Today, they're certain that you were taken and are among us against your will. They are demanding your immediate return. We've explained our situation, but they're adamant that we return you, unless . . ."

"Unless what?"

"Unless you told them you have an important mission here and will stay for a while voluntarily."

"Not a chance."

"That's what we expected you to say. As far as we know, there isn't much that the Planetary Alliance can do about your situation. The former ambassador, Mark Muller, assures us that the Alliance would not be inclined to intervene in the affairs of another planet, especially in any way that could be considered violent. Since we're a self-sufficient planet, they can't threaten us with a blockade or sanctions. The worst they can do is expel our current ambassador. I think we're heading for a standoff with the Planetary Alliance until we return you to them. For now, why don't we just focus on tomorrow? At least you have your reunion with Brenna Murphy to look forward to."

"I am not interested in attending the meeting tomorrow."

"What do you mean? Don't you want to be reunited with Brenna?"

"Of course I want to see my foster daughter again but not if the purpose of the reunion is to manipulate me."

"We're going to take you to the meeting anyway. You can refuse to speak or interact with others; you can do whatever you wish. Both sides know you're here against your will, so nothing will surprise us or the traditional Kelvonists. I do, however, think that Brenna would be devastated."

"I suppose that's true," I admitted. "I'll attend the meeting and cooperate to the extent that I deem to be ethical, but I must name one condition."

"Yes?"

"My namesake, Kelvoo Buchanan-Paige, must be there. I met with him briefly before I was forcibly presented to the worshippers. I trust him, and I must meet with him in private before I see anybody else."

"The human called Kelvoo is well known to us," Xavier replied. "Although he is affiliated with the traditionalists, we trust him too. While his role is largely ceremonial, he keeps in touch with us and has often sought ways to reconcile our differences and reunite our organizations.

"Kozoltoo has already informed us that Mr. Buchanan-Paige will be present because of your previous acquaintance with him. Remember that it's in the best interest of all parties to be as agreeable as possible under the circumstances. If you'd like to meet with human Kelvoo first, I'm sure I speak for both parties when I say I can guarantee that this will happen."

"That will be fine."

"Is there anything else we can do for you?" Xavier asked. "Apart from sending you home, of course!"

"Just one thing," I said. "I need time to mentally prepare for the meeting. I would like to return to my room for deep meditation and to analyze the situation. I require complete privacy and expect to remain undisturbed until tomorrow."

Xavier looked at the other board members. Some nodded and others shrugged. "Very well," he said, turning back to me, "but your room will be guarded by our staff and using electronic methods. Any attempt to sneak away will be futile."

"You have my word that no such attempt will be made."

"In that case, we'll see you at 07:00 tomorrow morning."

***

As I write this, I'm ensconced in my room with four fridgepacks of algel. I have no intention of meditating or preparing for the meeting tomorrow. Instead, I'm pouring all my energy into completing the story that I started writing last night.

I'm on a theocratic planet where I've been under the control of two religious factions that were founded upon the worship of a deity. To my absolute horror, I am the being that they worship.

These factions deny that they are religions, and they deny that they engage in worship, but I've lived and learned for long enough to know a religion when I see it—especially when my very life is the subject of its superstitions.

I have tried to convince the leaders of the Kelvonist Society and the Reformed Kelvonists to cease their efforts to have me lead the Terran humans. Using reason and logic, I have asked, pleaded, and demanded that I be returned to Kuw'baal or into the care of the Planetary Alliance. Unfortunately, reason and logic no longer apply on Terra. Instead, I find myself enmeshed in uncertainty, driven by the collective madness and superstition of billions of humans.

My "hosts" have assured me that I will be released at some point in the future, implying that this will happen sooner if I accept the role they have given me. I have no intention of leading the Terrans. History shows that the only results will be conflict, suffering and death.

I can't predict how this situation will end, but I think there's a high probability that I will be held on this tragic planet until my life is over.

Tonight, I intend to complete the account of my experiences to this point. As I did with my past autobiographical stories, I will try to write in a narrative style in a manner that will engage the interest of readers.

Tomorrow when I see Brenna, I'll try to transfer this story to her in the hope that she'll be able to leave Terra and, when it's safe to do so, share my written account as the cautionary tale that I intend it to be.

PART 2: BRENNA

FOURTEEN: TAVEUNI

I don't think I'm much of a writer. It feels weird saying that since I've spent most of my life teaching adults to read. My charitable foundation has introduced literature across the Planetary Alliance and, most of all, to the human outlier worlds of Exile and Perdition. That literature has included timeless classics, along with contemporary works from leading authors of our time.

Trying to write the following story fills me with anxiety. Some people call it "imposter syndrome." I've been asked to write a memoir many times by many people because of my unique connection with Kelvoo. I've pointed out that May knew Kelvoo at least as well as me. After all, Kelvoo raised both of us for a large portion of our childhood and teen years, and we both called Kelvoo "Pa" (our shorthand for "parent"). May argued that I should write the story since I was the one with Kelvoo when the Kelvonists took us. I don't know how interesting the story will be. Since I don't have a perfect memory, it's possible I haven't recalled the dialogue with 100 percent accuracy, so I'll just have to hope my best effort is good enough.

Brenna Murphy.

***

I was terrified when the group of Reformed Kelvonists raided the gathering and took Kelvoo away. During the brief battle, I was hit in the shoulder, which fractured a collar bone, and left me in intense pain. Night fell soon after, so it took hours for Kozoltoo's staff to search the grounds and the surrounding forest for the jamming devices that prevented our group from calling for help. It was after midnight when help arrived, and we were evacuated to the Kelvonist Society's headquarters. I was treated in the medical section before returning to the suite where I had stayed before.

The Kelvonists treated me like royalty. All my wishes were attended to immediately, except for my fondest wish, to be reunited with Pa and taken off Terra, never to return. Kozoltoo's staff must have viewed me as a spoiled diva with my constant demands to see Kelvoo, but they were always courteous toward me.

"We're doing everything we can to resolve this," Kozoltoo kept telling me. Sometimes I felt guilty for being so demanding, especially since the Reformed Kelvonists were the ones who took Pa, while the mainstream Kelvonists were trying to defend us.

Unlike Kelvoo, I don't have a perfect memory of the specifics, but I think it was two or three days after Kelvoo was taken when Maria came to my door. "Exciting news!" she said. "We're leaving in an hour, please make sure you're ready!"

"I'm not interested in going anywhere," I replied, "unless it's to see Kelvoo."

"That's exactly what we're going to do!" she said.

I asked Maria for specifics.

"We're going to a beautiful archipelago called the Viti Islands," she said. "It's in the tropics of Terra's southern hemisphere in our largest ocean, named the Pacific.'"

"Yes, I do have some grasp of basic Terran geography. I did live here for a few years, you know."

"Of course, Brenna! Sorry. Have you heard of an island called Taveuni?"

"No."

"Well, it's one of a few places on Terra that's set aside as a 'neutral area.' These areas allow groups of humans with opposing views to gather in a safe place for meetings, negotiations, signing agreements, and so on. Please forgive me if you already know that, but it happened long after you left Terra."

"Sorry, Maria. I'm extremely anxious about Kelvoo. Go on."

Maria explained that negotiations had been taking place between the reformers and the Kelvonist Society. The parties were going to reunite me with Kelvoo and try to figure out how to move forward.

Pollybot and I were waiting to board the transport half an hour ahead of schedule. Two hours after our departure, I felt a wave of relief as the trip progress display showed that we were descending toward the island of Vanua Levu. As we flew southeast, we crossed a line of coral reefs, followed by scattered agricultural land on the west side of the island. Rugged, forest covered mountains came next, forming a solid backbone along the east coast. We traversed a strait of sapphire water, which changed to brilliant turquoise in the shallows as we crossed over the shore of the much smaller Taveuni Island. We turned and landed at Matei on the northern tip of Taveuni, passing beaches of white sand, lined with Terran coconut palms. Hope filled my mind as I looked forward to being reunited with Pa.

The transport hovered outside a building marked "Reconciliation Center," and I walked in through the main doors with Maria and Pollybot close behind.

The lobby was full of people, chatting. I saw Kozoltoo in his robe and pointy hat, along with a couple of his staff, speaking with a man considerably older than anyone else there. I recognized several other Kelvonist Society staff members and many others who, I assumed, were associated with the Reformed Kelvonists. Drinks and snacks were being offered by servitor bots that made Pollybot look like the antique that it was.

A young woman approached me in the lobby. "You must be Brenna," she said, extending a hand in greeting. "I'm Tenisha Herzog and I've had the pleasure of getting to know Kelvoo recently."

"Oh, I recognize you, alright! You're one of the attackers who took Kelvoo from me!" I said, pointing a finger in her face instead of shaking her hand.

"I'm so sorry, Brenna," she replied. "If we had known you were in the group, we would've taken you with us."

"I seriously doubt I would have been any better off with your violent gang!" I replied.

"Well, at least we're all here today to figure a way out of this," she offered.

"Where's Kelvoo?" I asked, wanting to get down to business.

"Kelvoo's in a private meeting with Kelvoo Buchanan-Paige. I understand you both met with him at Kelvonist Society headquarters."

I wasn't interested in Tenisha's small talk. I was about to demand to see Kelvoo that instant, but Tenisha cut me off.

"Kelvoo is being informed that you've arrived. Please wait here for a few minutes."

I didn't have to wait at all. A side door opened, and there was Kelly. He beckoned me into the room, and I walked in with Pollybot right behind me. As soon as I saw Kelvoo, I moved as fast as my old bones would allow. Kelvoo strode toward me with upper limbs extended. I hugged Kelvoo despite the fact I was partly blocking one of Kelvoo's breathing inlets and a couple of vocal outlets.

"Oh, Pa! I've been so worried about you!" was all I could manage to say as we held each other.

I felt a joyful warmth with Kelvoo's clasper limbs wrapped around me and my head nestled under the base of Kelvoo's eye dome. My happiness was unexpectedly accompanied by tears. At that moment, I realized how tired I was from being constantly on guard since our kidnapping. I released my suppressed tension and gave in to my exhaustion as I cried without restraint.

I don't know how long I embraced Kelvoo, but the spell was soon broken. "We don't have much time, Brenna," Kelvoo said. "There are some things you need to know."

"What do you mean, Pa? Aren't we going to stick together now?"

Ignoring my questions, Kelvoo pulled out an Infotab.

"Brenna, before anything else, please accept a document transfer."

I pulled my Infotab from its holster and unlocked it.

"I've written my account of events since shortly before the upheaval, and up until last night," Pa said. "You now have a copy on your Infotab. Please share it with the Planetary Alliance, but ensure they keep it confidential. The story might aid their efforts to resolve the situation, but it could also put many humans in jeopardy, especially if Kelly's cooperation with us is revealed. The document must be kept secret until the safety of all the beings in the story can be ensured. Please provide my story to the Alliance the *moment* you are safely off this planet."

"You mean, the moment *we* are safely off this planet!" I said, not liking where the conversation was going.

Kelvoo held both of my hands and faced me. "Brenna, after speaking privately with Kelly and having some direct discussions with Kelvonist leadership, I have agreed to cooperate with both Kelvonist factions as they try to unravel the mess that's been created. However, my agreement is contingent on one condition: your immediate release and transfer to Kuw'baal, an outlier planet, or any planet or facility of the Planetary Alliance."

"Hell no, Pa!" I shouted. "They'll never let you go! How are you going to get by without me to stick up for you?"

"Brenna, I appreciate your concern, but I'll be able to take care of myself. The Kelvonists only want *me*, so we don't need to put you at risk by having you stay here. I love you and May more than anyone or anything else. That's why your safety is of the utmost importance."

"To hell with my safety!" I replied. "My life is almost over. I have no spouses and no children, and I have a skilled team running my foundation. I don't give a damn about any risks to me!"

"Brenna, there's more to it than that," Kelly said, touching my arm. "What happens if you stay here and neither of you ever leave Terra? How will your stories survive? The other worlds *need* to know what's happening.

"*This* world has gone mad!" he continued. "At least one of you must get off this planet and inform the Alliance of what's happening. Since the Kelvonists aren't going to let Kelvoo go, it's up to you, Brenna. Kelvoo has provided you with a detailed record. If you can get the information to the Alliance, perhaps they can use it to get Kelvoo out of here faster."

"So that's it?" I asked. "I'm just supposed to leave?"

"Pretty much," Kelly replied, "but please be assured that we have a plan, and it may require the services of your bot. We're asking you to leave Pollybot with Kelvoo."

"When would I have to go?"

"I'm so sorry, Brenna," Pa said. "An interplanetary shuttle is waiting for you outside."

"That seems awfully convenient since they didn't have a spacecraft available when we first asked to go home!" I replied.

"I know, Brenna. Remember that we're dealing with deceptive people. Superstition is based on deception, and the Kelvonists have embraced superstition entirely. Nevertheless, a shuttle is here, and our plan calls for you to board it."

"What? Right now?" I said, my voice cracking with emotion.

"Please transfer control of Pollybot to Kelvoo," Kelly said.

I turned toward Pollybot, which had been hovering behind me with its usual vigilance. "Pollybot, stay with Kelvoo," I commanded. I felt as if a part of me was being taken as Pollybot silently circled us and stationed itself behind Kelvoo.

"Brenna, please listen carefully," Pa said. "Once you're in contact with the Planetary Alliance, the Terran government will accept a brief call from you over its quantum entanglement network. During that call, provide them with a phrase that only you and I know. When they pass along the correct phrase to me, I'll know you're safe, and I'll start cooperating with the Kelvonists."

Pa leaned over, placing a vocal outlet close to my left ear. "Love above fear."

To confirm that I had heard correctly, Pa asked me to repeat the phrase in a whisper. I leaned close and whispered into one of Pa's auditory receptors, "Love above fear." As soon as the words left my lips, I broke down and cried. Any pretense of courage I had wanted to display vaporized. I embraced my beloved pa and sobbed.

Kelly backed away to give us space as we clung to each other. I felt as though I would never see Kelvoo again. Too short a time passed before I managed to get hold of myself.

"I love you Brenna," Pa said in an unusually halting voice. "I love you, and I love May every bit as much as if I were human and you were my biological daughters."

"I know you do, Pa, and I'm sorry if I ever seemed to doubt that. Thank you for raising May and me. We love you so, so much."

My eyes were blinded by my tears as Kelly held my shoulders and guided me out of the room. I may be old, and my memory might not be what it once was, but I remember the sound of every footstep as Kelly led me outside. I also remember the heat of the tropical sun beating down on me, the humid, salt-tinged air, and the relative coolness as we entered the shuttle.

Kelly guided me into my seat and fastened me in for takeoff. I blinked away my tears and saw the same kind of streaks on Kelly's cheeks as he kissed my hand.

"Please take care of Pa," I whispered.

Kelly nodded as he squeezed my hand and left the shuttle. Seconds later, the hatch closed, and the shuttle roared into the brilliant blue Terran sky.

FIFTEEN: SARAYA

The shuttle orbited around Terra until it was heading toward a jump point. I was struck by the silence, and when I looked out of the window, I was awed by the beauty of the fragile world below me. My tears stopped as relief set in. My relief soon gave way to guilt. *How awful of me to be relieved while Kelvoo is trying to survive the collective insanity of a world full of humans*, I thought.

As the shuttle headed away from the Terran North Pole, I resolved to make Kelvoo's freedom my sole mission. My work could wait, and the foundation could run without me. I was well past the average age for retirement anyway. For the past couple of years, May had become mildly annoying by describing how stress-free her life was after she retired but also how much busier her days had become as she pursued new interests and activities. There I was, about to embark on a retirement that would be anything but relaxing. I fully expected my mind to be consumed with extreme stress and worry about Pa.

My first step was to read Kelvoo's document on my Infotab. I was surprised to see how similar its style was to Kelvoo's other books, the main difference being that Kelvoo's newest story had not reached its conclusion. Finding the end of the story would be my goal. Getting Pa off that godforsaken planet to tell the tale would be the means to that end.

As the shuttle made its hours-long journey toward the jump point, I was able to set aside the worst of my worries and focus on reading Kelvoo's story. This was aided by the fact that I was alone in the passenger section since the entire vessel had been set aside for my removal from Terra. Somebody emerged from the cockpit infrequently to ensure that I was still present, though I would have been hard pressed to go anywhere else.

As I read Kelvoo's story, it was interesting to see Kelvoo's perspective on the preparation for the coming upheaval, prior to my arrival. I wasn't sure why Kelvoo included the upheaval in the story, but I supposed it was a much-anticipated event, which the Kelvonists took as a sign that they needed to take Kelvoo to fulfill their cockamamie prophecy. As I thought about it, I also realized that *Kelvoo's Testimonial* had an entire chapter about the first contact mission's survey of Ryla 6 and how they were able to predict the upheaval. I felt very old as I recalled that the Ryla 6 survey had happened during my childhood. I also wondered whether Kelvoo started the new story with the upheaval so that part of *Kelvoo's Testimonial* could be brought full circle. I felt sad as I wondered whether my dear pa was tying up loose ends as a way of saying goodbye due to the unthinkable possibility that Kelvoo's life was going to end on Terra.

I only skimmed the parts of the story that started with my arrival on *Platform 313* and ended with my separation from Kelvoo when the reformers "rescued" Pa. Not only did I already know those parts of the story, reading about myself has always made me feel embarrassed and self-conscious.

I read the final two chapters with intense interest, needing to know what happened after we were separated on Terra. I could sense Kelvoo's hope when the reformers described their movement as philosophical and non-religious, but I could feel Kelvoo's disappointment when the reformers turned out to be just a slightly different flavor of crazy.

The five-minute jump warning sounded just as I finished reading Kelvoo's story. The jump was uneventful, and soon afterward, I fell asleep, exhausted.

I was roused by an automated chime and announcement indicating that we were approaching Saraya. I had been expecting to be taken to a Planetary Alliance station in deep space or perhaps an embassy on Kuw'baal or my home planet, Exile.

I had visited Saraya twice before to attend interplanetary literacy conventions, but as we made a final, almost vertical approach, I could tell we weren't heading for the same continent that I had been to before. Still, the forests, mountains, beaches, headlands, and stunningly clear blue ocean seemed strangely familiar. I put the feeling down to similarities with my previous views of the Viti Islands on Terra.

The shuttle landed on a circular pad on top of a pillar that rose above the treetops of a dense forest. A raised path led to a group of glass buildings that were also built on platforms above the trees.

The hatch opened, and the pilot approached me from the cockpit. "Off you go, then!" he said.

"What? That's it?" I asked. "Where am I supposed to go? Is someone here to meet me?"

"Look, all I know is I was called up with no notice and told to bring you to these coordinates and then return. I don't know who you are, and I have no idea what you're supposed to do here."

I stepped out of the shuttle, expecting the pilot to accompany me until I could get my bearings. Instead, the moment I was a few steps away, the hatch closed behind me. I walked until I could see through the cockpit windows. I saw the pilot and someone whom I assumed was the copilot. Looking at them, I shrugged and mouthed the words, "What now?" That was when the engines, which had never been shut off, started producing a powerful downward thrust. The pilot just shrugged back at me, and the co-pilot waved goodbye as the thrust was increased and the shuttle lifted off, its exhaust nearly knocking me off my feet.

I felt utterly alone, with no possessions beyond my Infotab, but I wasn't afraid. I decided to walk toward the buildings to find assistance. Saraya's star, Sah, shone with intense light and heat, which was mercifully moderated by a cool breeze, tinged with a variety of pleasant natural fragrances. As I walked, I looked out toward the turquoise water, fringed by a white sand beach and a rocky, black headland beyond. For the second time, I had a feeling of déjà vu.

As I reached the edge of the walkway, a small white car dropped out of the sky, stopping just before it would have slammed into the landing pad, then settling down gently. A male Sarayan practically jumped out of the vehicle.

With their short bodies but long legs, Sarayans walk in a manner that I usually found graceful. The Sarayan who greeted me was anything but graceful, his gangly legs flailing about and the grey crinkly skin of his extendable neck smoothing out as he craned his head toward me. The nostrils in the middle of his face were flared, and his dozens of small, pointed teeth were visible as he panted with exertion.

"Ms. Murphy? Brenna Murphy?" he exclaimed as he sprinted toward me.

"Yes."

"My apologies, Ms. Murphy! I was informed of your arrival only moments ago!" he said as his robe flapped behind him. "I came as soon as I could!"

The deep blue side panels of the Sarayan's garment indicated a role in law enforcement. His medallion bounced on his chest, and he had to use one hand to keep his traditional Sarayan hat in place as he ran.

"That's alright. I was just taking a moment to enjoy the view," I said. "And please, just call me Brenna."

"Please come with me, Brenna," he said as he directed me toward the car.

I took the seat beside the Sarayan. The car lifted off and made a beeline for the top of the headland beyond the beach.

"I hope you had a pleasant flight," he said.

"Given my reluctance to leave Pa—I mean Kelvoo—I suppose it was alright, Mr. . . ." I paused to give the Sarayan a chance to introduce himself."

"I do beg your pardon, Brenna! I am Special Investigator Pelegran, but you can just call me Pelegran," he replied. "We're heading to the top of the cliffs up ahead. A long time ago, before the coup on Terra, the Terran High Commission was located there. That was where Kelvoo and the crew of the *Pacifica Spirit* stayed the first time we were graced with a visit from Kelvoo."

"Of course!" I exclaimed. "That's why this place looks so familiar. Kelvoo described it in a chapter of *Kelvoo's Testimonial.*"

"Yes, yes!" Pelegran replied. "The chapter was titled '*La Playa del Saraya*.' I'm told it means something like, 'the beach on Saraya' in one of the ancient Terran languages."

"Kelvoo was here a long time ago," I remarked. "I guess not much has changed, since Kelvoo's description still fits."

"With most of the city below the forest canopy, I suppose things still look quite similar from up here," Pelegran replied.

The car banked and turned, landing on the roof of a large, curved building, perched on the edge of the cliff. A cool wind blasted us as we made our way to a stairwell that led down into a large room lined with windows that overlooked the spectacular view of the shore below and the ocean beyond.

"So, Pelegran, why was I brought here?" I asked.

"Where were you expecting to be taken?"

"From what little I heard on Terra, I thought the Planetary Alliance was requesting Kelvoo's return, so I expected to be taken to an Alliance office or embassy."

"Well, space in this building has been provided to me for temporary use as a branch of the Planetary Alliance Investigations Division. I have been chosen to head up the investigation to try to ascertain Kelvoo's condition and precise location. I'll be assembling a team shortly.

"Saraya was selected to host the investigation's headquarters, partly because we're well equipped for this kind of work but also because we Sarayans are a neutral and relatively unemotional species. With Kelvoo being so beloved and so enmeshed in human history, our neutrality and careful, methodical approach serves to prevent us from making rash decisions."

"I hope you don't think a rescue mission would be rash."

Pelegran gave the Sarayan equivalent of a sigh. "I'm sorry, Brenna, but a rescue by physical intervention is out of the question. Under interplanetary law, Kelvoo's fame does not make Kelvoo any more important than any other individual. We can't risk armed conflict or increased tension with another world for the sake of one individual, especially if there is no evidence that the individual is under physical threat."

"What I'm gathering from you," I said with annoyance, "is that any attempt to get Kelvoo returned is going to disappear down a giant bureaucratic black hole."

"I'm sorry, Brenna. I have no doubt it seems that way to you. I can only assure you that we'll make every effort to extract Kelvoo. In fact, I suggest that we start immediately. Would you be kind enough to let me ask you an extensive list of questions?"

Pelegran's suggestion made me realize how distracted I had been after my unceremonious arrival on Saraya. "Oh, my goodness!" I blurted. "I have a document for you on my Infotab! Kelvoo transferred it to me just before I came here!"

"That seems like a good place to start," Pelegran replied.

I transferred a copy of Kelvoo's story to Pelegran, stressing how important it was to keep the contents confidential until Kelvoo was returned and the lives of others in the story were no longer in danger.

"There's something else we need to take care of," I said. "I'm supposed to place a call to the Terran government through the Planetary Alliance. I need to provide them with a passphrase that Kelvoo gave me. They're going to repeat the phrase back to Kelvoo, to prove that I am off Terra and safe."

"I wish I'd been told that," Pelegran replied. "Everything's been far too rushed and disorganized." He sighed again.

It took Pelegran twenty minutes of calling before he was connected to a human at Planetary Alliance headquarters who knew of the plan. From there I was patched through to the Terran government. When the connection was made, the screen revealed the face of former ambassador Mark Muller. I wanted to reach through the screen and smack the smirk right off his grinning mug.

"So, you have something to tell me?" he said.

"Do you mean something other than 'eff off?'" I asked, to Pelegran's horror.

"Something Kelvoo wanted you to pass along. You know, some sort of password," the ambassador said.

"Love above fear," I replied. "OK? That's the passphrase, 'love above fear.'"

"That's exactly the kind of wisdom I would expect from Kelvoo," he said.

"You'd better take care of Kelvoo!" I yelled. "If you don't return Kelvoo undamaged, I'll dedicate the rest of my life to destroying the lot of you!"

"I can see how upset you are, Brenna. Let me assure you that there will be no destruction of any being or anything else. There shall only be salvation, and it will come from Kelvoo."

"We're done!" I snapped as I stood up and walked away from the screen.

"Shall we get to work?" Pelegran asked as he terminated the call.

He began by skimming through Kelvoo's story, ignoring me completely.

"Fascinating!" he kept repeating in a soft voice, not taking his eyes off his Infotab.

I didn't know what to do with myself, so I wandered around the room. I pulled up a copy of Pa's first book on my Infotab and read the chapter that was set on Saraya, many of the events having taken place in the building where I stood.

I could picture the space filled with crew members from the *Pacifica Spirit*, along with the Terran high commissioner and various human and Sarayan dignitaries, as they hosted a reception for Kelvoo and the nine other kloormari in the group.

I was also able to visualize the art that had been displayed around the room and on the now empty walls as I read about Kelvoo's conversation with Lynda Paige. They had looked at an abstract painting. Lynda had seen mountains, rapids, deserts, lava, and crowds of beings among the swirls, shapes, and colors, but Pa only saw the swirls, shapes, and colors themselves. That was back before Pa had learned to imagine, which was a foreign concept to the kloormari. I wondered how Kelvoo would have interpreted that painting now, after the passage of so many years and experiences.

I walked over to the glass doors that led onto the deck and stepped outside into the cool breeze. I pictured Kelvoo's group drifting off into a meditative state under a starry night sky with

Saraya's moons passing overhead. That was when the effects of cold temperatures on kloormari physiology were discovered as the group lost consciousness and had to be carried inside and gradually warmed. Thanks to Kuw'baal's cloud cover and mild temperatures, no kloormari had ever been exposed to the cold before that first off-world trip.

I walked to the railing and looked back at the building where I noticed a large digital display of the current temperature along with the wind direction and speed. I wondered whether the kloormari hypothermia incident had been the reason for the display being installed.

Sah was getting low in the sky and casting a red glow as I looked over the railing and down to a line of beaches. The day after arriving on Saraya, Kelvoo and the other kloormari accompanied their human teacher, Sam Buchanan (Kelly's dad), to a nearby beach. As I watched the gentle surf roll onto the shoreline below, I wondered which bay they had visited.

I was so deep in thought that I hadn't noticed the arrival of additional staff. All were Sarayan except for one Bandorian and one human. They were examining something on their Infotabs—likely Kelvoo's new story, except for the human, who was leaning over Pelegran's desk and conversing with him. The man was tall, thin, and smartly dressed. His curly hair had a touch of grey on the sideburns, giving him an air of charm and sophistication without pretense. The man saw me looking at him, so he strode over and introduced himself as Guiseppe Smithers.

"Are you the token human investigator on the team?" I asked, intending to be witty, but as soon as I spoke, I worried that I had come across as sarcastic or condescending. Fortunately, Guiseppe showed no offense in his response.

"No, nothing like that," he replied. "I'm a hospitality consultant. I work with human visitors to Saraya. I coordinate their accommodations and meals, and I try to make them as comfortable as possible. I have been assigned to attend to your needs."

"So, you're the official 'Brenna wrangler,' is that it?" I asked, again realizing too late that my question was snarky. It occurred to me that I might have found Guiseppe rather handsome, and my sarcasm served to keep me focused on the investigation.

Instead of taking offense, Guiseppe chuckled. "I have had many job titles in a varied interplanetary career," he said. "'Brenna Wrangler' is a new one for me! Am I going to have my hands full wrangling you?" he asked, smiling.

So much for staying focused on the investigation, I thought, feeling a flush of embarrassment. At the same time, I welcomed the amusing distraction from a man perhaps twenty-five years my junior.

"May I show you to your quarters?" he inquired as he led the way down a corridor. "Pelegran and his staff are reviewing Kelvoo's document, then they'll have a meeting before they ask you a whole raft of questions."

My room was small but pleasant—a far cry from the luxurious suite at the Kelvonist Society's offices, but it was homier and more inviting. Guiseppe showed me the room's features, then gave me a tour of the shared kitchen and a supply room where I could pick up additional bedding, toiletries, clothing, and other basic items.

Guiseppe transferred his contact information to my Infotab and asked whether he could get anything for me. I thanked him and let him leave for the night, after which I made a snack in the kitchen before I went to my room.

I checked my Infotab for relevant news, only to find it pouring in from every news outlet, rife with speculation.

"Kelvoo Located on Terra!"

"Kelvoo on Terra—Abducted or Just Visiting?"

"Kelvoo—Terra's New God?"

"Kelvoomania Sweeps Terra"

"Terra in Uproar over Kelvoo"

These were just a few of the headlines that scrolled by. The stories all mentioned that I was on Terra with Kelvoo, so my relocation to Saraya was not yet public knowledge. I had no wish to deal with the press, so I was glad they didn't know my whereabouts.

I went to the supply room and picked out a set of pajamas and bathroom supplies. I wanted to sleep, but I knew that Pelegran would have questions for me. Bored, I walked along the corridor into the makeshift investigation headquarters where I saw all the investigators conferring while sitting on sofas arranged in a rectangle.

"Brenna!" Pelegran said when he noticed me. "I think we're ready to ask you a few questions." He glanced at his group for confirmation, and they nodded back.

"Alright, as long as it's just a *few* questions," I said. "I'm quite tired."

Pelegran invited me to sit in a large, comfortable chair next to him. Then he asked me to recount recent events.

As I told my story, I tried to touch on each detail, but I was frequently interrupted and asked to elaborate on every nuance. I was irritated at having to provide details that I thought were utterly irrelevant. Sometimes I was challenged on my recollection of events that were also covered in Kelvoo's story.

"Look," I said at one point, "I'm only a human. If there's a discrepancy between what I remember and Kelvoo's story, I suggest you rely on Kelvoo's perfect kloormari memory."

As the hours dragged on, fatigue weighed on me, my memory became increasingly inaccurate, and the investigators kept challenging me. Finally, exhaustion and frustration got the better of me.

"What's wrong with you people?" I shouted, to everyone's surprise. "Am I a suspect? Are you accusing me of lying?"

"Why would you think that?" Pelegran asked.

"Do you know how little sleep I've had lately? Do you have any idea what I've been through and how exhausted I am?"

"Brenna, I shall assume that your questions are rhetorical since I have insufficient information to answer them."

"I think we need to keep in mind the human tendency to lose concentration and become irritable and irrational when insufficiently rested," one of the other Sarayan investigators said.

I was hardly in the mood to be called irrational, but I was also too exhausted to protest. Pelegran apologized for his limited experience working with humans and then assured me that there were just a few more questions.

Half an hour later, I couldn't keep my eyes open, and I could barely form a basic sentence. Pelegran suggested that it would be counterproductive to continue until I could get a good night's sleep.

"What a brilliant deduction," I mumbled, which Pelegran took as a great compliment.

I slept through the few remaining hours of the Sarayan night and remained asleep until Sah was at its zenith the following day.

I put on a bathrobe that had been provided with the room, then went back to the supply room and found a Sarayan tunic with dark grey side panels, indicating my status as an off-world visitor. Back in the room, I changed into the tunic and put the clothes from the previous day, along with my pajamas, into the "refresh" hamper. Then I went into the kitchen and threw together a plate of food to ease my growling stomach.

I was startled by a voice behind me. "Did you sleep well?" Guiseppe asked.

"Very well, thanks," I replied. "And feeling much better too," I added, suddenly feeling guilty about not worrying more about Pa.

When I entered the main investigation room, some of the staff were in small groups studying data on display panels while others worked alone on their Infotabs. I greeted Pelegran and then apologized for not being at my best the previous night. I told him that I was ready for more questions, and he dived right in.

I was more engaged than I had been the previous evening and I endured being cross-examined by focusing on the overall goal of ensuring Kelvoo's wellbeing.

I had a few questions of my own. I asked how the investigators would be able to learn anything about events on Terra, given that the only quantum entanglement connection was to the Terran government, and the only other channel was via the few Terran embassies.

"We might have a few limited backchannels," Pelegran said, "though it's hard to tell what information is reliable." When I asked for details, his reply was vague.

"If such communication exists, I would not be at liberty to discuss it."

Pelegran also told me what he knew about the situation on Terra. The general population was growing anxious and restless. They wondered why Kelvoo had been presented to them and then vanished from view. Mainstream Kelvonists and the reformers were claiming that Kelvoo was fine, but both groups claimed to be hosting Kelvoo. One side said that Kelvoo was meditating and planning to emerge at an unspecified date while the other announced a future date for Kelvoo to address the people, with the future date being adjusted with each announcement. Some Terrans also speculated that Kelvoo had been brought to Terra by force. Protests had cropped up, but the gatherings had been peaceful so far.

"What should I do now?" I asked, looking around at the others, then back to Pelegran.

"Whatever you wish, Brenna," he said. "Please feel free to observe our investigation and to ask questions as we work toward Kelvoo's release."

I walked around the room, but I only saw investigators looking at screens with messages going back and forth. I asked a few what they were doing, but "gathering information," was all I got in response. All in all, I felt rather useless.

Guiseppe must have noticed me wandering aimlessly. "Would you like to get out of here and get some fresh air?" he asked.

"Yes puh-leeese!" I replied.

"I was thinking we could retrace the route of the tour that Sam Buchanan and the kloormari went on when Kelvoo originally visited here," he suggested. I was pleased to take him up on the offer.

Before we left, he handed me a long grey scarf made from a light, thin fabric. "If we get out of the car, you'll want to wrap this over your head and maybe even around your lower face a couple of times," he said.

When I asked why, he reminded me that I wouldn't want word of my location to get out. He assured me that no Sarayan would think it was their business to reveal information. "But it's the humans you want to be wary of," he said with a smile. "You wouldn't want some tourist recognizing you and ratting you out to the media!"

Guiseppe used his Infotab to sign out a car, which delivered itself to the rooftop landing pad. The clouds were scattered, and for a change, the wind was light, and the air was warm. The car lifted off, and Guiseppe guided it down toward the glass buildings and the large landing pad where I had been dumped the day before.

Guiseppe commanded the car to take a pre-programmed route. It descended close to the base of the pylon supporting the landing pad and made its way below the forest canopy, along a cleared route between massive tree trunks. The route had a great deal of traffic in both directions. "It's probably a little busier than when the bus took Kelvoo through here," he said as we passed some elaborate buildings and ancient ruins.

Several minutes later, we ascended back above the forest canopy. Guiseppe took the controls again as we flew through a steep-sided gorge with a fast-flowing river and a few flying reptiles below us. "This area's become a bit more built up than when Kelvoo was here," Guiseppe explained as I looked up to see towering buildings along the top of the cliffs. Despite the changes, I thought about how amazed Pa must have been, not only to see such things but also to be visiting another planet for the first time.

The river slowed and opened into a flat delta and then flowed into the ocean. We turned and followed the shore to a towering point of black rock that jutted into the sea below. Paths and caves were carved into the rock face where primitive Sarayans had lived hundreds of thousands of years ago.

We flew over the headland and then dropped into a small bay. "Is this where Kelvoo's group took the underwater tour?" I asked.

"That's right. The bus they were in was equipped to submerge. I wish I could show that part to you, but I don't know how watertight this car is, and I sure don't want to find out!" Guiseppe said with a laugh.

We circled the bay and then turned back around the tip of the headland, close to the surface of the crystal-blue water. *Kelvoo's Testimonial* describes tall waves with frothy spray being blown from the tips, but the water below us was calm with just a small swell breaking on the rocks.

"Where to next, madam?" Guiseppe asked in a posh tone, smiling. I asked him to take me to the beach that Sam Buchanan visited with Kelvoo's group.

When we landed at the edge of the sand, I took off my shoes and put on the scarf, wrapping it over my head, mouth, and chin. Naked Sarayans walked, ran, or lounged under Sah's rays while other beings reflected their species' modesty by being partly or fully clothed. I walked to the edge of the water, lifted my Sarayan robe just above my knees, and waded in. I let the gentle waves move the sand over my feet, enjoying the feeling, just as Pa had done so long ago. Guiseppe wasn't dressed for the beach, let alone for wading, so he waited on the shore.

"I guess you'll be wanting to return to base for an update," Guiseppe said as we walked back toward the car.

"If anything important happened, they'd call my Infotab, right?" I asked. Guiseppe assured me that Pelegran would do so. "In that case," I replied, "could we wait a while longer?"

"We can wait as long as you'd like."

We found a bench in a park beneath a shady grove of trees, close to where the car was parked. As we sat and watched locals and tourists strolling along the path that ran alongside the beach, we talked about our lives, our families, and our work, discussing just about everything except the investigation and the events that led up to it. At one point, Guiseppe received a text message from Pelegran, requesting an update on our whereabouts. Guiseppe replied to confirm that all was well as we exchanged a grin.

We were so engrossed in conversation that I hadn't noticed the dimming light until dusk set in, and a city light switched on above us. "Wow!" I exclaimed. "I didn't realize how late it is. I guess we'd better get back."

"Sure, but would you fancy a bite to eat first?" Guiseppe replied.

"I'd love that." I said, realizing how hungry I was.

Guiseppe took me to a human-owned restaurant with a lovely assortment of dishes from Alliance worlds with human-compatible cuisines. The lights in the restaurant were dimmed, but each table had a clear sphere at its center, filled with water and dozens of bioluminescent Sarayan water worms swimming around and casting a warm orange glow. We agreed that I could pull the scarf back from my face since the lights were dim enough that it would be difficult to recognize me.

Guiseppe and I sat at a cozy table for two and enjoyed a sumptuous meal with a glass each of Sarayan jadafruit wine. The wine was an exquisite blend of fruit and floral flavors tinged with afternotes of herbs and mineral ions. At least that's what the Terran portion of the label said, and my palate wasn't sophisticated enough to disagree.

"How are you holding up, Brenna?" Guiseppe asked as we enjoyed dessert.

"Considering the circumstances, I'm doing great, thanks to you, Guiseppe. But I also feel guilty enjoying myself while Pa—I mean Kelvoo—is stuck on Terra."

He nodded, then the conversation shifted to our shared fondness for Sarayan cuisine.

A few minutes later, Guiseppe received another message, inquiring about our location and when we could be expected to return. "I guess we'd better head back," I said.

When the car landed on the roof of the investigation headquarters, I looked up at the star-studded sky above and the bioluminescent ocean below. Along the coast, waving curtains of the aurora shimmered, then when I looked in the opposite direction, I saw Saraya's smallest moon rising in its low orbit, its oddly shaped mass turning end over end before it crossed the sky and dipped below the horizon two minutes later.

With the night air becoming chilly, we went inside. Guiseppe walked me to the door of my room where I hugged him and gave him a kiss on the cheek. "Thank you so much, Guiseppe," I said. "Thanks for such a lovely time and for distracting me from my worries for a while."

"It's been my pleasure," he replied. "Who'd have thought that the job of 'Brenna wrangler' could be so enjoyable?"

I started to ask myself, *should I? Do I dare?*

As I opened my door, I turned to look at Guiseppe, who was standing behind me, and I smiled. "Would you like to come in, just for a while?"

"Oh, Brenna," he replied, "that's a very tempting offer, but I'm sorry. My family is 'old school.' Our contract is far stricter than most, and my wife and co-husband would take issue with it."

My face flushed with embarrassment. "Oh, yes, of course. I'm Sorry." Earlier, we had discussed Guiseppe's family conglomerate, but I hadn't realized it involved restrictions on extramarital intimacy.

We said goodnight, and then I prepared to sleep, slipping into my freshly washed pajamas. *You're such an idiot!* I thought. *He was just doing his job, and you stupidly thought there was more to it. You're old enough to be his mother, for god's sake!*

As I lay awake, I decided to cut myself some slack. In my youth I had been in plenty of relationships, but they had always come to a quick end, usually by my own choice as I focused on my charity work. My "date" with Guiseppe made me consider how my life might have been different if I had become involved in an intimate family group. I wondered whether I might find a special person or two in my retirement years, but then I dismissed the thought, filing it in the "would've, should've" category as I drifted off to sleep.

SIXTEEN: MAY'S INTERVENTION

I awoke with a renewed determination to focus on the investigation and contribute however I could. As I dressed, I worried about seeing Guiseppe again and wondered whether things would be awkward between us. *You're an old lady*, I told myself. *Nothing should faze you. At your age you're supposed to enjoy making other people uncomfortable!*

I went to the kitchen and made myself breakfast with a mug of tea, put it on a tray, and then walked into the main office area. Guiseppe spotted me right away. "Brenna!" he exclaimed as he strode toward me. "I see you have your hands full." He motioned to take the tray.

"That's OK," I replied as I set the tray on a small round table beside the windows. I took one of the two chairs and invited Guiseppe to sit. "I hope I didn't make you feel awkward last night," I said, searching his eyes for an answer.

"I took it as a great compliment," he replied, smiling.

Oh, he's good at this! I thought, feeling relieved.

We made the usual small talk, then Guiseppe asked me whether he could take me anywhere or run any errands for me. I told him that I wanted to stick around and see how the investigation was going.

"OK," he said. "I'm going to leave and take care of some business. Give me a call if you need anything."

I finished breakfast and drank my tea while looking at the view. It was a windy day, and a wall of dark grey mist was rolling in from the ocean. The sea far below had lost its brilliance and was turning grey as the darkness advanced. The mist turned out to be a wall of torrential rain that drummed against the windows. I could no longer see the land or the sea, giving the sensation that the headland and the building were floating inside a layer of fog as thick as the clouds of Kuw'baal.

A servitor bot floated up to the table and offered to take the tray and dishes. I accepted, then for some reason, I asked the bot for its designation. "My Terran language designation is . . ." the bot began, followed by a string of alphabetical and numeric characters. It made me wistful as I wondered how Pollybot was doing and what possible service it could be providing to Pa. I reminded myself that it was silly to think of Pollybot as having any real intelligence, but I'd had such feelings ever since Kelvoo, May, and I came up with the name Pollybot and assigned it to our servitor unit, so long ago.

I noticed Pelegran at his desk. He turned around and saw me approaching. "Good morning, Brenna."

"Good morning. Any news about Kelvoo?" I asked.

"No. Just additional news about the overall situation on Terra."

I expected Pelegran to continue, but he just sat in silence. "Were you planning on sharing the news with me?" I inquired.

"No. It doesn't concern extracting Kelvoo from Terra, so I didn't think it would interest you."

I couldn't understand Pelegran's terseness, especially since he had practically been tripping over himself and apologizing for every perceived slight when we first met.

"Pelegran," I said, "I want to know *everything* about everything! When I first arrived, you and your team grilled me for hours, wanting every tiny detail. Why would you think that I wouldn't want the same level of detail, especially since the wellbeing of my own parent is involved?"

"My apologies, Brenna," he said. "We have passed the phase where we gather the most basic facts, and we're now meticulously gathering additional details. I should be more mindful of the differences between human and Sarayan mindsets and priorities. I will be pleased to update you now, if you wish."

"Please do," I replied.

Pelegran described reports of increasing turmoil among the Terran citizens and the intense debates inside the Kelvonist groups, or "sects," as he liked to call them. Sometimes it seemed that the sects were cooperating, but at other times, they would point fingers at one another and declare that they were the only true followers of the way of Kelvoo.

Rumor had it that Kelvoo had agreed to address the people of Terra. I assumed that Kelvoo must have done so after receiving my passphrase. Apparently, Kelvoo wanted to make a live broadcast, but the Kelvonists wouldn't allow it, not knowing what their reluctant god might say. When they recorded Kelvoo's speech, it was, as they had feared, a command for the Terrans to stop their worship, abandon all forms of Kelvonism, and stop wasting their time looking for divine guidance instead of thinking for themselves.

In response to growing insistence to see Kelvoo in person, the Kelvonists resorted to producing a false vid that simulated Kelvoo's movements and words. A Terran contact had reported that the message from "fake Kelvoo" was vague and consisted mostly of Kelvoo urging patience until the time was right to emerge from meditation and reveal all. Terrans who were familiar with vid and audio manipulation identified the broadcast as prerecorded and phony. The Kelvonists responded that the people who were crying foul were lying, leading to further divisions in their increasingly fragile society.

Pelegran told me that much of the information was still unverified, but his team's confidence was growing as other sources worked to confirm their findings.

"So, who are these sources?" I asked.

"I'm sorry, Brenna, but I'm not at liberty to say."

"Don't you trust me?"

"That is irrelevant. Whether I trust you or not, I'm prohibited from sharing that information outside of the investigative team and certain Planetary Alliance authorities."

"OK, how about this: Are your sources inside the Terran government? Are they from a Kelvonist sect?"

"I'm prohibited from sharing that information outside of the investigative team and certain Planetary Alliance authorities," he repeated.

Fed up, I turned and walked away, though not before urging Pelegran to keep me constantly updated.

For the rest of the day, I alternated between pacing, watching news on my Infotab, pacing, looking at the rain outside, pacing, eating to excess, pacing, chewing my fingernails, pacing, and badgering Pelegran and the other investigators for any tidbits of information. Guiseppe called me twice to check on me. I replied that I was fine, thanked him for calling, then ended the call abruptly, almost to the point of rudeness.

The rain continued through the following night. I got out of bed frequently, each time eating a snack, and pacing through the investigators' area, no doubt serving as a distraction to the night shift investigators, their grey Sarayan faces illuminated only by their Infotab screens and display panels.

The next morning, the rain had tapered to showers, but the headland and the buildings were still shrouded in mist. That entire day was a repeat of the previous one. Guiseppe offered to take me out and about. "There's a mountain about a hundred kilometers from here," he said. "Its peak is above the clouds and there's a nice restaurant there with some great human food. Why don't you let me take you there for lunch?"

I declined Guiseppe's offer and instead, repeated my routine from the previous day. Unfortunately, there was no news of any kind from Terra, so I ended up going to bed early, feeling frustrated and useless. There was a skylight over the bed. I overrode the nighttime opacity setting to keep the glass clear. The fog above me was illuminated by lighting along the paths outside the building. Over time, the fog dissipated, and gaps appeared. Moments later the brilliance of the starlit sky was framed in the skylight, with the billions of stars in the central disk of the galaxy, spanning the center of my celestial view. I don't know how much time passed before the larger of Saraya's moons crept into view and lit up the room. The change in the weather made me think that the following day would bring significant change to my circumstances. With that in mind, I closed my eyes and slept.

My slumber was ended by the brilliant light of a new Sarayan day piercing the skylight. I got dressed, filled a tray with breakfast, then walked through the work area to the doors leading onto the deck. Sah's orange rays beamed through the clouds on the horizon. When I stepped outside, there was no wind at all. The air was so crisp I could see slight condensation from my breath, but when I stood in Sah's direct light, it warmed me. I balanced my tray on the railing and ate while I stood there, comfortable in the increasingly warm air as I sipped my mug of hot tea.

As I stepped back inside, the office bot relieved me of my tray and dishes. I saw Guiseppe sitting at the small table where we had chatted two days before. He was with a woman whom I couldn't recognize since she was facing toward Guiseppe and away from me. Both of them were eating breakfast.

As I approached, Guiseppe looked up and grinned. "Brenna! I would introduce you to our guest, but I'm sure that won't be necessary."

I recognized my sister before Guiseppe finished his sentence. I was so delighted and overwhelmed, I just stood there for a moment, staring.

"Well, the least you could've done would've been to call me!" May said, smiling.

She stood up, and we embraced one another. "Oh my god, May! I'm sorry!"

"Which god are you talking about, Brenna? I hope you haven't started worshipping Pa!"

I told May that I didn't want word to get out about my removal from Terra. I admitted that I could have called her privately, but I had been so focused on following the investigation.

I released my grip on May and backed up a step, holding onto her forearms. "You look great!" I said.

"And you look like you were just shot out of an airlock!" she replied. We both laughed.

"So, how did you find out I was here?" I asked.

"The Planetary Alliance let me know. In fact, they're the ones who arranged for me to come here. They figured you could use a break."

"More like they figured I was being a pain in their posteriors!"

"Well, they might have dropped a few hints in that regard," she said, grinning. "So, Guiseppe said he's become known as the Brenna wrangler."

"Oh, he's been trying alright," I said as I shot a smile at Guiseppe. "I guess they invited you here because they needed to pull out the big guns."

"Well, today you're going to give yourself and the investigators a break!" May said. "Guiseppe told me about the places he's shown you, and I wanted to see them for myself. The three of us are going out on the town today, and I won't take no for an answer!"

"I don't know, May. Don't you think Pa would want me to keep on top of the investigation and help where I can?"

"Hell no! Brenna, don't you think I'm just as worried about Pa? Believe me, I haven't had a good night's sleep since we found out you and Pa were taken. But what's the point of standing around here if we're just getting in the way? Pa wouldn't want that at all, and you know it!"

I couldn't argue with May. We all climbed into a car, and we had a wonderful day in some beautiful Sarayan weather. As Guiseppe took us back to the places he'd shown me before, and to many new sights, May and I spent much of the time talking about Kelvoo and the situation on Terra.

When we were at the beach, I made sure to wear the scarf over my face, but we were confident that May wouldn't be recognized. I asked Guiseppe to excuse us for a few moments, then I invited May to wade with me. Guiseppe kept a close watch over us, but when we were out of earshot, I told May about my foolish advance toward Guiseppe.

"Who can blame you?" she replied. "He's gorrrrrrrgeous!"

"Shut up!" I said, embarrassed but laughing.

"You shut up!" May replied, laughing as she jabbed her index finger toward me.

I kicked some water toward May, which splashed her more than I had expected. She kicked back, soaking me with a wall of water. When I reciprocated, my foot flew up, and I let out a shriek as my center of gravity shifted, and I fell flat on my back in the knee-deep water.

I flopped about in the waves until I flipped onto all fours and tried to get up. Guiseppe came running, shedding his shoes as he waded in. He and May each grabbed one of my arms, pulling me onto my feet and guiding me ashore. By then my scarf had fallen around my shoulders. May howled with laughter. I did too, between my coughs and sputters. Guiseppe just shook his head, then retrieved his fancy shoes.

I couldn't put the sodden scarf back over my face, so we made our way back up the beach and found a secluded spot where I wouldn't be recognized. While we waited for our clothes to dry, May asked me about my time with the Kelvonists on Terra. Her questions were very specific regarding locations and landmarks, which made me suspicious.

"You're up to something, aren't you, Sis?" I asked.

"You know me. I'm always cooking something up," May replied with her signature wicked smile.

"How long are you planning to stay?" I asked.

"For as long as it takes. Hopefully, not long at all."

We spent the late afternoon and early evening at the delightful mountaintop restaurant, where Guiseppe had offered to take me a couple of days earlier.

As Sah was setting and the car descended toward the rooftop landing pad at the investigation office, Guiseppe asked whether we were ready for our chat with Pelegran.

"What chat?" I asked.

"Didn't I mention it?" Guiseppe said. "Sorry about that. He wants to talk to all three of us."

May was silent, indicating she was aware of some sort of plan. I shot her a dirty look.

As we left the car and made our way down the stairs, Guiseppe entered some text into his Infotab. Pelegran was waiting for us in the group of armchairs and sofas. Guiseppe took a chair while May sat on a sofa and patted the cushion next to her. I reluctantly sat beside May, waiting for some kind of intervention along the lines of, "We love you very much, but . . ."

Pelegran nodded toward May. "Come with me, back to Perdition," May said, looking into my eyes. "There's an interstellar transport in orbit, and a shuttle can take us there in two hours. Please come with me."

"No!" I replied. "I need to stay here and help the investigation! What if some news comes in?"

"We'll establish a direct quantum entanglement connection to May's home," Pelegran said. "News will be provided instantaneously, and you can still communicate directly with us."

"But I need to be part of this! I need to help!" I replied.

"Brenna, your presence here has not been helpful. You've been a distraction, which has the potential to hinder our important investigation," Pelegran said without a hint of emotion.

"What are you saying? That I'm in the way?" I asked, realizing immediately that I didn't want to know the answer.

"Yes, Brenna. That's exactly what I'm saying."

"Wow! Well, there's no slap in the face that stings quite like Sarayan bluntness!" I said, feeling hurt to my core.

Guiseppe shifted uncomfortably. "Pelegran's statement was, perhaps, a bit harsh," he said, touching my shoulder but stopping short of disagreeing with Pelegran's sentiment.

"Come back with me, Brenna," May pleaded.

"I can't impose on you like that," I replied, my mind still reeling. *Leave? Now?*

"There's no imposition at all! Tristan, Ndugu, Beth, and Simone love you. Your nieces and nephews adore you too. We've set aside a room for you, and you can come and go as you please."

"Exactly how many nieces and nephews do I have now?" I asked.

"Hell if I know! I lost track years ago," May replied, which made me smile.

"It sounds as if I don't have a choice."

May, Guiseppe, and Pelegran didn't reply. They all just gave me a look that confirmed my fears.

"Fine!" I exclaimed, letting out a sigh and throwing my hands up, knowing they were right. I stood and brushed some remaining beach sand off my legs. "Might as well get on with it."

May and I went to my room and stuffed my few possessions into a bag. I left the scarf behind. "To hell with it!" I said. "I'm not hiding any more. I don't care if the entire sector knows where I am and what I'm doing!"

Later that night as the transport pulled away from Saraya and headed to a jump point, May and I reclined our seats to get some rest after our eventful day. "I knew it! Right from our time on the beach, I knew you had something up your sleeve." I said.

"What do you mean?" May asked.

"Getting me to leave Saraya, obviously."

May turned to face me. "Well, if you think that's the only thing I've been plotting, you've seriously underestimated me, Sis!"

SEVENTEEN: MAY'S MADNESS

I slept until the jump announcement was made. When the actual jump happened, I was dozing off again, but I didn't find the weird sights, sounds, and feelings of the jump particularly disturbing. I was too tired to think about it.

I was fully awake during the approach to orbit around Perdition. May yawned, stretched, and rubbed her eyes.

"Alright May, what's the plan?" I asked.

May looked around to see how close other passengers were, then lowered her voice. "I'm going to launch my *own* investigation," she said.

"Oh, sure you are!" I replied, raising my eyebrows and giving her a "side-eye" look.

"Just watch me," she said.

"What can *you* do?" I asked. "Pelegran's team has access to every available resource and communication channel. They're doing everything they can to get Pa out of there."

"Really, Brenna, do you honestly think they're doing *everything* they possibly can?"

"Not even close," I admitted with a sigh. "OK, so where are you going to magically come up with the investigators, the contacts, and the leads? Neither of us have ever done that kind of work."

"You'd be amazed what money can buy!" May replied.

"Look, I know your family conglomerate has enjoyed plenty of success, and Pa has been more than generous with us, but you aren't *that* rich!" I said, speaking a bit louder than I intended.

"Shh! Let's keep it down," May admonished. "From the moment word got out that you and Pa were on Terra, I launched a fundraising campaign for my investigation. Within two days we had millions of contributors and over two billion SimCash units. The donations are still rolling in. I can't wait to see how big the pot is when we get home!"

"So, what are you going to do if all that money isn't spent?"

"It's OK. Anything that isn't used will be returned to the donors."

"Well, I doubt the Planetary Alliance investigators will be happy when they find out about it."

"Oh, they spotted my fundraiser right away. I got a call from one of their bureaucrats. They don't like it, but they said they can't stop me from doing my own work, as long as it doesn't interfere with theirs."

I couldn't get my mind around what May was telling me. Her ambition was inspired, but her assumption that she could make a difference seemed to take a lot of confidence that I certainly didn't share.

"OK, so where are you going to find the experts to help you?" I asked.

"Who needs experts?" she said, smiling. "It's contacts, Sis. It's about having the right contacts."

"Well, sure, but how are you and your contacts going to gather information from Perdition?"

"Oh, I'm not going to be on Perdition when this plan goes into action!"

I started to think that May was just playing some sort of weird game. "Sure, May, so what are you going to do? Sneak onto Terra and save Pa?" I asked with a sarcastic chuckle.

She didn't answer. My heart started racing, and the blood drained from my face as I turned to look at her. Her devilish smile told me everything I needed to know.

"Are you out of your goddamn mind?" I hissed. "How . . . who'd be crazy enough to take you there?"

"Contacts!"

May's hand was on the armrest between us. I grasped her wrist and leaned toward her, staring into her eyes. "What contacts?" I asked slowly, enunciating each word.

"Well . . ." she said, blinking and smiling with mock innocence, "I might happen to know someone who might happen to know someone who has a contact in the Brotherhood."

"The Brotherhood? Are you out of your effing mind?"

"Shhhhhhhhhh!" May replied, holding a finger over her lips.

My outburst caught the attention of dozens of other passengers. They looked over at us, then chattered with their companions. A couple of them pointed in our direction. Up to that part of the trip, I had gone unrecognized. *So much for being anonymous*, I thought as I tried to come to grips with May's madness.

Our conversation was cut short when a chime sounded, indicating that shuttles from the surface were approaching to take us to Perdition. Eager passengers rose to line up by the docking bay doors, to get aboard the first shuttles. Being in no rush, we got out of our seats, but we hung back. May used her Infotab to summon one of her family's cars to the spaceport.

May gripped my arm, just above the elbow. "Listen, Brenna. My spouses and kids know that I'm fundraising for an investigation, but I haven't mentioned anything about going to Terra. Not a word of this to *anyone*, at least not yet, OK?"

"That's fine with me. I don't want to be the one to tell them they have a nutcase for a spouse or a lunatic for a mom! But mark my words, May. I'm going to talk you out of this insanity."

We boarded the second group of shuttles, and we were in the spaceport about twenty-five minutes later. After we were processed through customs, we settled into May's car and headed to her home.

Following a couple of minutes of silence, May looked over at me. "I can see the wheels turning in your brain," she said. "What are you thinking?"

"I can't even begin to tell you! There are so many holes in your plan, I don't know where to start!"

"Can you give me a single example?"

"Sure. How about the fact that you haven't set foot on Terra since you were a kid, and everything's different now? How would you even find your way around?"

"Well, Sis, that's where *you* come in," May said, smiling.

EIGHTEEN: MONEY

Months passed while I was at May's home. Pelegran and I fell into a pattern where I called him every morning or evening, depending on the differences in the time of day between Saraya and Perdition. There was frustratingly little news about Kelvoo, or even the situation on the ground. Protests on Terra ebbed and flowed in intensity, and conspiracy theories abounded. I was heartened to learn that some Terrans were expressing doubts about Kelvoo's divinity, but I worried that instead of blaming the Kelvonists, they might think that Kelvoo had intentionally misled them.

I spent a lot of time with May and her spouses. When her children, grandchildren, nieces, and nephews visited, I spent more time with them than I had imagined I'd be capable of enduring. Sometimes when a plethora of grandchildren were over, the constant shrieking and frenetic activity exceeded my tolerance, and I'd have to escape to my room. Most of the time, though, I liked watching how the members of a large, loving family enjoyed one another's company, supporting and challenging each other. I was treated with respect, kindness, and love, and I was very happy for May, but her vibrant family life made me miss and appreciate Pa more than ever. My life floated along on undercurrents of worry and sadness. As my despair and frustration grew, May's plan sounded less absurd with each passing day.

During those months, May would work for a few hours each day in a room that served as her personal office. Her family knew not to disturb her "investigative research." When we spoke in private, she rarely mentioned her wish to go to Terra, but I spent plenty of time thinking about it and how we could pull off such an insane plan.

One afternoon, I called Pelegran from May's courtyard garden when it was early morning on Saraya. He told me about a violent skirmish between staunch traditional Kelvonists and a group of doubters who believed that Kelvoo was a fraud who had led Terra astray. Clubs had been wielded, rocks had been thrown, and severe injuries had resulted.

Pelegran told me that the Planetary Alliance was starting to worry more about Kelvoo's safety and had stepped up its demands for the Terran government to release Kelvoo immediately. The Terrans simply ignored the demands. "There's nothing else we can do at this point," Pelegran said when I pressed him.

"What are you saying?" I demanded. "Are you suggesting that Kelvoo's death is an option?"

"Yes."

"What?" I must have looked apoplectic, because he hurried to explain.

"Look, Brenna, I'm sorry about my Sarayan bluntness, but Kelvoo's death is a possibility. You should prepare yourself for such an event. The hard truth is that the Planetary Alliance can't jeopardize interplanetary relations over the life of a single being no matter how prominent that individual may be."

After Pelegran terminated the call, it took a moment for my stunned silence to transform into seething anger. I stormed into the house and found May reading in a recreation area.

"Let's do this!" I said. May knew exactly what I was talking about.

The next day, May told her unsuspecting family that we were going to a deep-space command post in a few days where we would meet with her private contacts who were returning from Terra. She told them we would be incommunicado for several days. May's story wasn't a *complete* lie. We were going to deep space, we were meeting a contact, and we would certainly be unable to communicate for a while.

When the time came, May took a family car, which drove us to a remote location about 120 kilometers from her home. We touched down in a clearing beside a wooded area. A well-dressed middle-aged man emerged from the forest and introduced himself as Desmond Cipollone. Our "friend" pulled out some tools and a reprogramming device and got into our car. He modified the car's log so it would show that it took us to the spaceport, then automatically returned home.

We each retrieved a small travel bag from the car and then watched it speed away. I felt alone and extremely vulnerable with the stranger, even though I had expected him, as an associate of the Brotherhood gangs, to be scruffier and cruder than he was.

Desmond led us into the forest where a mini shuttle was hovering, ready to go. "You must be May," he said to me.

"No, I'm Brenna."

"Oh, sorry. I was told that May was the younger one," he replied, smiling.

"Nice try," I said, not about to fall for his flattery.

He turned to May. "We need to take care of phase one in advance," he said.

May used her Infotab to transfer the first payment to Desmond, then we got into the shuttle. It followed a standard traffic path to an orbital departure location and was given automated clearance to ascend into orbit. The shuttle met up with a mid-size interstellar transport that had a cargo airlock barely large enough for the shuttle to park inside.

The four Brotherhood crew members were as disheveled and impolite as I would have expected, but they went about their tasks with little fuss. During the three-hour trip to the jump point, May and I were provided with Terran-style clothing, so we could blend with the population. Then, when May transferred an astronomical amount of SimCash to Desmond, he gave each of us a bag of gold metallic pieces, telling us we had one hundred each. Each piece was about the size of my thumb and around two or three millimeters thick. Two small silvery squares of metal were embedded in each of the larger gold pieces.

"What are these?" I asked.

"Gold chips," May said. "Money."

"Money? You mean like coins or paper that humans used in ancient times?"

"Yep. SimCash doesn't work on Terra since they aren't connected to that system."

"Why didn't I see this stuff when I was with the Kelvonists?"

"I don't know. Did they ever take you shopping?"

"No, we never quite got around to it," I said, which made May smile. She turned to Desmond.

"Your people use gold chips on Terra, right?"

"Oh yes!" he said, grinning. "A little hard currency goes a long way outside of the Alliance worlds! We use it whenever we trade with Terra."

"What kinds of things do you trade with Terrans?" I asked.

"You wouldn't want to know," he said, still smiling.

After the jump, May and I looked through a window, gazing at Terra as the transport sped toward orbit. "From up here, you'd never imagine the craziness going on below," I said. "It looks so beautiful."

"Saraya looks nicer," May replied.

"Hell, even Perdition looks nicer," I added, "but it's still a beautiful world—at least from a distance."

As soon as orbit was established, May and I boarded Desmond's shuttle in the cargo airlock. We made our way to Terra's surface with just a few jolts in transit as the small vessel punched through the atmosphere's outer reaches. We descended into a scrubby, isolated semi-desert area. "No need to attract attention," Desmond explained. "Terra doesn't have much need for orbital tracking, but there's no sense taking chances."

We proceeded at a low altitude for almost two hours before merging into a standard traffic stream as we closed in on our destination. The arid scenery gave way to grassland, then fields, and finally, forest. As we crested a hill, we saw a lake below with a river flowing from the far end. Homes and other buildings were on the river's right bank, forming a village, with farms and forests farther to the right. The left bank was parkland with the Kelvonist Society's towering headquarters perched on its soaring pillars. Kozoltoo's home and the golden-domed temple were at ground level just beyond. The long pond resembled a moat, snaking its way beneath the edge of the headquarters and along the base of the supporting pillars.

Desmond had the shuttle touch down beside a path that was across the river from the Kelvonist headquarters, a short walk from the village.

"Well, ladies, that's it for me!" Desmond announced as we removed our bags from the shuttle. "Just one more matter to take care of."

May pulled out her Infotab and transferred another fortune in SimCash. Desmond checked the amount on his Infotab. "Forgive me for asking," he said, "but you would like someone to pick you up, along with your mysterious extra passenger, when you're done?"

"Of course," May replied. "We'll pay for our safe return when we're picked up."

"Oh, it doesn't work that way. We require a deposit for such services," he said, naming a new astronomical sum.

"You're thieves; that's what you are!" May exclaimed as she transferred more SimCash.

"M'ladies," Desmond said with fake charm, "if 'twere up to me, I would have brought you here in exchange for nary but your delightful company. But, alas, my Brotherhood masters must extract their kilogram of flesh from every one of us!"

"Do you think you're funny?" I asked. "Especially after what your people did to Kelvoo on *Jezebel's Fury*?"

"That was a long time ago, well before *my* time," he replied in a more serious tone. "Things have changed, and we must all do what we can to survive."

Desmond passed a handheld device to May. "Open the lid and press the button when you're ready for pick-up. Be sure you're in exactly the same location forty-eight Terran hours later for your extraction. Good luck," he added as the shuttle's hatch closed and he soared away.

We were weary and hungry as we trudged into the village. The time at May's home on Perdition would have been close to midnight, but it was mid-morning in our location on Terra, and we hadn't slept since the start of the journey.

As we walked along the riverside path, the most astonishing sights were the images of Kelvoo wherever we looked. Metal posts lined the railing along the riverbank, supporting banners that hung over the path. Each bore an image of Kelvoo's upper torso and eye dome, backlit with a brilliant white light that appeared to flow directly from Kelvoo. While the pictures on the banners were the same, the text was different on each one.

"Kelvoo is Here!"

"A Joyous Return!"

"Prepare for Salvation!"

"Terra's New Era!"

"Celebrate!"

I can't describe how weird it was to see images of praise depicting a being that I simply knew as Pa. Adding to our unease, we also saw "Where is Kelvoo?", "Free Kelvoo!", and "Liars!" scrawled over some of the banners and other signs along the way. The graffiti was just one sign of the unrest that presented a growing danger to Pa.

On the far side of the river, we looked up at the Kelvonist headquarters. When Kelvoo and I had been in the building, surveying the scene below, everything looked so serene. From my new vantage point, the towering building was impressive and ominous. *What the hell have we got ourselves into?* I wondered as the enormity and the risks of our mission hit home.

A young man approached. "You look as if you might be lost," he said. "Are you looking for something in particular?"

"How do we get to Kelvoo Buchanan-Paige's place?" May asked.

"You're joking, right?" the young man said. "You can't just walk up to the front door of the richest person on the continent!"

"Please forgive my sister," I replied. "We're not from around here."

"I wondered about your accents," he said. "Where are you from?"

"Australia."

"Oh? You aren't reformists, are you?" he asked, his eyes narrowing with suspicion.

"No! Never!" I exclaimed, trying my best to look affronted. "We want to get away from them! That's why we're visiting this place. We're thinking of moving somewhere where people are better grounded."

"Well, you can't do much better than here! So, where in Australia are you from?"

May and I responded simultaneously.

"Queensland."

"Perdition".

"Yes! Uh, Perdition in Queensland," I said, scrambling to maintain my composure.

"Hmm . . . I've heard of Perdition the planet, but I've never heard of an Australian city with that name!"

"Oh, um, I wouldn't call it a city," I said. "It's just a tiny hick town off the traffic routes. It's got nothing but dust and a whole lot of alligators."

"Don't you mean crocodiles?"

"Yeah, I guess. Same difference, right?"

The man stared at us as if we each had two heads.

"Sorry if we're not making much sense," I said. "We haven't slept for a long time, and we're starving! Is there a place nearby where we can buy a meal?"

"Sure. Take the next path to the right. Go up the little hill to the main path and, you'll see a place on the corner."

"Thank you. You're so kind."

"Oh, it's no problem, but I wouldn't suggest you try going to the KBP compound. They won't let you get anywhere near it!"

"KBP?"

"As in Kelvoo Buchanan-Paige. Wow! You two really aren't from around here!"

"Good to know!" I replied.

"OK, take it easy you two. May Kelvoo's blessings be upon you!" he called out as we walked away.

"Yeah, yeah, you too!" I said.

"How did that man know my name?" May asked.

"What do you mean?"

"You know, when he said 'May, Kelvoo's blessings be upon you.'"

"He didn't mean 'May,' as in your name!" I said with slight annoyance. "He meant the other kind of 'may.'"

May smiled knowingly. I was in no mood for jokes, but I appreciated her attempt to be lighthearted in the face of an increasingly overwhelming situation.

We turned up the path on our right and passed more signs of Terra's obsession with Kelvoo. A display panel on the side of a building showed images of children playing beside a lake and others gathered around a campfire. "Support Kamp Kelvoo!" the text read. "Summer fun and learning under Kelvoo's kind, watchful eye!"

We found the restaurant right away. A sign shone through the front window, with Kelvoo's image and text indicating that the business supported Kelvoo's charitable causes—whatever they were. A bot showed us to a small table on a patio under the broad, leafy branches of two large trees. The coolness of the shade was a welcome respite from the increasing heat of the day. The bot brought us glasses and a water dispenser. The ice-cold water was refreshing, both physically and mentally.

We ordered our meals and enjoyed the authentic Terran cuisine. A different bot approached us and asked whether we required anything further. When we declined, it quoted a price, which meant nothing to us. "Please place currency on the detector," it said, extending a tray toward us.

May reached into her bag and produced a gold chip. "Will this cover it?" she asked as she placed it on the tray.

"Unable to process," the bot replied. It lowered the tray and tilted it until the chip slid onto the tablecloth in front of May, then requested payment again. May reached into her bag and pulled out a second gold chip. She placed both chips on the tray, but the bot had the same reaction.

"I'm sorry, but I don't know what you want," May said after the third request. "How many gold chips do you need?"

"Stand by," the bot replied as it glided into the restaurant. May put one of the chips back in her bag. A few seconds later, a woman who appeared to be in her mid-forties strode toward us.

"Sorry to bother you ladies," she said. "There seems to be a problem with our pay bot. Perhaps I can take your payment."

"Will this be enough, or do you need more?" May asked, holding up a gold chip.

The woman gasped, and her mouth fell open. "A gold chip?" she sputtered.

May nodded. "Yes."

"Is this some kind of prank?"

"I hope not."

"We sell meals here, not luxury cars!" she said. "I'd have to sell half my business to give you change for that amount!"

"Sorry," I said. "We're visitors. From Australia."

"More like from another planet!" she replied, which made me extremely nervous.

"We're from a small place, and we aren't familiar with your big city ways," I said, realizing how stupid I sounded, given that we were in a small village at that moment.

"Sorry about that," the woman replied, "though the last time I checked, we use the same money in every corner of Terra!"

"What should we do?" May asked.

The woman calmed down, seeming to take pity on us. Perhaps she thought we were two old ladies in cognitive decline—two extremely *wealthy* old ladies in cognitive decline.

"Well, dear," she said to May, "why don't you take that gold chip to a bank and have them exchange it for some smaller denominations? While you're at it, you might want to deposit most of the amount. It really isn't wise to carry that much cash with you!"

"Where can we find a bank?" I asked.

The woman pointed to a blue building a short way along the main path. We thanked her and said we'd let her know once we had taken care of things. We didn't fully understand the purpose of banks, but I had read something about them from pre-SimCash times. May figured that my knowledge made me an expert, so she handed her chip to me, and I walked to the bank while she waited at the table.

A large image of Pa hung over the bank's entrance. As I entered, a reception bot inquired as to my business there. "I would like to exchange one gold chip for smaller denominations," I said. *Whatever denominations are,* I thought.

A man in Terran business attire emerged from an office. "Good day, madam," he said. "How may we help you?"

"My sister and I were at the restaurant down the path, but this is all we have to offer as payment," I explained, holding up the gold chip. "We need to exchange it for smaller pieces."

"Yes, of course! Do you have an account with us?"

"I don't think so."

"Well, if you'd like to keep your funds on deposit with us, we can offer an excellent rate of return."

I had no idea what the man meant, but I played along. "Yes, that sounds fine," I said, "as long as I can keep enough to pay for the meal."

"That's wonderful, ma'am! All I need is your ETCI data."

"ETCI data?"

"You know, your encrypted Terran citizen identification data. Please send it to me from your Infotab."

I felt as if the walls were closing in. I tried to retain my composure amid visions of being arrested and thrown into a Terran correction center for fraud.

Coming up with a ruse, I pulled out my Infotab and looked at the screen. "Oh, dearie me! It looks as though I have my sister's Infotab by mistake. She . . . she must have mine! Oh, I'm so stupid!" I stammered. "I'll tell you what, I'm going to run back to the restaurant and swap my Infotab with hers. I just need two minutes, and I'll be right back!"

"Would you like me to accompany you?" the man asked. "I'd advise against carrying that much money around!"

"No!" I said, louder than I intended. "I mean, that's very sweet of you, but I don't want to waste your time." He seemed to be intensely interested in my gold chip and was probably worried I wouldn't return. "I know!" I said, "Why don't I leave this little chip with you, and I'll be right back?"

I grabbed the man's hand and pressed the gold chip into his palm. He just stood there, astonished. "Be right back," I said in a singsong voice as I made my way through the main doors and back onto the path.

I broke into the closest thing to a run that my old legs would permit. When May saw me approaching, I mouthed the words "We need to go!" as I pointed at a side path that led between a few houses. May shrugged in confusion. As I approached the table, I reached into my bag, pulled out one of my gold chips, and placed it on the tablecloth. Then I grabbed May's wrist, almost dislocating her shoulder as I pulled her to her feet.

"We need to run! Now!" I hissed.

Fortunately, May was the only patron on the patio. Neither the restaurant's owner nor any of her bots or staff were in sight as we hightailed it down the side path and toward a wooded area a few houses away. My heart was pounding out of my chest as I expected the restaurateur, the bank manager, or a law enforcement officer to pounce onto us at any moment.

By the time we reached the tree line, we were gasping for air. We looked back down the path from just inside the trees. Sure enough, a law enforcement vehicle was touching down outside the restaurant. The restaurant owner came out and spoke with the officer, followed by the banker, who jogged up from the bank. All three of them were looking around, making me hopeful that they hadn't seen where we had fled.

May and I crouched down. "We haven't broken any laws, have we?" May whispered, her body trembling beside mine.

"Hell if I know," I said, "but we sure looked suspicious!"

"I guess we're down to only a hundred and ninety-nine gold chips now."

"More like a hundred and ninety-eight, since I gave another one to the man in the bank. Still, I don't think a lack of funds is going to be much of a problem for us!" I scowled. "That Brotherhood grifter could at least have told us how much those chips are worth on Terra!"

Once we caught our breath, we decided to walk deeper into the woods. There wasn't much undergrowth, so it was easy to move between the trees. We came upon a winding, well-maintained gravel path and soon noticed other paths. There were also display panels on posts, explaining the local flora. Some of the panels had Kelvoo stickers on the sides, perhaps added by children. Thankfully, no other people were around. We found a bench and plopped ourselves down on it.

"Oh, Sis," May said. "I'm sorry I talked you into this. What a stupid idea! I should've listened to you." Seeing she was on the verge of tears, I put an arm around May's shoulders.

"It's alright May, really. It's not over yet, and at least we're doing *something*. Besides, look at the good we've done!"

"What are you talking about?"

"We just made a restaurant owner and a bank man very, very rich!"

My comment broke our pent-up stress, at least for that moment, and the woods echoed with the cackling of two old bats, screeching with laughter.

NINETEEN: TOURISTS

After our close call with the law, May and I spent the day lying low in the park, crouching behind bushes at any sign that somebody was approaching. We had nothing to eat, but the park was equipped with water dispensers and public lavatories.

At dusk, we sheltered inside a gazebo. Graffiti had been added to the interior walls. Most of the text praised Kelvoo, but some suggested conspiracies and calls for rebellion.

After dark, we sat in a corner of the gazebo, huddled under a blanket we had found abandoned in the woods. The blanket was filthy, but the night was chilly. As fugitives—or at least a couple of suspicious-looking old ladies—we didn't have a wealth of options. It felt odd to be carrying an almost inconceivable amount of money with no practical way of putting it to use. Again, I cursed the Brotherhood.

We must have slept for only an hour or two before the dawn light pierced the treetops. The cold made my joints ache as if my bones were broken, but we knew we had to get moving before any visitors arrived. May and I looked like hell. Our disheveled hair must have made us appear like a couple of eccentric hags.

As we dragged our carcasses to an upright position and limped around to warm up, we discussed our plan of action. All we could come up with was to put some distance between the village and ourselves and try to convince people to help us by befriending them.

"Oh, sure! That'll be easy, given how attractive and put together we are right now!" I said. We were both too exhausted to find any amusement in my words.

We left the park and got back onto the main path on the far side of the village. We didn't notice the car above us until it dropped straight down just a couple of meters from us. We were too startled to move.

The car hovered beside us as its lone occupant retracted the roof. "You ladies still seem to be lost," said the young man we had encountered the day before.

"We're fine!" I replied, avoiding eye contact.

"I'm not so sure about that," he said. "The scuttlebutt is that you're either confused and in need of professional help, or you're a couple of scam artists, flashing gold chips in people's faces for some reason."

We started walking again, but the man drove his car alongside us as we walked.

"What do you want?" May asked.

"I was going to ask you the same question," he replied. "In fact, I was going to ask whether you still want to go to the KBP compound."

I stopped walking and turned to him. "Are you offering to take us there?"

"Possibly."

"That would be very kind of you," May said, flashing a smile.

"Alright then. Why don't the two of you hop in? I can't take you inside the compound, but I can take you to one of the entrances. I can't guarantee a security guard is going to let you in, though."

"We'll deal with that," May replied.

When we took our seats, the car ascended about one hundred meters, then hovered as the young man turned toward us. "OK, let's get this straight," he said. "We're just going to make a quick stop at the enforcement office, so they can ask you a couple of questions and make sure you're on the up-and-up, then we'll carry on to the compound."

"No!" I shouted. I was terrified, but I did my best to project outrage and anger. "What we're doing is nobody else's business! Put this car down, and let us out!"

"What I was *going* to say," he replied with an evil smile, "is that we might skip the whole law enforcement step if you're willing to part with a gold chip."

"But we only have one left!" May lied, quite convincingly.

"Perfect!" he said, then we started on our way.

The compound was farther away than we anticipated. After forty-five minutes, the car rounded a hill, and we saw a collection of buildings in the woods below. The compound stood inside a high fence that formed a circle, perhaps a kilometer in diameter. We saw the pale blue outline of a dome, delineating a forcefield over the entire compound. No paths led to the fence. Even if we had known the location of the compound, we would have had to trek through kilometers of hilly forest, only to arrive at an impenetrable fence.

There were three entrances to the compound, equally spaced around the dome. Each entrance was at least fifty meters above ground, perched atop pillars that stood just inside the fence. A small building and a landing pad were located at each entrance, with each building intersecting the forcefield.

The car landed on the outer edge of a landing pad. A large sign was posted outside the building, bearing the words, "Service Entrance." The man held out his hand for payment.

"How do we know you aren't going straight to enforcement as soon as we get out?" May demanded.

"Hmm . . . do I want enforcement to know I took a bribe from two fugitives?"

"We aren't fugitives," May retorted as she pressed a gold chip into his hand. "We just have private business here and that's none of your concern."

"OK, you two have a good one, whatever that is," he called out as he sped away.

"We walked to the building, opened the door, and entered a long, rectangular room, that appeared to be a waiting area. A bench ran along the outside wall, and a counter lined the opposite wall. A glass barrier ran along the length of the counter, separating the waiting area from an office where an imposing guard sat, staring at his Infotab screen. Yet another portrait of Kelvoo glowed on the wall behind him.

"How do you do?" I said when he looked up from his screen.

"Oh, fine, fine," he said. "What brings you here today?"

"My sister and I need to speak with Kelvoo Buchanan-Paige."

"For what purpose?"

"It's a personal matter."

"Look, ladies, Mr. Buchanan-Paige has plenty of admirers. If you'd like to leave your names and contact information, his assistant can get in touch with you."

"We're not admirers, sir," I said. "Kelly and I are friends, and I have information he needs urgently!"

"What's your name?"

"It's . . . Gwen."

"Gwen who?"

"Gwen Murray. But that's not important! Kelly won't know that name, but if you send him a picture of me, he'll know exactly who I am."

The guard held up his Infotab and pointed it at my face. Then he tapped the screen a few times. I was hoping he was transmitting my image to Kelly, as I had requested.

"Have a seat," he said.

As soon as we sat, the guard made a voice call on his Infotab.

"Dispatch," a woman's voice said.

"This is security calling from the service entrance of the KBP compound," the guard replied, staring at us. "I have two older ladies here who are trying to gain access to Mr. Buchanan-Paige. One of them claims to know him, but her story doesn't add up."

"No!" I shouted, then I silenced myself, not wanting to alarm the person on the other end of the call.

"OK, hold them there. We'll send officers over. They might be a couple of suspicious characters who were in the village yesterday."

When the guard ended the call, we jumped to our feet. "Why the hell did you do that?" I shouted.

"Kelly's going to be furious!" May said. "This'll be the last day you work here!"

I walked toward the outside entrance, only to hear a click come from the door. I pushed and pulled it and threw my weight against it. "Did you just lock us in here?" I yelled. The guard merely smiled. "Let us out!" I shouted.

"I could, but where would you go? It's an awful long way down, and I wouldn't want to see you make a jump for it."

May and I paced back and forth in the narrow space. We were distraught and furious, not just with the guard but also with ourselves and our absurd scheme. We pounded on the glass at the counter, but the guard was indifferent to our protests.

We gave up when we saw a law enforcement vehicle approaching. I slumped onto the bench, devastated that our journey was at an end, when a familiar voice came from the guard's console on the other side of the desk.

"Pete!" the voice said. "Do you still have that lady at the checkpoint? The one whose image you sent to my assistant?"

"Yes, sir! In fact, enforcement just landed to have a little chat with them."

"What? No! Hell no!" Kelvoo Buchanan-Paige said, sounding almost as panicked as we were. "Take them inside! Hide them! Do whatever you have to do, but don't let enforcement see them! I'll be right up!"

By then the two officers were halfway between their vehicle and the entrance. The guard tapped a panel, and a door opened at the far end of the waiting area. "Hide!" he snapped, with a mixture of anger and embarrassment as he hustled us through.

We crouched behind a desk just as the officers arrived at the entrance. Fortunately, it was still locked. The officers knocked on the glass, and the guard made his way back to his console and unlocked the door.

"We're here for the two little old lady troublemakers!" one of the officers said in an amused voice as they entered.

"Yeah, sorry, Mike," the guard replied. "It was all a misunderstanding. Turns out they're friends with the boss, so I let them through."

"Aw, that's OK, Pete," the officer replied. "Mind if we come inside and take a quick look around?"

"Why would you want to do that?"

"Just standard procedure. C'mon Pete, you know that."

I wished we were in a better hiding place. The small desk we were hiding behind was in clear view of the entrance to the security counter. I could hardly breathe out of the fear that gripped me.

"Dispatch said something about a couple of suspicious characters," the guard replied. I assumed he was trying to help us by stalling the officers.

"Yeah, two elderly women," the officer said. "It's weird. They showed up in town yesterday, claiming to be visiting from Australia. That raised suspicions that they might be reformist agitators. Then they went to a restaurant and tried to pay for their meals with a gold chip!"

"What? No kidding."

"Yep! So, the restaurant owner sent one of them to the bank, but when she got there, it was like she didn't even know how money works! Then she panicked and took off. Next thing you know, they both vanished! Something's not right about those two. I figure they're either cuckoo old biddies or criminal masterminds." The officer chuckled.

It was nerve wracking and strange to hear someone talking about us just a few steps away. Despite my fear, I took great offence at the "cuckoo old biddies" remark, preferring to be seen as a criminal mastermind.

"Anyway, Pete," the officer said, "let us in so we can take a quick look and then be on our way."

We were spared when Kelly came charging into the room from the far end of the building. He looked right past us, striding toward the counter. "Good morning, officers," he said, standing behind Pete.

"Oh! Good morning, Mr. Buchanan-Paige," an officer said.

"Great to see you, sir!" the other added.

"Is there something I can help you with?" Kelly asked.

After Officer Mike explained the situation, Kelly nodded. "Oh, I see. Well, there were two ladies here, but they're not the ones you're describing. They're old family friends from Vancouver Island. They've come for a little visit, and they're in my home now, getting settled in.

"Yeah," Pete said, "sorry to have wasted your time."

"Is there anything else you gentlemen need?" Kelly asked. "I really must get back to attend to my guests."

"No, no, we're good. Sorry for the misunderstanding," Officer Mike said.

"No need to apologize," Kelly replied. "Good to see you're alert and on the ball!"

When the officers left, May and I, still crouched behind the desk, smiled up at Kelly as he walked over to us, but he didn't smile back. "I need the two of you to keep your mouths shut!" he said. "The three of you," he added, turning to Pete, "will come with me right now!"

"Sir, there's no one else on duty here," Pete said. "The next shift doesn't start for twenty minutes."

"Don't worry about it. Shut this entrance down and come with us."

After Pete went to the console, manipulated some controls, and turned off most of the interior lights, we hurried through the building and exited onto the side of the landing pad that was inside the forcefield. Mindful of Kelly's stern look, we all stayed silent as we got into a car, and Kelly drove into the compound. The compound was well treed, but I managed to spy a few rooftops through the canopy. We descended and entered a garage, then walked into a small but stylish house.

Kelly showed us into the living room. "Pete," he said, motioning toward a sofa. "Have a seat. We'll be right back."

Kelly took May and me back into the entryway. "Brenna, what the hell?" he asked as he stared at us in astonishment.

I was so overcome that I wrapped my arms around Kelly and pulled him close. I rested my head on his chest, comforted by his warmth and the sound of his heartbeat. I was about to cry with relief, but he was having none of it. He grasped my upper arms and pushed me away, holding me at a distance.

"Who's this?" he demanded, looking at May.

"That's my sister, May."

"Please tell me the two of you were brought here against your will."

We looked at each other.

"Are you out of your minds?" he exclaimed.

"Yes," was all I could say.

"Are you trying to screw up everything I've been trying to do?"

"No."

I felt heartbroken. I thought Kelly would be happy to see me again, but as he seethed, the folly of our plan hit home once again. *Didn't you realize Kelly would have his own plan?* I asked myself. *What made you think you could burst onto the scene without messing things up?*

Kelly led us back into the living room. May and I sat together, and Kelly took a seat beside Pete, putting a hand on Pete's shoulder as he looked into his eyes.

"You've never seen these two people," he said. "You don't know them, you wouldn't recognize them if you saw them again, and we never had this conversation. Is that clear?"

"I guess so," Pete replied, "sir."

Kelly stood and tapped his Infotab screen. A small panel opened in a wall, and a drawer with a thick metal front extended out. Kelly retrieved a gold chip from it, just like the ones we had in our bags, then placed the chip in Pete's hand. Pete's jaw dropped, and his eyes practically bulged out.

"I'm going to say this again, Pete. You don't know these women, you wouldn't recognize them if you saw them again, and we never had this conversation. Is that clearer now?"

"Yes sir! Clear as day! Never seen them, wouldn't recognize them! I don't know anything about this, sir!"

"I don't want you mentioning this to anyone. Not your coworkers and not even your family. Not another soul!"

"No sir! Not another soul, sir!"

"Excellent. I've always seen you as one of my most trustworthy staff, Pete. When are you due to be moved up to the next pay level?"

"Um, I guess about ten months from now, sir."

"No, that doesn't sound right. How about we make it effective today?"

Pete's jaw dropped again, then a broad smile crossed his face. Kelly stood, followed by Pete. Kelly extended his hand, and Pete shook it vigorously.

"Alright, take the car, and back to work you go!" Kelly said. Pete practically levitated out of the room.

Then Kelly turned back to May and me. "Now, where were we? Oh yes," he said as his voice changed to a low growl. "What in bloody hell are you doing in my house, on my planet, and in the middle of my plan to save Kelvoo?"

TWENTY: AN UNWELCOME REUNION

May and I spent the next hour recounting our story and our frustration at the Planetary Alliance's inaction. As we spoke, Kelly's anger subsided, but he still made it clear that our plan was childishly naïve at best and counterproductive and dangerous at worst.

"I don't think you realize how lucky you are that you didn't get caught. It's also damned fortunate that my assistant passed along your image from security," Kelly said. "I almost didn't recognize you. Have you changed your hair or something?"

"Yeah, sure, Kelly! I added all this dirt and threw in a few twigs and insects for effect. Pretty stylish, huh?" I replied, pointing to my filthy, windblown locks.

For the first time since he saw us at the service entrance, Kelly smiled, albeit briefly.

"So, what would've happened if we'd been caught?" I asked.

"You would have been used as leverage."

"Leverage?"

"Yes. To convince Kelvoo to play along with the Kelvonist scheme and become the supreme being they're looking for."

"What do you mean? They'd threaten our lives? Lock us up? Torture us?"

"These are desperate people. The situation here is getting out of hand. The Kelvonist leaders will do anything to avoid the wrath that's going to rain down on them once the public reaches the limit of their tolerance. Kozoltoo, Tenisha, and their disciples will do whatever they can to change Kelvoo's mind.

"Here's the thing," Kelly continued. "I'm on the outs with the Kelvonists. My influence and access are close to zero these days. They suspect I'm on Kelvoo's side, and they're right, but they also resent me negotiating the agreement that released you and got you off this planet. The moment you were away safely, Kozoltoo regretted it. Essentially, he saw you as a bargaining chip that I threw away."

"And now I'm back," I said.

"Yeah." Kelly sighed. "You and another bargaining chip," he added, looking at May.

"Would you like us to leave?" May asked.

"No. You're here, and you're in no immediate danger. There's also no safe or easy way to get you off Terra."

I decided that, for the moment at least, I wasn't about to tell Kelly about the device that Desmond had given us to summon a ride off the planet.

"You might be staying for a long time," Kelly continued, "so you'd better make yourselves comfortable. I'm guessing you might like to bathe and maybe get a little sleep?"

"Thank you, Kelly," I said. "I'm sorry we dropped in on you like this," I added, mustering a smile.

"I'm glad to see you again," Kelly said. He gave me a warm, comforting hug, then sniffed and stepped backward. "Have a nice, warm bath," he remarked, his smile easing my embarrassment.

Kelly opted not to give May a hug. Instead, he bowed toward her. "Delightful to see you again, May," he said, referring to a time on Terra long ago when May was a child.

"Could you please show us to our room?" I asked.

"You can have whichever rooms you want. You're in one of my guest homes. This house is at your disposal for as long as you're here." He turned his head to the side. "Stanley!"

A servitor bot glided into the room and hovered beside Kelly. "This is Brenna, and this is May," he said, extending a palm toward each of us. "Follow their commands until directed otherwise by me." He turned to us. "Make yourselves comfortable, and get some rest. If you get hungry or thirsty, Stanley can bring you whatever you need. Tomorrow, let Stanley know when you're ready, and we'll get together. We have a great deal of catching up to do!"

Kelly's guest house was welcoming and comfortable. May and I chose a bedroom and bathroom each. I had a long, hot shower with a sonic field deep-clean option. The filth ran down my body in rivulets of muck. The shower also helped me release the tension of the last few days, along with a flood of tears as exhaustion got the better of me.

I wrapped myself in one of the sumptuous bathrobes that were hung on the door and put my head inside a dryer pod just long enough to stop my hair from dripping onto the floor. I was still wearing the bathrobe when I laid on top of the clean, luxurious bed. Although my hair was damp, I fell asleep the moment my head touched the pillow.

I slept through the rest of the day and the following night. When I woke, I could hardly move, feeling even sorer and stiffer than after the night in the gazebo. I hobbled into the living room where I found May sprawled on a sectional sofa, reading her Infotab.

"Kelly has an InfoServer that's compatible with our Infotabs," she said. "He's got a great selection of novels, especially the old classics!"

"That's nice," I replied. "What are you reading?"

"It's called *Love Beneath a Sarayan Moon*. It's about a forbidden relationship between a Sarayan diplomat and an outlier human princess."

"Is it any good?"

"No, it's totally cheesy, but it's good for a laugh. Listen to this. 'What is that?' Princess Cassidy exclaimed as Vazdor doffed his robe. 'That's my shnuzle,' he replied. 'Surely you have seen an unclothed Sarayan male before.'

"'Why, no!' the princess replied. 'At least not in such an imposing state! Oh my!' she stammered as she flushed with embarrassment, wishing she could avert her eyes, but she was mesmerized by the spectacle before her, burning with a flaming desire she could never have imagined."

Stanley floated into the room, interrupting our study of sophisticated literature. "Brenna and May, I have informed Mr. Buchanan-Paige that you are both awake. Mr. Buchanan-Paige has invited you to join him for breakfast in one hour. Do you accept?"

"Yes," I replied.

"Invitation accepted. Confirmation has been sent to Mr. Buchanan-Paige."

"Stanley?" I said.

"Yes?"

"Do you have to call Kelly 'Mr. Buchanan-Paige'? Can we use something shorter?"

"What designation do you wish to assign to Mr. Buchanan-Paige?"

"How about just Kelly?" May said.

"Please confirm that this unit should refer to Mr. Buchanan-Paige as 'Just Kelly.'"

"No," I said, "use designation 'Kelly.'"

"How about 'Kelly Baby?'" May joked.

"Or 'Kelly Roll!'" I added.

"Kelly Bean?" May suggested.

"Yes!" I replied. "Assign designation 'Kelly Bean' to Mr. Buchanan-Paige."

"Confirmed," the bot said. "Kelly Bean has replied and will see you in fifty-nine minutes."

The bathrooms were stocked with an assortment of beauty products. May and I weren't familiar with the Terran brands, but we used them to the best of our abilities to make ourselves presentable, or at the very least, less haggard.

We had no idea what we were going to wear, so we looked through the bedroom closets for something to throw on. When we emerged empty handed, we were delighted to see that Stanley, or some other entity, had cleaned and smoothed our clothes from the previous day and hung them on a rack at the foot of our beds.

When the time came, Stanley led us along a covered walkway into the main residence. Kelly's home had a minimalist elegance. Fine art was displayed in each room, but not to excess. Terran music played softly as Stanley led us to a table.

"Good to see you looking like your old selves!" Kelly said.

"Yes, 'old' is correct," I retorted, "and feeling older every day!"

Kelly chuckled as we sat down to a wonderful assortment of exotic fruits and delectable pastries.

When we were finished, Kelly led us down a hallway and into his office. A woman was working in front of several large display panels, speaking instructions into a control console. She was impeccable—impeccably dressed, impeccable figure, impeccable posture . . . uncannily perfect looking.

"Good morning, Inga," Kelly said. Consumed by her work, Inga merely nodded in reply. "She's my eyes and ears," Kelly said. "She's also the one who sent your image to me yesterday. She had been watching the vid feed of your conversation with Pete at the service entrance. It caught her attention enough that she interrupted me to show me your image. She's an incredible multi-tasker and totally indispensable! Best of all, she won't be taken in by the Kelvonist nonsense. She's on our side. She's the one you can thank for saving you."

Inga was still engrossed in her work, so we assured Kelly that we would thank her at the earliest opportunity as we followed Kelly to his section of the spacious office area.

Kelly's semicircular desk was surrounded by monitors, floating virtual displays, and holographic projectors. The setup reminded me of action vids that showed control centers used by villains to cause planet-wide mayhem. Kelly pulled up two chairs and invited us to sit on either side of him.

"So, let's talk about Kelvoo," he said.

"When's the last time you saw Pa—I mean Kelvoo?" May asked.

"You don't have to correct yourself," Kelly replied. "The last time I saw your pa was yesterday evening, though only for a short time."

"How's Pa doing?" I asked. "Did you tell Pa we're here?"

"Where's Pa being kept?" May added. "Somewhere close by?"

"Take it easy, you two! I didn't see Kelvoo in person," Kelly said. "Kelvoo is being held in the Kelvonist headquarters across the river. They won't let me close to the place. Let me show you how I was able to see your pa."

Kelly gestured toward a symbol on a virtual display. A live vid feed appeared, showing the inside of a room, viewed from a corner close to the ceiling. Kelly tapped a different symbol on a physical panel. "Show me Kelvoo," he said.

The cam that was providing the feed drifted across the room, then panned in the opposite direction. Right in the center of the shot was Kelvoo. Tears sprang to my eyes at the sight of Pa after so many months. Kelvoo was kneeling at a desk, reading text on an Infotab. "This is how I'm able to see Kelvoo," Kelly said.

"Oh, Pa!" May exclaimed, in a teary voice. "So, you have control of a cam at the Kelvonist Society?"

"It's more than a cam. It's none other than your old, faithful Pollybot."

"Pollybot!" I exclaimed. "So, that's why you wanted me to leave Pollybot with Kelvoo!"

"That's right. When we met in the courtyard at Kozoltoo's residence, you'll recall that I removed the surveillance code from Pollybot. When I pulled the offending sub-processor module, I replaced it with a module with code that can be updated or replaced remotely. Over time, we've been coding the module to increase Pollybot's capabilities. Now we can view or listen to whatever Pollybot sees and hears in real time.

"And you can talk to Pa?" May asked.

"I can, but I almost never do. Lots of signals are being broadcast out of the Kelvonist HQ, but I'm concerned that they'd be more likely to detect transmissions *to* their location. Early on, Kelvoo and I agreed that we would speak with each other in emergencies only.

"I also slipped some micro cams into Pollybot's accessories compartment. Whenever the coast was clear, Pollybot would sneak into offices or boardrooms and place a bug there." Kelly tapped an arrow symbol on a monitor. The view changed from Kelvoo to the interior of Kozoltoo's office. Kelly tapped the symbol again and again, the view from a different spy cam appearing each time. There were many views of places I didn't recognize.

"Have any of the bugs been found?" I asked.

"Just one. And you should have seen how Kozoltoo's people reacted! They blamed the reformers. The reformers denied it, and it took a long time before things settled down between them.

"A couple of other bugs have malfunctioned or been broken, but we still have pretty good coverage. They're nearly impossible to detect." Kelly's excitement increased as he talked about the technical details. "The bugs are powered by ambient light. They're as thin as a human hair. When they're stuck on a surface, they analyze its colors and patterns and change their surface to blend in perfectly."

"You must have some talented techs in your staff!" I said.

"Staff? No, my only staff are security for the three entrances and Inga. She's the expert who creates surveillance gear and programs sub-processors for me. That stuff's way over my head!"

"You have no other staff? Who runs your business empire? And who takes care of your investments and properties?"

"Bots and AI systems. It's all automated. I'm just here to make key decisions. Sometimes it feels as though I'm the one working for the bots and AI!" Kelly said with a laugh.

"Don't you get lonely?" May asked.

"Oh, yes. Sometimes. It's not like I didn't have a huge social circle in my youth! I had more lady friends than I can count," Kelly said, a wistful look in his eye, "but I realized that many of them were more interested in my wealth and fame. I was so nervous about being used and betrayed that my defenses were always up. Over time, I isolated myself more and more. Now I'm kind of a recluse."

"I'm sorry that May and I showed up unannounced. You must feel as if your privacy is being violated."

"Not at all, Brenna. I like it," he said as he took my hand, "but right now, my only concern is keeping you safe."

Kelly switched the display back to Pollybot's view of Kelvoo. We sat and watched for several minutes.

"So, is there any kind of plan for getting Pa off Terra?" May asked.

"Yeah, but it's not much of a plan. I've got what is perhaps the fastest car on the planet. It was custom built on Bandor." Kelly was proud of his car, and he described it in great detail, getting more excited as he went. My eyes glazed over after the first thirty seconds, his words nothing but technical gibberish to my ears.

As Kelly waxed on, I leaned over to May, whispering, "No wonder he's single!" She struggled to keep a straight face.

After about a minute, Kelly caught himself. "Anyway, I won't bore you with further details," he said, "but I also have an interstellar transport hidden elsewhere on Terra. I bought it from a Sarayan manufacturer."

"OK," May said, "but with Terra being isolated for so long, how did you manage to get anything from the other worlds?"

"Money," Kelly said, rubbing his thumb and fingers together. "Money and contacts. If you have enough of both, you can make things happen."

"And who exactly are these contacts?" I asked.

"I'll give you one guess."

"Damn it!" I replied. "Is there no place in the whole universe where the Brotherhood *doesn't* have its sticky fingers?"

"Not that I know of. Anyway, do you want to know the plan or not?"

"Sorry, Kelly. Yes."

"We're going to wait till there's an opening. Then we'll grab Kelvoo, take off in the car, get to the transport, blast our way to a jump point, and get into Alliance space as fast as we can."

"That's it?"

"That's it," Kelly replied, "unless you can suggest something better."

May and I certainly didn't have anything, so the three of us spent the next four hours chatting and watching Pa, who kept reading an Infotab. From time to time, Kelly worked at his console, dealing with his business issues as they came up.

We were interrupted when Stanley glided in. "Excuse me, Kelly Bean, would you like today's lunch to be brought here for you and your guests?"

Kelly frowned in confusion. "Kelly Bean?" he exclaimed as May and I nearly doubled over with laughter.

TWENTY-ONE: MASSACRE

Several days passed without incident. Kelly would leave the compound for a few hours each day, dealing with business or personal matters. Guests would also visit but usually in the business center, which was well removed from the residences. May and I couldn't go anywhere. Inga had set up a connection between our Infotabs and the vid feed from the spy cams, so we spent most of our time watching Pa on our screens.

The day after we got there, May and I stopped at Inga's desk to thank her for alerting Kelly to our presence when we first arrived at the compound.

"There is no need to thank me," she replied, barely looking up from her display panels. Inga's cold demeanor struck us as odd, making us wonder whether she was displeased by our presence.

"Do you think there might be something going on between her and Kelly?" May asked once we were well out of earshot. I merely shrugged in reply.

As the days passed, we watched the Terran news broadcasts. The content was under tight government control, full of praise for Kelvoo. The broadcasts included news of the unrest and protests, always depicting the Kelvonists' opponents in a negative light.

Since well before our arrival, Inga had set up AI software to monitor communication across Terra. Talk among government departments, the Kelvonist factions, and protesters was constantly monitored and analyzed.

May was worried about her family on Perdition and what they might do if she didn't contact them soon. The last thing we needed was to draw attention to ourselves by being reported as missing. I had similar worries about the associates in my foundation. Kelly was working on a plan to get a short, untraceable message out, conveying our assurance that we were safe and letting our families and friends know that our work was taking longer than anticipated. Kelly's plan turned out to be unnecessary, however, as events on Terra took a sudden turn.

***

On the morning of our eighth day at Kelly's home, Inga informed Kelly that the AIs had detected a change in the quantity and tone of the chatter they had been monitoring. The threat of increased unrest and violence was on the rise, and there were vague implications that the risks to Kelvoo's wellbeing were growing. Kelly cancelled or postponed his upcoming meetings, then sat us down and gave us the news. We asked for specifics.

"If I get any more details, you'll be the first to know," he assured us. "So far, there's nothing specific or credible, just patterns being picked up by the AIs. They're predictive of increased societal instability." Kelly advised us to keep our belongings close in case we needed to act fast.

"Act fast to do what?" I asked. "Rescue Pa or flee Terra?"

"Either or both," he said with a nervousness I hadn't seen in him before.

May and I packed our travel bags and kept them with us. Every hour or so, I checked my bag to ensure that the vast fortune in gold chips was still present, as if they would go anywhere.

Around midday, the three of us watched a live broadcast showing several thousand protesters swarming the grounds at the base of the Kelvonist headquarters and the adjacent temple. I looked at my Infotab and saw Kelvoo walk to the wall of windows to watch the gathering crowd. I flipped through the vid feeds from the Kelvonist headquarters and watched Kozoltoo's staff looking at the spectacle below. I also noticed people who looked like enforcement officers on the outdoor decks, lined up along the railings.

It seemed to me that the enforcement officers may have been carrying weapons, but they were far in the background of the vid image, so it was hard to see them clearly. I asked Kelly about it.

"Here on Terra?" he said. "I seriously doubt it."

"Free Kelvoo!" the protestors screamed. "Down with Kozoltoo! Liars, liars, liars!" At one point, they broke into a protest song.

> We're taking back the power.
> The people now demand
> to hear the word of Kelvoo
> the time for truth's at hand!
>
> Your lies and your deception,
> we shall no more allow.
> Free Kelvoo! Free Kelvoo!
> Free Kelvoo now!
>
> No longer shall you keep us
> from our savior's guiding light.
> Let it shine so bright upon us.
> Let the truth and love take flight.
>
> We must overthrow the tyrants
> who broke their sacred vow.
> Free Kelvoo! Free Kelvoo!
> Free Kelvoo now!

When the song was over, a blue orb of light shot up from the crowd.

"So much for Terra being free of weapons!" Kelly exclaimed as the ball of plasma impacted the edge of the headquarters, shattering a section of the glass wall and sending shards tumbling into the pond at the base of the pillars. On my Infotab, I saw Kelvoo jump when the projectile hit the building. The vid feed from Pollybot was focused on Kelvoo, but part of the main office area was visible through a glass wall in the room where Kelvoo was located. A cloud of dust and debris billowed into the edge of the frame after the plasma hit.

Outside, all hell broke loose as my earlier suspicion was confirmed. The enforcement people on the deck opened fire on the crowd below. Plasma and incendiary grenades followed, raining down on the protestors. The three of us watched in horrified silence as the broadcast showed screaming people running from the scene. Some protestors were struck by plasma rounds from behind, landing face down with charred holes in their backs. When most of the fleeing people were past the broadcast camera, a woman ran by, engulfed in flames and screaming. A child, perhaps seven years old, wandered toward the camera, covered in lacerations and bleeding from his neck before collapsing. I felt like retching, so I turned away and looked out a window with my hand clamped over my mouth. I closed my eyes and tried to concentrate on controlling my rapid, shallow breathing, but I couldn't block the sound of mayhem from the broadcast.

"We need to get Pa out of there now!" May shouted.

"That's not going to work," I said as I saw Kozoltoo run into Kelvoo's room, accompanied by five officers.

"We need to get you somewhere safe," Kozoltoo said. Pollybot followed as Kelvoo was led into the hangar and loaded into a transport, accompanied by Pollybot and the five officers. A few minutes later, the vid feed fritzed and vanished.

"Out of reception range," Kelly said. "Damn it!" He slammed his fist on his console. "They must have left the area."

We sat in stunned silence, then Kelly sighed. "The irony is ridiculous. The Kelvonists wanted Kelvoo to usher in a new era on Terra. Well, they've got a new era, alright! Now that weapons are among us once more, there's no turning back. Starting today, the whole planet's on a track to hell. Again."

An hour later, Kozoltoo made a public statement, his face grim. "It is with deep sorrow that I stand before you today," he began. "I am sorry that the Kelvonist Society has failed to produce Kelvoo for all these months, but I'm even sorrier that our species has reignited its murderous ways. As I have said all along, Kelvoo has returned to lead us into the future, but Kelvoo has also required time to study, to meditate, and to prepare to assume such a role.

"The time for Kelvoo's emergence was at hand, then evil anti-Kelvoo protesters opened fire on our headquarters. We had no choice but to quell the uprising, and we deeply regret the loss of life. All lives are precious, even the lives of those who hate Kelvoo and the coming new era that Kelvoo represents.

"I have been in an emergency meeting with Kelvoo, during which Kelvoo insisted that I reach out to the leader of the Reformed Kelvonist Movement and bring her into the meeting via a live vid feed. Under normal circumstances, I would avoid communication with our rivals, but I am not one to question Kelvoo's wise counsel. I am moved beyond words to announce that we have reached an accord with our reformist brethren.

"While today's events have been tragic, they have also inspired a breakthrough—not only by healing the rift between Kelvoo's followers but also because they have brought about something wonderful."

Kozoltoo's grim expression transformed into joy. "It is my great honor to turn things over to our new friend and ally from the Reformed Kelvonist Movement, Tenisha Herzog, so she can announce a momentous breakthrough. May Kelvoo's blessings be upon her."

The broadcast switched to a vid feed from Tenisha Herzog. I noticed sloped windows in the ceiling behind her. Pa's story had described such windows in the reformists' Australian office.

"It is with great honor and utmost humility that I make this historic announcement," Tenisha began. "Kelvoo, our divine inspiration and guide, has decided to address the citizens of Terra, even though the timing is not ideal. As undeserving as humanity is today, Kelvoo believes that Terra has suffered enough, and the time for our healing has arrived. Kelvoo will make an address tomorrow from the main Kelvonist Society guidance center at 17:00 in the Kelvonist HQ time zone.

"Let us put aside our differences!" Tenisha beamed into the camera with unabashed joy. "Let us move past today's tragic events and advance as one people under one leader with one purpose!

"Let us turn toward one another today with love in our hearts as we look forward to tomorrow and the wonders it holds for all of us. May Kelvoo's blessings be upon us all."

After the announcement, the Terran media buzzed with excitement. Interviews with random citizens reflected nervous anticipation and hope for great things to come. May and I were nervous too but not with a great deal of hope. We couldn't imagine Pa saying anything in public that would please the Kelvonists.

That night the AIs monitored the media and private communication channels, ever vigilant for new developments. I fell asleep, but I was jolted awake several times by terrible dreams as visions of the protest and the dead and wounded men, women, and children replayed in my mind. With sleep being an ineffective escape from the dreadful memories, I woke hours earlier than usual.

I tried to read a book on my Infotab, but I couldn't concentrate. I kept flipping through the vid feeds, checking for any signal from Pollybot. In the pre-dawn hours, the feed was restored. I watched Pa inside a transport as it landed in the hangar in the Kelvonist headquarters. My pa was led back inside the building. Pollybot's feed showed metal plates covering the sections of the exterior wall where the glass had been blown out. Pa entered the same room as before, then entered a meditative state.

Like me, May couldn't sleep either. She wandered into the kitchen, then brought a snack to the living room, surprised when she saw me. I told May about the restored vid feed, then we watched Pa on our Infotabs for a while.

Just after first light, Stanley glided in. "Kelly Bean is awake and in his residence's kitchen area," the bot announced.

Kelly was preparing a light breakfast of fruit, cereal, and pastries. "Care for a bite?" he asked. Kelly arranged some food on a second plate and brought it out for May and me to share as we sat at the console in Kelly's office.

On various feeds, we saw one of Kozoltoo's staff bring a fridgepack of algel to Kelvoo. That's when I noticed that Kelvoo's algel dispenser was no longer in the room. When Kelvoo asked where the dispenser was, the staffer explained that it had been removed while repairs were made to the building, adding that it required maintenance.

"What kind of maintenance would an algel dispenser require?" Pa asked.

"I have no idea," she replied. "That's just what I was told."

After Kelvoo consumed the algel from the fridgepack, the staffer returned to remove the empty food package.

About twenty minutes later, we saw Kozoltoo arrive at his headquarters and then stride toward the hangar with six employees in tow. The spy cam in the hangar showed a vessel arriving and its occupants disembarking. Three minutes later, Kozoltoo reemerged with a woman and twelve others accompanying him.

"Is that—" An AI sounded a chime on the console, interrupting my question.

"Event of interest. Event of interest," the AI announced. "Tenisha Herzog has arrived at Kelvonist Society headquarters and is interacting with Kozoltoo."

"Is this the first time the two of them have met?" May asked.

"No, they've met before but never in the inner sanctum of the Kelvonist Society's headquarters," Kelly replied.

We watched as Kozoltoo held his office door open for Tenisha to enter, then motioned for Tenisha to have a seat. The twelve staffers walked away, leaving the large main area empty, presumably to give maximum privacy to their leaders.

Kelly displayed the feed from Kozoltoo's office on a large monitor directly in front of us. "Now, *this* is going to be interesting," he said.

TWENTY-TWO: A BLAZE OF GLORY

As Kelly watched the meeting between Kozoltoo and Tenisha, May selected the same feed, so she could view and record it on her Infotab. The following includes a transcript of the conversation.

Kozoltoo (KZ): So, Ten, I never did get around to congratulating you. How long's it been?

Tenisha Herzog (TH): Since the old man died? Must be about two months to the day.

KZ: Natural causes?

TH: Yeah, pretty much.

KZ: Pretty much?

TH: Look, Koz, he was on the way out, so let's just say natural causes with maybe just a smidgen of help to speed it along.

KZ: Did the board take long to name you CEO?

TH: Nah. I just acted like it was supposed to happen automatically. There wasn't much debate, since my "rescue" of Kelvoo from your clutches, put me closer to our "savior" than any of them had ever been.

[*TH and KZ laugh*]

At that point, Kelly sent a message to Pollybot asking it to relay the audio of the meeting to Kelvoo as it happened. "Transform audio to ultrasonic frequency band," Kelly commanded. May and I knew that Pa's kloormari hearing would pick up the meeting, but nearby humans wouldn't be able to hear the ultrasonic audio. We saw Pa move closer to Pollybot and appear to listen intently as the relayed audio began.

KZ: Anyway, thanks, Ten, for going along with the unity plan.

TH: Well, we have to be pragmatic considering our friend's emergence this afternoon. I just hope we're not going to have to "play nice" for too long.

KZ: Oh, I'm sure we'll find some reason to divide again in no time. It's strange—when your people decided to splinter off, I thought it might be the end of Kelvonism.

TH: Yeah, who'd have thought the competition would boost the public's engagement?

KZ: [*Laughs*] Not to mention financial contributions!

TH: What a strange business we're in!

KZ: It's the people who are strange. We're just giving them what they want. I've studied these kinds of movements throughout history. You've got to go back centuries, but it worked then and it's sure working for us now!

TH: So, are you saying our friend is right? Are we religions now?

KZ: I don't know. What does that word mean, anyway? You can call it religion, spirituality, faith. Who knows? I prefer "philosophy," but it's just semantics. The people want it, and we're just their humble servants.

As we watched and listened, Kelly shook his head. "Those bastards! I knew they were grifters from the get-go. Look at how much they're enjoying it. Son of a bitch!"

I looked at the monitor that showed my pa. Pa's hand paddles were raised. Pa was curling and uncurling them while looking directly at them. It was an action I'd never seen before.

TH: So, I know it's terrible to say this, but it seems like the protestor who took a shot at this building, kind of did us a favor.

KZ: A favor? How so?

TH: By forcing us to get moving and get our kloormari friend in front of the followers. I know you've been getting defensive weapons from the Brotherhood, but how did a protestor get hold of a blaster?

KZ: What makes you think that was a protester?

TH: What do you mean? Was it—No!

KZ: Yep! Just a low-level staffer with a troubled background. He didn't get along well with the others, and he had a bad attitude. We gave him a blaster and told him to blend in with the crowd and take a potshot at the corner of the building. We promised him a promotion and heaps of cash.

TH: OK, I'm getting a little uncomfortable with this. How do you know he's not going to blab to someone?

KZ: He's the first one our enforcement officers took out when they fired back.

TH: You killed him?

KZ: Oh, heavens no! It was my people. I didn't do it *personally*. Like I said, he was a troublemaker with a bad attitude.

Anyway, it worked! We needed an excuse to get Kelvoo in front of the people, so we had to make it happen. If anything goes wrong, we can say it's because we were forced to bring Kelvoo out before the time was right.

TH: Wow! Well, I agree we had to force the situation. The unrest was getting out of hand. If it was any worse, the people would be out for blood. *Our* blood! Still, I can't help thinking we've gone too far.

KZ: There's no doubt about that, but there's nobody to blame except our kloormari friend. What can I say? I really believed in the prophecy, but since our friend wouldn't cooperate, what else could we do? We sure as hell couldn't just tell our followers, "Oops, we were mistaken. Turns out Kelvoo's just another kloormar!" After that, one thing led to another, and one lie fed into the next one. We've been tap dancing our way from one excuse to the next, but at least it's going to stop today.

TH: [Takes a deep breath] OK, I've heard parts of the plan, but why don't you tell me the whole thing, step by step? We're going to have to be on the same page."

"I don't like the sound of this," Kelly said to May and me. "Let's get to the car. If we see an opening, it might be our last chance to grab your pa and get the hell out of here. Are your things ready to go?"

As we grabbed our bags, I felt myself trembling as a sickening feeling came over me.

"Inga, keep a comm lock on our Infotabs," Kelly said. "If I give the go-ahead, drop the entire forcefield, so we can fly out as fast as possible. Also, on my signal, send the spy cam transmissions in a tight beam between here and the Kelvonist HQ so we can keep monitoring Kelvoo if we need to get over there."

"Affirmative," Inga replied as the three of us strode to one of the compound's hangars. I set my Infotab to show Pollybot's view of Kelvoo while May's device received the meeting between the Kelvonist leaders. There was little sound from Pollybot's position, so we watched the vid of Kelvoo from Pollybot while we listened to the meeting.

KZ: Alright, so you probably know that Kelvoo was captured and tortured during the civil war.

TH: Obviously.

KZ: But Kelvoo wasn't the only kloormar in captivity.

TH: I would think not.

KZ: Medical research was conducted on some of the unfortunate kloormari.

TH: That's sickening.

KZ: Certain drugs were concocted and tested on the kloormari. One of the drugs was a combination of vinamibefentyn and enzymes that affect kloormari muscle tissue.

TH: I hate vina. I've seen the effects of vina addiction. It's a lifelong nightmare even after just one dose!

KZ: Well, this combination will put a kloormar into a catatonic state for several hours, but it also stiffens their muscles. The researchers were able to move the kloormar's limbs, and they would remain in that position, all stiffened up. They could pose the kloormar in a standing position, and the kloormar would remain standing until the drug wore off or they were pushed over. Of course, the side effect was an addicted kloormar who would be in intense pain without further doses of vina.

We arrived at Kelly's customized car. "Let's climb in, so we're ready to go," he said. As we continued watching Pollybot's feed inside the car, I reminded myself that the bot was relaying the conversation to Kelvoo in real-time. Kelvoo's limbs were moving sluggishly and Kelvoo was observing them. Kelvoo was clearly having difficulty moving.

TH: OK, Koz, I'm not sure what vina has to do with our friend. Please don't tell me you're using research gathered by war criminals!

KZ: Our friend's breakfast included a strong dose of the vina cocktail. Kelvoo will be feeling the effects by now.

"Those effing bastards!" May yelled. "What the hell are they doing to Pa?"

"Damn it! It's the drugs! That's why Pa's having trouble moving!" I shouted.

"Shhh! We need to keep listening," Kelly said.

TH: So, how does this tie in with the plan to present Kelvoo to the people?

KZ: Our friend will be unresponsive soon. When that happens, my closest staff will put Kelvoo in a crate, and take it into the guidance center. We're going to pose our friend, standing on the altar with hand paddles wrapped around the railing. We'll use some glue if required.

Staggering toward the door, Pa exited the room into the main area, close to Kozoltoo's office. Kelvoo crouched down and limped toward the hallway outside of Kozoltoo's office. As the drug took effect, one of Pa's legs started to drag. "Pollybot, follow me at floor level," Pa said.

Pollybot descended, limiting our view to Kelvoo's lower limbs and feet.

TH: And how exactly is a catatonic Kelvoo going to address the crowd?

KZ: The speech has been pre-recorded. Our experts have used the best audio processing tech to simulate Kelvoo's voice patterns. The address won't start until our friend is far enough above the crowd that nobody will be able to tell if Kelvoo's vocal outlets are moving.

TH: Are we sure your people can pull this off without a hitch?

KZ: We're sure enough. History tells us that, when humans really want to believe something, they'll find a way. If anyone claims to find flaws in our plan or if they say we faked the events, we'll double down and accuse them of spreading lies and being enemies of Kelvoo. Believe me, it won't go well for them!

Pa stumbled and fell to the floor but was still able to crawl along using clasper limbs and shorter arm and leg movements. I watched with a sense of helplessness and dread.

"Damn it!" May exclaimed. "Why are we just sitting here? Isn't there something we can do?"

"I don't know what that would be," Kelly replied. "We'll have to wait until Kelvoo is presented at 17:00. Then we'll grab Kelvoo from the altar and get the hell off this planet."

"But Pa's going to be dependent on vina," I said.

"I'm sorry Brenna," Kelly replied. "Even if we could take Kelvoo immediately, that's already happened."

We watched in horror as Pa continued crawling in the direction of Kozoltoo's office.

TH: So, Kelvoo's speech is going to tell the people to follow us, right?

KZ: Right. The recording will start with Kelvoo talking about you and me and having worked with us since coming to Terra. Kelvoo will say that the Kelvonist and Reformist leaders needed to learn the "new ways" and, after much study and consultation, are now ready.

Next, our kloormari friend will admonish the people for trying to rush the day of advancement and for the protests and violence. Kelvoo will tell them that this great day almost didn't come because of their impatience and opposition.

Finally, Kelvoo will say, "There is but one way to release my power and endow humanity with the love, joy, and enlightenment within me. The time has come for me to transcend my corporeal presence and move to a new dimension of existence. Accept my sacrifice as my gift to humanity."

"A new dimension? Sacrifice? What are they talking about?" I asked.

"And why in the hell is Kelvoo crawling to Kozoltoo's office?" Kelly added.

"Could Pa be going somewhere past the office?" May asked. "What's at the end of that hallway?"

"An exit onto the deck outside," I said as I recalled the building's layout.

The realization that Kelvoo was trying to escape hit us simultaneously. All three of us gasped.

Kelly smacked a button above the car's windshield, and the hangar door started to rise. It was painfully slow.

TH: So, is that when the anti-matter comes into play?

KZ: You got it. It's embedded deep inside the altar top. When the recording ends, Kelvoo will be a couple of thousand meters above the crowd. That's when the magnetic seal around the anti-matter will deactivate.

TH: Wow! What's that going to look like?

KZ: Like a blaze of glory. A brilliant blaze of glory!

"They're going to kill Pa!" I cried. "No! No! No! No!" May reacted in a similar way. I felt terrible for Pa, who was hearing the same conversation, repeated by Pollybot in an ultrasonic range. Pa seemed to find new reserves of energy, crawling faster along the hallway outside Kozoltoo's office.

When the hangar door was halfway up, Kelly slammed the car forward, scraping the undercarriage along the hangar floor to squeeze through the gap. We flew up at a steep angle and turned.

"Inga!" Kelly shouted into the car's console. "Drop the forcefield, and transmit in the direction of the Kelvonist HQ now!"

The faint blue of the forcefield over Kelly's compound flickered and dissipated just before we would have collided with it. As the car sped toward the Kelvonists' headquarters, my eyes and May's were glued to the vid feed on my Infotab as we all listened to the meeting.

TH: So, a flash of white light with a shock wave and a big bang?

KZ: That's what I'm told. When it happens, don't look in Kelvoo's direction. There's a possibility of permanent eye damage for anyone who looks directly at the flash.

TH: Bloody hell! Will people be blinded?

KZ: It's possible. We'll claim they were fortunate. We'll say that, after witnessing the miraculous transformation of Kelvoo's power into blessings upon humanity, there's no longer any need to see anything else. We'll elevate them to a special status and make sure that they and their families are taken care of for the rest of their lives.

We watched Pa crawl along the floor past the glass wall of Kozoltoo's office. Pa's limbs were increasingly limited in their range of motion. I wondered whether Pa was in pain, since each movement seemed to be an intense struggle.

Tenisha was seated with her back toward Pa. Kozoltoo was on the other side of the desk, facing Tenisha, deep in conversation with her. Pa was able to stay low enough to crawl past the glass wall, undetected. Pollybot followed, gliding along the floor right behind my pa.

"How much longer till we get there?" May asked.

"Ten minutes, maybe twelve, tops," Kelly replied. "I'm pushing it to the limit."

Kelvoo reached the door to the deck but was too low to trigger the door sensor. "Pollybot, follow at standard height," Kelvoo said. As the bot rose, the sensors detected its presence, and the door opened. We saw sunlight and the vast deck beyond.

"C'mon Pa! Keep going!" I shouted when Pa's body was halfway through the door. "We're almost there!" May joined me in our unheard encouragement as the car sped between hills and over treetops.

TH: It's so damned sad it's going to end this way for our friend.

KZ: Yeah, I was fond of Kelvoo. I mean, not as fond as when I thought Kelvoo was the savior!

TH: I'll bet you were furious when Kelvoo wanted nothing to do with saving Terra! I know how betrayed *I* felt.

KZ: Furious doesn't even begin to describe it! Still, over time, despite our friend's obstinance, I grew to like Kelvoo, the plain old ordinary kloormar.

TH: Things would have been so much easier if Kelvoo had just played along.

KZ: For us or for Kelvoo?

TH: Both!

KZ: My biggest regret was letting Kelvoo's foster daughter, Brenna, leave Terra. We could've used her to our advantage when we were trying to convince Kelvoo.

TH: Why'd you let her go?

KZ: It was that damned Buchanan-Paige twit! He thought it'd be a good idea to let her go. We also had a deal with Kelvoo to cooperate and make a statement if Brenna was freed.

TH: So, why didn't Kelvoo make a statement?

KZ: Oh, we got a statement alright—to abandon Kelvonism! We couldn't broadcast that! After that, it was just more of the same from our too-logical friend.

When Kelvoo's legs and Pollybot were clear of the doorway, and the door closed, Kelvoo turned toward the railing.

"No, Pa!" I shouted. "Don't go that way. That's right outside Kozoltoo's window!"

"How much longer?" May demanded.

"I don't know! Maybe six minutes," Kelly said.

Pollybot was positioned beside the edge of the deck when Kelvoo reached the base of the railing. On the Infotab screen, I saw pa lying on the deck. Farther back I could see through the side window of Kozoltoo's office. Kozoltoo was at his desk, facing Tenisha. If he turned to his right, he would see Kelvoo on the deck.

"Lift this limb, Pollybot" Kelvoo said, waving an arm, "and hook it over the railing at the elbow closest to my hand paddle." Pollybot followed Pa's order. Pa repeated the command concerning my pa's leg on the same side. Pollybot struggled to lift the much heavier leg but managed to get the lower knee over the railing.

"What the hell is Pa doing?" May asked.

Kelvoo started pulling from the limbs that were on the railing and pushing off the deck with the other arm and leg.

"Maybe Pa is trying to stand," I said.

When my pa's body was almost level with the top of the railing, the horrifying realization hit May and me. "Oh no! Oh, hell no! No! No! No!" I cried.

"What the hell's going on?" Kelly demanded.

"Danger! Stop your action!" Pollybot said. "Danger! Stop your action!"

When Kozoltoo and Tenisha heard Pollybot's alarm through the glass, they jumped up and ran to the window.

"Oh no!" Kozoltoo shouted.

"Kelvoo! For eff's sake, don't!" Tenisha screamed. Kozoltoo called for security as he ran into the hallway.

Pa's nearly limp body was balanced on top of the railing when Kozlotoo and Tenisha rushed out onto the deck. As Pollybot screamed its warning and Kozoltoo reached out to grab Kelvoo, May and I watched in horror as Pa tumbled over the railing.

TWENTY-THREE: BEYOND THE BRINK

Pollybot moved sideways, hovering 500 meters above the ground on the far side of the railing, still repeating its warning. As the bot panned down, I dreaded what we would see. May and I gasped when we saw Pa lying on a narrow service catwalk a meter below the deck, with one arm and one leg hanging over the edge.

As we raced toward Pa, Kelly tapped an icon on the console. "Pollybot, silence!" he commanded. The bot ceased its strident warning. "Relay my voice to Kelvoo!"

"Voice relay open," Pollybot replied.

"Kelvoo, it's me, Kelly! Can you hear me?"

"Kelly? Where are you, Kelly?" Pa replied, the words slurred.

"Don't move, Kelvoo! We're coming for you! We'll be there in a couple of minutes!"

Pollybot's vid feed showed security personnel arriving at the railing, brandishing blaster rifles. They lined up along the railing on either side of Kozoltoo and Tenisha, peering down at Kelvoo. They could hear Kelly telling Kelvoo to hang on.

"No, Kelly, turn back! It's over for me!" Pa said.

"Pa!" May shouted over Kelly's shoulder. "Please wait! I'm here with Brenna. We're coming, Pa! Hold on!"

"We're almost there, Pa!" I shouted, my voice breaking with emotion.

"Brenna? May? No! It's too dangerous! You must go!" Pa shouted.

"What the hell are those two doing on Terra?" Tenisha asked Kozoltoo.

Kozoltoo ignored her. "If a vehicle comes here, shoot it down!" he said to the enforcement officers, who unslung their rifles and scanned the horizon.

"Leave!" Pa slurred. "Flee Terra! Go now!"

"Hold on, Kelvoo," Tenisha pleaded. "We'll send a hoverlift to get you down from there."

"It's too late," Pa replied. "If any of your people come close, I'm going over."

"But why, Kelvoo?" Kozoltoo asked. "Why are you doing this?"

"Because I know your plans for me today. You're going to make me a martyr for your misguided cause."

"Kelvoo, how could you think that? We would never do such a thing! We love you!"

"I heard you in your meeting moments ago. I heard the whole conversation."

"But we never said such a thing!"

Using the kloormari abilities to remember everything and to imitate voices and sounds flawlessly, Pa repeated part of the conversation to Kozoltoo and Tenisha in their exact voices.

"So, is that when the anti-matter comes into play?" Pa said in Tenisha's voice.

"You got it. It's embedded deep inside the altar top. When the recording ends, Kelvoo will be a couple of thousand meters above the crowd. That's when the magnetic seal around the anti-matter will deactivate," Kelvoo repeated, just as Kozoltoo had sounded.

"Wow! What's that going to look like?" Kelvoo continued.

"Like a blaze of glory. A brilliant blaze of glory!"

With no adequate rebuttal, there was utter silence from the Kelvonists on the platform.

From inside Kelly's car, we saw flatter land up ahead, just beyond a hill.

"We're almost there! Just over this next hill!" Kelly said, forgetting that his voice was being broadcast by Pollybot.

"No! They'll kill you!" Pa said. "Turn around! It's over!"

Undaunted, we continued toward the Kelvonist headquarters at top speed. We couldn't help noticing the increasing traffic around us. The time for Kelvoo's public appearance and grand finale was still hours away, but vehicles of all kinds were heading toward the temple, to stake out the best positions. Kelly's car weaved around many others until it found an altitude between layers in the traffic pattern.

Dipping down just above the treetops, we finally crested the hill. Straight ahead was the village, the river, and the towering headquarters beyond. I looked for the Kelvonists along the railing and my pa just below them, but we were still too far away to see such details.

May and I glanced at the feed from Pollybot and saw Kelvoo struggling to move a lower limb, using it to edge closer to the rim of the catwalk.

"Damn it! If you're going to die, at least die for a purpose!" Tenisha screamed at Kelvoo in desperation.

"Why waste your life right here and now?" she asked. "You can heal humanity, Kelvoo! Your life can be given for the greater good!"

"Don't think about yourself, Kelvoo!" Kozoltoo bellowed. "Think about humanity! Do what's best for humanity!"

"That is exactly what I'm doing," Pa said in a fierce voice, no longer slurred.

At that moment, we were close enough to see the Kelvonists along the railing and their rifles pointed at us. We were also close enough to see Pa falling, falling, falling to the ground below. May and I screamed, and Kelly angled the car into a steep dive.

May and I stared in horror at my Infotab, which showed Pollybot descending, unable to match the speed of Pa's freefall. From the bot's vantage point high above, we saw Pa's limbs spread apart. "That's it, Pa!" I said, sobbing. "Keep your arms and legs and claspers spread out! It'll slow you down!"

Pa adjusted the angle and position of limbs and hand paddles as if to change trajectory.

"Hit the water, Pa! Oh god, Pa, please hit the water!" May shrieked.

"Danger! Stop your action!" Pollybot said, adding to our screams.

Seconds after the splash, Kelly slammed the car to a stop on the bank of the moat, directly below the deck of the headquarters where the security officers couldn't see us. Kelly leaped from the car, ran into the moat, and waded forward to Pa's limp body; its limbs bent at unnatural angles. I saw a clasper limb drifting near the opposite bank, torn from Pa's body by the impact.

May and I followed, slipping on the muddy bank as Kelly waded back through the thigh-deep water and muck, towing Pa's body. We each grabbed one of Pa's upper limbs and tugged while Kelly pushed Pa's lower limbs forward, slipping on the filthy mud that was clinging to his legs.

Farther down the path on the opposite side of the moat, several of Pa's devotees came running. They must have seen Pa's fall. "No, it can't be!" one of them cried in denial of the horrible scene they had just witnessed.

As the others closed in, we slid Pa's mud-caked body onto the flat grass. Kelly grabbed Pa under the arms, and May and I each took a leg as we muscled the limp, crumpled mass onto the floor in front of the car's rear seats. Seconds earlier, Pollybot had reached ground level and had stopped sounding its warning, somehow aware that an end had been reached. The bot glided into the car behind us and hovered, as if in a silent vigil.

I looked back over my shoulder where a worshipper had found Pa's detached clasper limb next to the far bank. He jumped into the water and picked it up. When he was back on the bank, he lifted Pa's limb over his head, crying hysterically toward the sky as a crowd gathered around him.

"Give us Kelvoo! We must have Kelvoo!" people screamed as they waded across the moat toward us. May and I slammed the car's hatch shut. The last thing we saw was the beginning of a riot around Pa's clasper. A woman tried to pull the limb from the hysterical man's grip. Nausea almost overcame me as more crazed worshippers joined the fray, trying to take the sacred relic, or perhaps just a piece of it, for themselves.

The car rose and Kelly guided it around the pillars that supported the building and back out into the light. The officers along the railing opened fire, balls of plasma whizzing past us. We flew over Kelvonist worshippers, who must not have been aware of the unthinkable fate that had befallen their assumed god. They scattered in terror, fleeing the fiery blue projectiles.

I looked behind the car and saw scores of vehicles emerging from the hangar in the headquarters. By then we were over the temple and had clear air above us since all approaching traffic was landing around the perimeter. Kelly commanded the car to rise, then he accelerated at full power. Seconds later we were high above the scattered clouds and racing toward the ocean, leaving a nightmare scene of devastated people.

TWENTY-FOUR: TAKING FLIGHT

The vehicles that the Terran government and the Kelvonists had were no match for Kelly's customized car, which soon outpaced them. As we neared the coast, some vehicles approached from ahead, trying to cut us off. The car's sensors picked them up well in advance. With some minor course adjustments, Kelly easily avoided them. When we were over the ocean, we descended and flew just ten meters over the waves to make it difficult for others to detect us.

Right after we took off with Pa, Kelly commanded the car to stow the rear seats, leaving a small area of open floor. As May and I knelt beside Pa, I pulled a bottle of water and two washcloths from my bag. May and I washed the mud from Pa's body as best we could. Our beloved pa was a mess, and it filled us with anguish. Pa's eye was split open on one side between two rows of triangular segments. Milky blue circulatory fluid seeped from the split and oozed from the joint where the missing clasper limb had been attached.

Without warning, a clod of mud was ejected from one of Pa's respiratory inlets, followed by a gurgling sound and then ragged breathing.

"Pa's alive!" May exclaimed, laughing and crying at the same time.

"Kelly! Kelly! It looks like Pa survived!" I shouted.

"What? After *that* high a fall?" Kelly turned back to look at us, a huge smile illuminating his strained features. "That's unbelievable!"

"What should we do?" I asked. "Should we get medical help or just get out of here?"

"I'm for getting out of here," Kelly replied. "We're maybe fifteen minutes from the transport and then we'll launch immediately. We should be able to jump less than an hour after that. No medical facilities on Terra can deal with traumatic kloormari injuries. Even if they could help, they'd just keep trying to make Kelvoo a god or a martyr, and who knows what they'd do to us!" He looked at the rearview scanner display. "Besides," he added, "we're still being pursued, though they're a good ten minutes behind us."

Kelly's logic was solid, and I felt foolish for even suggesting we stay on Terra.

May and I tried to rouse Pa, shaking Pa's shoulders. "Pa! Pa! It's Brenna," I said into one of Pa's auditory receptors. "We're leaving Terra! Hang in there, Pa! It's going to be alright!"

"Forget it," May said. "Pa's unconscious because of the drugs. It's probably going to be hours before Pa wakes up." Our dread about Pa's vina dependency remained unspoken.

I tried moving one of Pa's lower elbows. It took some effort, but the elbow bent and then remained in position, confirming the effect of the drugs that Kozoltoo had discussed with Tenisha. Pa was lying flat on the floor, which blocked half of Pa's vocal outlets and one respiratory inlet. May and I moved Pa's limbs to put Pa into a recovery position, lying on one side. We rubbed Pa's arms and shoulders. "Hang on, Pa. We're nearly there," I said.

"It's going to be alright, Pa. We're here for you. We love you," May added.

"ETA is five minutes," Kelly said into the console. "Is the vessel prepped and ready?"

"Affirmative," a robotic voice replied.

The car was closing fast on a small group of islands. It slowed as it approached a beach, then the scene became dark as the car flew through a tropical forest. It stopped in front of a rock face, which slid to one side, revealing a small tunnel. We flew a short way through the tunnel, which opened into a large underground hangar. A midsize interstellar transport was waiting in the center of the circular pad, its rear hatch open. Kelly maneuvered the car through the hatch, straight into the transport's cargo bay.

"Welcome to Plan B," Kelly said. "This facility's been prepped for some time now, for exactly this kind of event."

As we opened the car's doors, two bots emerged from their wall-mounted stations in the cargo bay. Kelly and I moved Pa out of the car and then the bots carried Pa into the pilot's compartment. A frame for securing a kloormar's anatomy was located right behind the main console. The bots placed Pa on the frame and fastened the restraints. Seats were positioned on either side of the frame, where May and I secured ourselves. Kelly took the pilot's seat and busied himself with the controls as the ship came to life.

"Alert!" the robotic voice said. "Unknown vehicles above. Analysis suggests vehicles are conducting grid pattern search."

"Damn!" Kelly shouted. "We must have been tracked all the way to the island."

He fastened himself in. "Open iris," he commanded. Sunlight poured in as the roof over the landing pad opened like the pupil of a human eye. On a monitor we saw two cars passing, perhaps one hundred meters above us.

Kelly tapped a control on the transport's console, and the vessel ascended. Once we were just above the trees, the transport's nose tilted up just as the two cars closed in. A moment later, with a great roar, the transport sped past the cars and into the blue Terran sky. No more than fifteen seconds passed before the sky turned indigo, then black, with Luna on our left and thousands of stars punctuating the velvet black sky.

We were accelerating at a tremendous rate, but like Kelly's fancy car, the transport was equipped with the finest inertial dampening technology, giving us a smooth ride.

"Are we safe now?" May asked. "Is anyone chasing us?"

"No," Kelly replied. "Because of its isolationism, Terra only has a handful of interstellar transports. We're good from here. We just need to get into open space to execute a jump."

May and I turned our attention back to our pa, who was held upright in the frame. Pa's circulatory fluid had stopped leaking, apart from a bluish trickle from the eye. A drop of the fluid dripped from the base of Pa's eye dome, giving the appearance that Pa was weeping. I dismissed the thought, chiding myself for assigning human traits to a non-human species—something Pa often advised against.

Just before we reached a suitable jump location, Pa seemed to stop breathing. "Pa! Pa!" I shouted. "Hang on! We're almost home!" Pa started to breathe again but in a rasping, irregular way. May and I each gripped one of Pa's hand paddles.

"We're going to jump in thirty seconds," Kelly said, turning to look at us. "I've programmed an offset from the standard location, a little closer to Kuw'baal, to avoid materializing into another interstellar vessel."

Kelly's update barely registered with me as I rested my cheek against Pa's shoulder.

"Here we go!" Kelly shouted.

The jump was short and uneventful. When we materialized, the perfect, pure white sphere of Kuw'baal loomed ahead of us. A Sarayan warship was stationed in the distance behind us and to our left. It diminished in size and disappeared in seconds as we accelerated from the jump point toward Kuw'baal. A moment later, an angry Sarayan's voice blared from the comm unit.

"Unmarked transport, unmarked transport, this is Sarayan warship *Krantoz*. Identify yourself immediately!"

"*Krantoz, Krantoz*, this vessel has no designation," Kelly replied. "My name is Kelvoo Buchanan-Paige. I'm on a rescue mission and require emergency clearance to proceed to Kuw'baal. I have three other souls on board—Kelvoo of Kuw'baal, Brenna Murphy, and May Murphy."

"Unmarked vessel, clearance denied. Decelerate to an immediate stop relative to the *Krantoz*."

"*Krantoz*, this is a medical emergency. We have just rescued Kelvoo from Terra. Kelvoo is in grave medical distress and requires immediate treatment."

As we continued toward Kuw'baal, a rapidly growing speck appeared between us and the Sarayan ship. "Unidentified vessel, this is fighter *Keta 332*. Continue steady on your present course and prepare for visual inspection."

The small fighter craft pulled alongside on our left and matched our speed. We could see the Sarayan pilot inside the transparent cockpit as the fighter closed to within five meters of us. The pilot stared at us for a few seconds, then rotated the fighter and moved away, back toward the *Krantoz*.

"Unidentified vessel, this is the *Krantoz*. What is the nature of Kelvoo's medical distress?"

"Severe physical trauma due to a fall from a great height."

"Unidentified vessel, proceed along your current course at maximum safe speed. Does your comm system accept standard Alliance auto-nav coding?"

"Affirmative."

"Sending approach parameters, coded priority one."

"Received and activated," Kelly replied, glancing at his console and making adjustments. "Thank you, *Krantoz*."

"Thank you, Mr. Buchanan-Paige. Please share with Kelvoo our sincere wishes for a quick and full recovery.

"You hear that, Pa? They're glad to have you back," May said, rubbing Pa's shoulder. Still unconscious, my pa was completely unaware of the situation. Thankfully, Pa was no longer leaking circulatory fluid and was breathing more steadily, but the rasping sounds were louder and quite disturbing.

I turned to May. "I'm glad they're happy to have Pa back, but I guess *we* don't even get a mention!"

"Nah! Compared to Pa, we're nothing more than a blob of algel!" she replied.

"That's OK. I could do without the attention," I said. Inside, I was a mess. We had to *hurry*!

We heard further conversation between Kelly and the Sarayans. All traffic had been cleared for the approach to the kloormari village beside Newton. We would be landing on an emergency pad on the roof of the kloormari hospital where medical personnel were standing by.

For the final ten minutes, we watched the growing orb of Kuw'baal in silence, all three of us too exhausted to speak. As we drew closer, I saw many of the ark platforms in orbit, looking like a glowing string of jewels adorning Kuw'baal. On our final approach, we tore through the planet's dense clouds, then flew over Sam's Lake and the village stream above the algel falls and then straight down to the hospital roof. A group of medical staff was waiting there with hover clamps ready.

Kelly opened the rear hatch as the transport settled onto the pad. Then he released the magnetic latches holding Kelvoo's frame to the floor. The emergency workers attached a hover clamp to each side of the frame and lifted it out, then pulled the entire assembly into the hospital. The three of us and Pollybot followed.

The medical team was connecting sensors to Pa even as they rushed down a corridor. When they passed through a set of double doors, a kloormari staffer told us that we could go no farther. "Let's get you all somewhere comfortable while we see what we can do for Kelvoo," the staffer said.

The staffer led us into a private "human-friendly family room" that was well appointed with sofas, chairs, a cot, and windows that looked out over the kloormari village and the city of Newton beyond.

I took a seat on a sofa, and Kelly sat beside me. "How're you holding up?" he asked, putting a hand on my shoulder. "I don't know," I replied. "So much has happened. I don't know what to feel until we find out how Pa's doing."

"Is the being with the designation 'Kelvoo' broken?" Pollybot asked as it hovered in a corner. We were startled, having rarely heard an older technology bot take the initiative to speak.

"Yes," Kelly replied.

"Is the being with the designation 'Kelvoo' repairable?" Pollybot asked.

"We're waiting to find out," I replied, my voice cracking with emotion. The bot seemed to be expressing genuine concern, but I reminded myself that I was projecting human feelings onto a machine.

May walked to the window and placed an interstellar call to her family while she looked outside. Her co-wife, Simone, was at home with their husband, Tristan. May and Simone's other husband, Ndugu, and their other co-wife, Beth weren't at home. I couldn't see May's Infotab screen, but the audio was clear in the otherwise silent room.

"May! Glad you could call," Simone said. "We were wondering how long you'd be. We were starting to worry. Hang on a sec." We heared Simone shouting. "Trist! Trist, get over here. May's calling!"

"Hiya, honey!" Tristan said a few seconds later. "How's the investigation? Do you have news about your pa?"

May closed her eyes and nodded at the screen. "Honey? Are you OK?" Tristan asked. May shook her head as tears escaped from beneath her eyelids.

"Where are you, May? Can we come and get you?" Simone asked.

May took a deep breath to calm herself. "I'm on Kuw'baal, and I'm fine. I'm here with Brenna."

"Kuw'baal? Why Kuw'baal?" Tristan asked.

"You're probably going to be hearing a whole lot on the news broadcasts any time now," May said. "I wanted to let you know what's happening before you hear some warped version of it on the news." She took a deep breath. "Brenna and I have been on Terra for the last several days."

"Terra? Honey, what the hell? Terra?" Tristan exclaimed. "How did you—were you kidnapped?"

"No, Trist. Please, just listen! We met up with Kelvoo Buchanan-Paige. You remember who that is, right?"

"Of course," Simone said. "Everyone does."

"Well, anyway, we found Pa and we all took off for Kuw'baal."

"What? You mean you rescued your pa from Terra?" Simone asked.

"Yes, well . . . kind of. Things didn't go well, and Pa was seriously injured. We jumped straight to Kuw'baal. Brenna, Kelly, and I are at a hospital—"

"Kelly?"

"Kelvoo Buchanan-Paige. We call him Kelly. Anyway, we're at a hospital on Kuw'baal. They're working on Pa now. We're just waiting for news."

"OK, but you and Brenna are alright?" Simone asked.

"Yeah, we're OK."

"So, what happened? Tell us everything!"

"I can't. Not right now. Call Doogie and Beth and let them know. Oh, and prepare yourself for the media. All of you need to work out how you're going to handle them. Feel free to tell them anything I've already told you."

"OK. Will we see you soon?"

"I think so. I'll call you when we know more. Gotta go. Love to everyone. Bye."

After the call, May and I didn't know what to do with ourselves. We took turns pacing and gazing through the window. At one point, the kloormar who showed us into the room stopped by to ask Kelly to move his transport off the roof. "Oh no! I left the rear hatch wide open!" he exclaimed.

When he returned, he was carrying our bags. May and I were relieved when we checked our bags and found that they still contained our remaining gold chips. Crime was almost non-existent on Kuw'baal.

After he returned, Kelly checked his Infotab. It didn't take long for him to find breaking news about the rescue of Kelvoo from Terra.

"The Sarayans probably released the news," he said.

It wasn't long after the first news broke when we saw media vehicles buzzing around the hospital. The security window didn't allow anyone to see in from the outside, so we were safe for as long as the hospital staff could keep our presence under wraps.

Occasionally, a hospital employee would poke their eye dome or head into the room and ask us whether we needed anything. Each time we asked for an update about Kelvoo, they assured us that we would get one as soon as there was news to share.

"I can't help thinking about what we could have done differently," I admitted to Kelly. "I should have insisted that we leave your home earlier. If only we had got to Pa a couple of minutes sooner."

"No, Brenna," he replied. "If anyone's to blame, it's me. In the rush to rescue Kelvoo, I should have asked Pollybot to relay my voice in the ultrasonic range, just like the meeting we were monitoring. That way, Kozoltoo and the others wouldn't have heard. They wouldn't have known we were on the way, and they wouldn't have been prepared to shoot us down. That's why Kelvoo rolled off the catwalk. It was to save us. How could I have been so stupid?"

Kelly's feelings of guilt brought me back to reality. He was the last person I would blame for what Pa was going through at that moment. "It's alright Kelly," I said, taking his hand. "Pa would say that guilt isn't warranted when our intentions are good, and we don't have the ability to foresee the future."

We waited in silence after that, each of us lost in thought.

After night fell, we stared at the lights of the village and Newton and the illuminated path and landing pad over the mineral plain. About an hour after midnight, the door opened, and a human male in business clothes appeared. He introduced himself as Samir Sondheim, a representative from the Planetary Alliance consulate.

"The Alliance has asked me to pass along some unfortunate news to you," he said in a somber voice. My heart skipped a few beats as I prepared for the unthinkable. "I know the timing is terrible, but I'm told I have a legal obligation to notify the two of you as soon as possible," he continued.

"Not a good time?" I asked. "A legal obligation? So, you're not here to tell us that Pa—I mean, Kelvoo—is gone?"

"Oh, heavens no!" he said. "I don't know anything about Kelvoo's condition. I've been ordered to give you notice that a warrant has been issued for your arrests. You have charges pending against you for interfering with an interplanetary investigation."

"Yeah, no kidding!" I exclaimed, having known all along that our good intentions wouldn't go unpunished. "As you can probably guess, May and I have a few other things on our priority list at the moment!"

"Believe me, I didn't want to do this," the man replied. "I'll leave the three of you alone now. The good news is, out of respect for what you're going through, the matter isn't going to be pursued until the present situation is resolved.

"Good night, and best wishes for a positive outcome," he added as he excused himself.

It wasn't long after that when a kloormari doctor entered the room. "Kelvoo will see you now," the doctor announced.

TWENTY-FIVE: INTO HISTORY

May, Kelly, and I stood, and started to follow the doctor, along with Pollybot, but the doctor held up a hand paddle to stop us. "I'm sorry, only immediate family are permitted inside."

"That's OK," Kelly said, stepping back. "I'll stay and keep Pollybot company."

I braced myself for what I might see as we entered the room, but I was relieved at Pa's appearance. Pa was squatting in a typical kloormari resting position, partly supported by a metal frame. A few medical sensors were attached to various parts of Pa's body. As we entered, Pa stood, using the frame for balance. When Pa's arms extended toward us, we rushed over, then stopped short and gave Pa a gentle hug, to avoid knocking Pa over. We held our pa close, resting our heads on Pa's shoulders, nestling carefully against the eye stalk.

"We love you, Pa," I said.

"We're so happy you're going to be alright," May added.

"I love you too. More than any language can express," Pa replied in a weak but steady voice.

May turned to the kloormari doctor who was standing in a corner beside a floating display panel. "Is Pa—I mean Kelvoo—still feeling the effects of the drugs from Terra?"

"The drugs that caused Kelvoo's catatonic state and muscular rigidity have been fully metabolized and eliminated; however, Kelvoo's circulatory system still contains a high concentration of vinamibefentyn," the doctor replied.

"When will Kelvoo experience withdrawal from the vina?" I asked in the most clinical tone I could muster.

"If Kelvoo were human, withdrawal would start in approximately six weeks. The interval is shorter in the kloormari, typically six to eight days. You do not need to be concerned about that."

"What were Kelvoo's injuries?" May asked. "What did you do to treat them? How long will Pa need to recover?"

"Kelvoo's injuries are extensive and Kelvoo's internal organs have ceased functioning. Regarding treatment, we replaced Kelvoo's circulatory fluid and repaired Kelvoo's structural anatomy where we could. For the most part, our treatment has consisted of making your pa as comfortable as possible."

The doctor's words, delivered in a tone that was uncharacteristically sympathetic for a kloormar, jolted me to my core. *We don't have to be concerned about vina withdrawal? Treatment has mostly been about making Pa comfortable?* My mind raced to come up with a different interpretation, but May reached the same conclusion.

"What are you saying? How long does Pa have?" she asked.

The doctor's body and eye dome turned to face Pa. We broke off our embrace. Pa held my hand in one paddle and May's in the other, then Pa's eye dome tilted down. "My time has reached its end," Pa said.

My head was spinning. *Should I scream? Should I cry? Should I be sad or angry?* I didn't know what to feel or what to do. May and I just looked at Pa in stunned silence.

"How . . . how much longer?" I asked.

"Based on what the doctors have told me, I have approximately thirty-five minutes remaining," Pa replied. "Doctor, is that still accurate?"

"Yes, give or take five minutes."

"You see," Pa continued, "my internal systems are shutting down. My body's regenerative capacity can't keep pace. As one system reaches a critical point, others will kick in to compensate. It's a cascading shutdown." Pa's eye dome motioned toward the floating display panel beside the doctor. "The white line is tracking my remaining reserves. You can see how it's been trending lower. When it reaches the solid red line at the bottom, my life will end."

The clinical, matter-of-fact description from Pa was almost unbearable. It was also undeniably typical and quintessentially kloormari.

"Are you in pain?" I asked. Inwardly, I cursed myself for asking the question too casually, without the level of emotion it deserved.

"Yes," Pa said, "but it's manageable. When I was captured in the Terran civil war so long ago, and I was held in captivity and tortured, I coped by learning how to shift and distribute pain throughout my body. My pain is under control now. It also became much more bearable when the two of you walked into the room."

This whole conversation is wrong! I thought. *Why are we being so damned casual? We're talking about Pa dying! What's wrong with us?* I suppressed my thoughts, fighting back tears.

"What can we do to help?" May asked.

"I'd like the two of you to hold me, please," Pa said. "It helps to take the pain away. Please hold me close and hold me tight. There isn't much time, and there are things I need to tell both of you."

Pa moved from squatting to a kneeling position. May and I knelt beside Pa and held on tight. My face was buried under Pa's eye dome. I pictured myself being full of love and pouring that love through my arms into Pa. I also imagined the pain that Pa was feeling, and I visualized pulling that pain out of Pa and into my own body. The thought of Pa being gone from my life forever was beyond my comprehension, and I would have gladly given up my life so that Pa could go on.

"The first thing I need to say," Pa began, "is that I have no final words for the public. I'm sorry to burden you with this now, but I'm sure you're aware that there will be immense interest in my passing. Beings across the entire sector of the galaxy are going to want to know my last words. They, and especially humans, will be looking for words to which they can assign profound significance. As we all know, my statements would be interpreted, twisted, and misconstrued to suit the goals of those who would quote my words and claim to know the 'true meaning' behind them. For that reason, I have no final words. And you can quote me on that!"

"Next, I don't want anyone—especially the two of you—to think that I condone suicide. I'm deeply concerned that you might have seen my intentional fall as a means for me to escape a difficult personal situation. Other than being terminally ill and dying to avoid suffering, suicide solves nothing. As I learned when my human mentor, Sam Buchanan, took his own life, suicide only transfers the pain to others. When I made myself fall from the Kelvonist headquarters, it was to prevent evil, power-hungry people from using my already imminent death to plunge an entire planet deeper into ignorance. My survival, even temporarily, was as much a surprise to me as it must be to you.

"I'm so sorry that this is the way my life will end. I hope you'll both be able to forgive my actions at some point."

My heart shattered with the thought that my wonderful pa would ever feel a need for my forgiveness. I was reminded of the time after my rebellious years when I left Pa and May on Kuw'baal to start my charity work on the outlier worlds, and I had asked for forgiveness for all I had put Pa and May through. With that in mind, I repeated the response that Pa had given to me.

"My dear, dear Pa. There is nothing to forgive." I hugged Pa tighter and May did the same.

"My dear, sweet girls," Pa said, "be kind to each other. Life is precious, family is important, and love is everything. Under normal circumstances, I never would have known these things, but the circumstances of my life have been anything but ordinary. I had my first taste of love and family when our kloormari group was abducted by the Brotherhood, and we were held captive on *Jezebel's Fury*. When my baby, Sam, was murdered, I began to understand the value of life.

"As tragic as those times were, something wonderful— something incredible—came from them. I met the two of you. Raising you, through all its highs and lows, was my most precious experience. Seeing you grow and make lives for yourselves—May, with your big, wonderful family, and Brenna, with your selfless devotion to your vital charitable work—has filled me with joy and admiration. You have added dimensions to my life that I never would have known.

"There's just one aspect of knowing you that has filled me with dread—something most humans fear deeply. With the lifespan of a kloormar being so much longer than a human's, there was a strong likelihood that I would outlive both of you. The thought of losing either of you was so unbearable that I had to push it to the back of my mind whenever it presented itself. As the being who helped raise you for part of your childhood and through your formative teen years, it's good and right that I go before you. I hope you'll find some small comfort in that."

At that moment, I was desperate to find adequate words. I wanted to match the depth and eloquence of Pa's expression of love for us, but the enormity of the situation was far too much. May and I just snuggled in closer and we both whispered, "I love you, Pa," over and over again.

At one point as I shifted position to tighten my grip on my wonderful pa, I glanced at the display panel. The white line had descended and was bouncing just above the red line. *This is it*, I thought. *This is when it ends.*

I buried my face into Pa's shoulder. "I love you, Pa", I said, breaking into a sob.

The feeling of Pa's body changed. It lost its tension as Pa's muscles relaxed beneath my grip. The last breath left Pa's respiration inlet as if Pa were sighing. A short, unremarkable beep came from the display panel.

That beep is indelibly imprinted in my brain. That beep marked the passing of my pa. It marked the moment when the time of Kelvoo passed into history.

TWENTY-SIX: NOT MUCH LIKE PA

May and I retreated to Pa's house on the island in the lake. With nowhere else to go, Kelly came along and took up residence in a guest room. When we left the hospital, the Planetary Alliance representative, Samir Sondheim, advised us that we would be given our privacy for the rest of the day and the following day. After that he would visit us to sort through "all of the relevant business matters." He told us that a travel exclusion zone would be established in a fifteen-kilometer radius around the house to ensure our privacy in the coming days.

Pollybot continued to exhibit unusual behavior. "Where is the being with the designation 'Kelvoo?'" it asked after we arrived at the house.

"I don't know. Probably still at the hospital," I replied. Since Pa's remains hadn't been released to us yet, I didn't know where they were.

"Is the being with the designation 'Kelvoo' repairable?"

"I don't want to talk about it now," I said. "Ask me later."

Hours later, Pollybot asked the same questions again and I delayed answering, not wanting to be bothered by what I assumed was a defective bot.

Early the next morning as I got out of bed after crying into my pillow for most of the night, I walked into the main living area and took a seat beside May on a sofa. Kelly was sitting in a chair, drinking coffee. Pollybot glided in.

"Is the being with the designation 'Kelvoo', repairable?"

"No Pollybot! Alright? Kelvoo isn't repairable," I said with weary exasperation.

"Is the being with the designation 'Kelvoo' dead?" Pollybot asked.

"Yes," May replied. "Our pa—the being with the designation 'Kelvoo' is dead."

"Understood," Pollybot replied. "Transferring documents to Infotabs in possession of beings with designations 'Brenna' and 'May.'"

May and I stared at each other, then grabbed our Infotabs and discovered the reason for Pollybot's odd questions. A treasure trove of personal messages had been recorded by Pa with the stipulation that they be released to the intended recipients upon Pa's death. Pa had been recording messages almost every day since I was taken from Terra to Saraya. Some messages were for me, some were for May, and still others were for both of us. I won't disclose the content of the messages to my sister or me due to their deeply personal nature, but I will say that they were heartfelt and a source of great comfort and emotional healing.

Pa mentioned other messages that would now be in the hands of Pa's closest kloormari friends as well as friends and acquaintances of all species on various worlds. Kelly came into the room to say he had received two messages from Pa. He shed a tear as he read them.

One of Pa's messages was composed shortly after I was taken to Saraya. It was sent to a variety of officials with copies to May and me. It conveyed Pa's wishes concerning any memorials or other events that marked Pa's passing. The message acknowledged that some species, especially humans, would feel a need for a memorial to provide closure.

My wish is that no memorials or ceremonies are to suggest that I am special, heroic, or in any way elevated above other beings, kloormari or otherwise. I request that no monuments to me be constructed. The places where I lived, the sites at which significant personal events occurred, and my place of death are not to be set aside or given any special designation, other than their inclusion in historical notes. In other words, any actions, places, or things that might attract misguided praise of me must be avoided.

My remains are not to be present at any official functions. My wish is for Brenna Murphy and May Murphy to

dispose of my remains wherever, and in whichever manner,
they see fit.

May and I spent the rest of the day reading Pa's messages. We
read some of them silently to ourselves, and we read others aloud
to each other. We also chatted at length with Kelly, who had
risked so much to help us. In his own way, Kelly was as lost as we
were. He had left everything he had ever known on Terra, though
he did have a stash of gold chips and other valuables hidden in
his car, which was parked next to the house. Kelly did not
envision ever returning to Terra.

When he wasn't talking with us, Kelly wandered through the
house and the surrounding area, sometimes tidying up, other
times just thinking. A couple of times he took his car or Pa's
hoverlift off the island and explored the surrounding area.

When he returned from one outing, he described a beautiful
spot up the side of the mountain across the lake. There, he saw a
stream cascading down the mountainside, just before it became a
waterfall that fed the lake. We had all been through trauma to
varying degrees, and it was comforting to see Kelly find brief
moments of peace and contentment.

That evening, we ate some instant meals that were stored in
the guest kitchen and then retired to our rooms, emotionally
exhausted.

The next morning, my Infotab chimed. It was our friendly
neighborhood Planetary Alliance representative, asking for
permission to stop by.

"Sure, why not?" I replied. I requested that he give us an hour
to finish breakfast and make ourselves more presentable. Exactly
one hour later, an Alliance car landed outside, and I met our new
acquaintance at the door. "Come on in, Mr. Sondheim," I said.
"Are you here to arrest us and take us away?" I added, a touch of
sarcasm in my voice.

"No, Ms. Murphy. I'm on your side, and I'm only the
messenger. And please, call me Samir or Sam, if you'd prefer."

"OK, Samir, I'm sorry. We're going through a few things here."

"I can't begin to imagine what this is like for you," he said.

"Thanks, Samir, and please dispense with 'Ms. Murphy.'" I invited Samir in, and he sat with us.

Samir suggested that we not worry about being arrested. "Any such notions have been delayed until your pa has been laid to rest and the present situation is dealt with," he assured us. Samir also explained the desire of the Planetary Alliance leaders, various levels of government, and hundreds of organizations to pay their respects to Kelvoo and to offer their condolences to us. He told us that the Alliance was in the preliminary stages of planning a public memorial, and we would be consulted every step of the way to ensure the event was in keeping with Kelvoo's wishes and ours.

"I assume you read the memo from my pa and you know that it was Pa's wish to avoid anything that would lead to more hero worship," May said.

"Of course, May," Samir replied. "The ceremony will be low-key and humble to reflect your pa's personality and values. The next few days will be busy. My assignment is to facilitate the process for you. We need to complete a series of forms and legal documents, and we also need to arrange for your pa's remains to be transferred to your custody or handled for you as per your wishes."

"What if we don't want to cooperate?" May asked. "Haven't our lives already been turned upside down?"

"Then I'll do what I can to accommodate you. If you choose not to provide any input, the Alliance will do things as they see fit. Based on my experience, I think you'll find that if you keep busy, it will alleviate your grief by giving you something else to focus on. Having a say in the process may also help you avoid feelings of helplessness."

"We probably could use the distraction for a few days," I said, and May nodded in agreement.

For the next seven days, a steady procession of well-wishers and dignitaries visited the house, offering their condolences. Kelly volunteered to serve as our "gatekeeper." He did an excellent job of scheduling visitors while also allowing all three of us to have some time to ourselves. I was grateful to have Kelly there. After all we'd been through, he felt like part of the family.

Many of Pa's kloormari friends and associates stopped by the house. For the most part, their expressions of sympathy were perfunctory and seemed to be scripted. This was not due to any flaws in their character; it was just a reflection of kloormari psychology, its basis in logic, and its lack of sentimentality. They knew Pa's loss would leave a void, but they also acknowledged that nothing could be done about it. Nevertheless, I appreciated that they had gone out of their way to try to comfort May and me in accordance with human custom.

Pa's fellow kloormari survivors from *Jezebel's Fury* were a different story. Having endured their abduction and the shared emotional trauma, they were fully capable of empathy. Their condolences were deep and sincere. I could tell that the loss of their friend was very painful to them, and I wondered whether they viewed the development of their emotions as a blessing or a curse.

May kept in touch with her family, with much back-and-forth about whether they should attend the memorial and, if so, which of them would be able to make the trek. May convinced all of them that they should stay at home and look after one another. I think May saw Pa's death as something very personal and, since most of our relationship with Pa preceded May's family life, she wanted to mourn the loss in private.

I wouldn't say that we were pressured by the organizers, but May and I were certainly "encouraged" to speak at Pa's memorial. We politely refused every time, not wanting to be drawn into a maelstrom of publicity and never-ending attention.

When the day came, May, Kelly, and I were taken to the memorial by Samir in a car owned by the Planetary Alliance. The organizers selected the place where the stream flowed from Sam's Lake above the kloormari village and Newton. The site was selected due to its significance. It was the place where Pa and K'tatmal placed the remains of Pa's first close human friend and Kelly's father, Sam Buchanan. The memorial was scheduled to start early in the Kuw'baal afternoon. I had warned the organizers about the risk of adverse weather during that part of the day, but they said logistical constraints left no other choice.

The car crested the rockfall and the hill above the village. The lake, nestled in the bowl-shaped valley, appeared on our left. The stream exited from the lake below us, flowed a short distance to our right, and then disappeared into a steep gorge. The valley had changed due to the recent upheaval, the colors of its newly exposed mineral deposits more vibrant than ever.

Viewing platforms, bleacher seating for thousands of guests, and the main stage hovered over the stream. Cars and buses arrived near the top of the hill on the village side of the valley, and hover devices shuttled mourners to the grandstands or other platforms. A hundred or more vid cameras from all the major broadcasters hovered overhead.

"So much for a low-key event," I remarked to Samir. He didn't reply.

Samir took us to the viewing stand for family, close friends, and dignitaries. Kelly sat with us because I had designated him as my personal guest. I wondered how he felt, sitting there in the location where his father had been laid to rest.

We watched as mourners arrived. The majority were humans. The next largest group was kloormari, and only a handful of guests of other species were present. This reflected the significance that humans attribute to death and their deep-seated fear of it. Other species tended to treat the death of another as a termination of their relationship with that being. They usually didn't see much point in marking the occasion.

The ceremony started with a chorus of fifty singers, performing a song that had been written for the occasion.

Life is like a river
with many twists and bends.
It carries every one of us
until our journey ends.

The wealthy and the powerful,
the poor and needy too,
are swept along like all the rest.
The same as me and you.

> We search among the rapids,
> for heroes who will lead,
> and guide us through the tempest,
> in times of pain or need.
>
> But if you search inside yourself
> with honesty, you'll find,
> your own true hero lies within
> your heart and soul and mind.

When the choir finished, I felt relieved that the song could be applied to any being, rather than naming and praising Pa specifically.

The song was followed by speeches. In keeping with Pa's wishes, the speeches avoided suggesting that Pa was special, heroic, or above other beings; however, some speakers added a personal note to their presentation, including anecdotes about the impact Pa had on their lives. Some of the stories told by humans had humorous elements, and some of them strayed into excessive praise. I had to remind myself that I was witnessing human nature, and I too would have trouble restraining myself if I had to speak at a memorial for a being who I admired deeply.

The songs that were sung and the words that were spoken that day were thoughtful and moving, or at least they were supposed to be, but I realized I wasn't responding as I "should" have. I just felt numb. I looked over at May and Kelly. Both of them were sitting upright, stone-faced and seemingly unmoved, but when I looked at Samir, he was close to tears more than once. Behind us, I heard humans sobbing or sniffling. *How strange it is that people who have never even met Pa are so moved by this spectacle. Why in the hell aren't we?* I wondered.

I believed that Pa would have understood my feelings, and the thought caused something to shift inside me.

Three more speeches remained in the program when I looked over and saw the sky darkening above the far side of the lake. The darkness approached and then ploughed into the proceedings in the form of a wall of wind and intense rain.

"I warned them," I muttered.

May, Kelly, Samir, and I, along with others in our section, were not impacted too badly since we were in a structure that had a roof. Unfortunately, the mourners in the bleachers and the participants on the stage, including the choir, were windblown and drenched. Undaunted, they carried on, though I got the distinct impression that the speeches were sped up just a little bit.

The storm ended just as the ceremony did. Samir guided us to the car, which had positioned itself at the edge of the platform. Along the way, many strangers offered their condolences. We thanked them accordingly, and I could feel their sincerity. Nonetheless, it was a relief when the car door closed, and we were on our way back to the house on the island.

When we arrived and Samir left us, we collapsed onto the sofas. "So," I said, "what did we think of that?"

"I think they did a good job," Kelly replied.

"Yeah," May added. "They did a good job. Whoever they were remembering must have been remarkable. I'm just not sure who it was."

I nodded. "It didn't sound much like our pa, did it?"

TWENTY-SEVEN: PACHELBEL'S CANON

Pa's remains were delivered to the house the morning after the memorial. Samir arrived with a kloormari coroner. May and I were afraid to look at Pa, not knowing the condition of the body, but the coroner wouldn't release Pa's remains until we both made a positive identification and signed the transfer.

I felt queasy as we walked into the back of the coroner's transport where a black bag lay on top of a hover stretcher. The coroner opened the bag enough to expose the body. It had been cleaned and prepared to look much better than we had feared. Pa's eyelid, pouches, respiratory inlets, and vocal outlets were closed. Pa's arms and legs were straight, and Pa's remaining clasper limbs were folded inward. Pa looked relaxed and peaceful. If Pa hadn't been lying flat, I would have thought Pa was in a deep meditative state. In fact, the body appeared so lifelike I almost expected Pa to wake up and start chatting with us. I leaned over, kissed Pa's closed eyelid, then turned away. May did the same.

"Where would you like us to place Kelvoo's remains?" the coroner asked. May and I hadn't considered the logistics of receiving Pa's body.

"We should get a sheet from the linen closet," May suggested. Kelly volunteered and soon returned with a clean bed sheet. We took Pa's hoverlift and maneuvered it close to the rear hatch of the transport. May and I placed the sheet on the lift's deck. Then we backed away and watched from a distance as Kelly helped Samir and the coroner to fully open the body bag and move Pa onto the sheet. They folded the sides of the sheet over to cover Pa. Then the coroner gave Kelly some adhesive tape.

"We can take it from here," Kelly said. Samir and the coroner offered their condolences, wished us well, and then left.

With the greatest of care, Kelly wrapped tape around the sheet at Pa's eyestalk, torso, waist, and ankles, making a tight-fitting burial shroud.

"We're lucky that Kelly is here with us," May said.

"He's wonderful," I replied. By then I had no doubt that Kelly had become a member of our family.

A few days prior, May, Kelly, and I had talked about an appropriate location to place Pa's remains. Kelly showed us the beautiful spot that he had mentioned earlier when he had some time alone to explore the area near the house. We visited the place and agreed it would be suitable.

When Kelly finished wrapping Pa's body, we sat outside for a while, reminiscing and talking as we looked at our shrouded Pa laying on the hoverlift. The sky was still being kept clear of traffic, and I was grateful for the lack of prying eyes during such a private time.

"Shall we get this done?" I asked after a lull in the conversation.

We rode the hoverlift as Kelly guided it over the lake to the bottom of the waterfall. Then we rose close to the falling water, feeling a light spray when the shifting breeze blew toward us. Pollybot hovered parallel to us, staying farther away from the falls.

As we rose higher, May and I looked at the lake below and its island with the house on it. I took in the flat area across the lake where Pa and I had gathered clay to repair the house after the upheaval. I recalled ending those strenuous days, caked in mud from head to toe. Beyond the lake, was the grove of k'k'mos plants where we harvested the long, spiky leaves. Pollybot had helped us to pull the fibers out of the leaves and mix them with clay along with kobo juice to create the ksada mixture that we slathered onto the walls of the house. Repairing Pa's house was exhausting, filthy work, but as I looked back, I felt a new appreciation for those few days of shared goals and closeness with Pa.

As the hoverlift continued to the top of the lower section of the falls, the wind buffeted us. There, the stream tumbled over rocky ledges in a series of rapids and small cataracts. At the base of the highest section of falls, the water flowed into a hidden area, then reemerged, shooting out between two pillars of rock. When we rose above the pillars, we could see the area, which was only visible from above. There we saw a spot that held a small pool of water with a tiny gravel beach on either side.

Kelly lowered the hoverlift into the little alcove on the mountainside, and Pollybot followed. The area was sheltered from the wind, and it felt inviting and tranquil. Kelly left the lift hovering over the pool, and we stepped off onto the beach, which was no more than three meters wide and just over a meter from the rock face to the water's edge. In one swift movement, Kelly slung Pa's shrouded body over his shoulder, stepped onto the beach, and then laid Pa on the gravel.

May and I sat on either side of Pa. I rested a hand on the shroud somewhere around Pa's shoulder.

As we sat in silence, I thought about the death of my biological parents. My dad, William Murphy, was simply known as "Murph" to his crewmates on *Jezebel's Fury*. He had taken May and me with him on *Jezebel* "for an adventure," not long after my mom, Sally, had fallen ill and died. I was only ten when my dad was arrested, tried, and executed along with *Jezebel's* captain and the other crew members. May, my birth parents, and I had been illiterate and poor back in the pre-Correction days. Life had often been short and cheap in the outlier colonies, but the grief that May and I had felt at the loss of our parents had been deep and damaging.

The death of Kelvoo, the kloormar who had taught us, raised us, and loved us so much was also profoundly emotional, but at our advanced age, we were much better equipped to process it and move forward, just as Pa would have wanted.

I thought about Kelly. His mom, Lynda, had left his alcoholic father before Kelly was old enough to understand what was happening. Lynda lived into her nineties, but Kelly said he hadn't seen her since his teen years. He had insisted that Lynda evacuate from Terra when the civil war was starting. He told her that he would follow on the next shuttle, but instead he remained to fight the Terran government as an underground rebel.

A few days earlier, Kelly had told me that, since he hadn't seen or spoken with his mother for so long, he didn't know what to feel when word of her death reached him on Terra. Although Kelly hadn't had much contact with Pa, I wondered whether Pa's death had opened unresolved issues for Kelly, concerning his mom's passing.

"I guess we should say something about Pa, but I can't come up with any words," May said.

"Me neither," I replied. "I'm not even sure what I'm feeling right now."

"You know," Kelly said, "as a kid, I resented being named 'Kelvoo.' I didn't like that my parents gave me a kloormari name. I know that your pa was my dad's best friend, but by the time I was old enough to understand, my mom had already left my dad and taken me with her. To me, my father was just a drunk who selfishly killed himself, and I didn't want to be named for a friend of the dad that I resented so much.

"I didn't meet your pa until I was thirteen. That's when I first saw the two of you, at that reception for your pa at the university. Your pa took a moment to talk to me. I wasn't receptive, but I could see that your pa was very kind.

"I didn't fully appreciate Kelvoo until I was in the resistance during the Terran civil war. When I was with the unit that broke into the prison and rescued your pa, I spent a moment guiding your pa to safety. Knowing the hell your pa had just been through, that moment helped me appreciate your pa's courage and strength.

"Please don't think I'm trying to worship Kelvoo like those fools on Terra. I know it's the last thing you or your pa would want. All I'm saying is that, after all this time, I'm glad my parents named me Kelvoo. It makes me feel proud now but also humble, if that makes sense."

Kelly's words were simple and moving. "Thank you, Kelly," I said as I touched his arm. "Your tribute to Pa was better than anything I would have come up with." That made him smile.

"Let's do this," May said.

Kelly removed his footwear and rolled up his pant legs. We also took off our shoes, then Kelly picked up the shroud at the end where Pa's eye dome was. He waded into the pool backward, dragging Pa's body down the slope of the beach. May and I grasped the fabric on either side of the shroud near the upper part of Pa's legs as we helped slide the shroud under the water.

Unlike the difficulty Pa and K'tatmal once had while trying to give Sam Buchanan a similar sendoff, Pa's denser kloormari body sank as soon as most of the air escaped from inside the shroud in the form of large bubbles. When Pa's body was lying in knee-deep water, it sank part of the way into the gravel of the streambed. As our feet disturbed the gravel, we stirred up a layer of silt that clouded the water and blocked our view of Pa. We waded out and waited for a couple of minutes as the cloud of silt flowed in the gentle current of the pool to the place where the water exited between the rock pillars. We saw that Pa had sunk farther into the gravel due to the natural movement of the water as it pushed more gravel over Pa's remains.

As we stood on the beach in our bare feet, I knew that Pa would be completely buried in a few minutes. The moment felt right to hear a piece of music that was significant to Pa. Pa had "sung" the classical piece of human music as a tribute to Sam when Pa and K'tatmal had buried him.

"Pollybot," I said, "please play 'Pachelbel's Canon.'"

Pollybot rose to a point several meters above the center of the pool and then the music started.

We bowed our heads and listened as the music grew in intensity, its volume rising above the rush of the water as the stream entered the pool from above and poured out into the falls below.

I had expected to cry during that part of our plan, but my eyes were dry. I wondered whether something was wrong with me, but as I searched my emotions, I discovered feelings of peace and, on some level, joy. I was happy to have had the opportunity to spend my formative years under the care of a being as loving and intelligent as my wonderful, incomparable pa. My heart swelled with gratitude for Pa's love and patience with me, even through my rebellious years when I was the cause of so much hurt to Pa and May.

I stole a glance at May and Kelly. They also seemed to be at peace as we took those precious minutes to reflect on the profound effect that Pa had on us.

As the music swelled, it filled the air and reverberated off the mountainside, and my heart soared with love and appreciation.

As the final strains of "Pachelbel's Canon" ended and the last echoes faded, I gazed into the pool and realized that the streambed had claimed Pa's body, its nutrients to be returned to Kuw'baal's natural environment. We had honored Pa's memory in keeping with the traditions of Pa's home village, dating back to a time long before the kloormari had ever conceived of the stars and galaxies beyond their planet's clouded sky.

The time for mourning had ended. We would still grieve the loss of Pa and would think about Pa every day, but we would also take the strength that Pa had given us. We would heal and continue with our lives as Pa would have wished.

For billions of beings, Kelvoo was a symbol of courage. Someone who was humble and wise and a great inspiration. Kelvoo was even a god figure to many, which I found so tiresome.

For May and me, standing barefoot on a gravel beach tucked into the side of a mountain in the wilds of the kloormari home world, Kelvoo was so much more than wise, inspiring, or even godlike.

To us, Kelvoo was just our pa, and that was worth so much more to us than anyone else could ever imagine.

EPILOGUE

Our final business on Kuw'baal was to deal with Pa's house and the huge fortune in gold chips that May and I still held.

We decided to donate Pa's home to a new Planetary Alliance charity for the reintroduction of Terrans to the range of cultures on the other planets. Pa's house would be a place for Terran delegations to stay and learn about who Kelvoo really was—just an ordinary kloormar who lived in extraordinary times and circumstances. I think Pa would have been pleased to see the house being used for such a purpose, despite claiming to have little attachment to inanimate objects.

May learned a bit about banking when she visited the only branch of an interplanetary financial institution on Kuw'baal to have them open an account for her. The staff advised her that they typically dealt exclusively with governments and large corporate organizations. They wondered what kind of business she would have that couldn't be served via standard SimCash transactions. They nearly had a conniption when she pulled out 197 gold chips to deposit. A flurry of high-level consultations and permissions settled the matter. Once the vast fortune was safe, she worked to distribute its value back to the millions of beings who had donated funds to May's investigation.

The Planetary Alliance authorities were kind enough to wait until May and I returned to Perdition before we were charged with interference in an interplanetary investigation. The entire case was controversial and highly sensitive. On the one hand, public sentiment was clearly with us, but at the same time, the investigation had been based on Saraya, which gave the Sarayans the authority to decide how to pursue the matter. With their penchant for following the letter of interplanetary law, the Sarayans insisted that we be charged and, if required, put on trial.

In the end, a trial proved to be unnecessary. Pa's old friend and legal expert, K'tatmal was kind enough to represent us. With K'tatmal's advocacy, we weren't required to go anywhere to turn ourselves in. Instead, an officer and an Alliance prosecutor visited us in May's home. We all drafted an agreed-upon statement of facts, and May and I pled guilty in exchange for a modified sentence.

Our one-year term of house arrest in May's home allowed the Sarayans and the Alliance to signal that justice had been served, while causing only moderate outrage from our growing legion of supporters as the details of our Terran escapade emerged. Every so often, we would record statements indicating that we were satisfied with the verdict and the sentence, and that the public need not be concerned for us.

While monotonous at times, our incarceration in May's home provided a welcome break for two older ladies who'd had enough adventure to last the rest of our lives. Our confinement was anything but solitary, with May's spouses going about their daily lives, along with a steady procession of children, grandchildren, nephews, and nieces coming and going, just like they had during my previous stay. I came to embrace the exalted role of Auntie Brenna, and all the love from May's beautiful family.

With the currency he had stashed in his escape car, Kelly bought a home—several properties, in fact—not far from May's place. Like May and me, he was hailed as a hero. He did his best to keep a low public profile, which proved more difficult since he didn't have the "luxury" of imprisonment like Brenna and I did. Nonetheless, he made time to visit us every day.

During one of his early visits, May asked Kelly about the fate of his guards and Inga, his assistant. "I left Inga with instructions that she was to follow if I died or left Terra," he explained. "My guards and their families will be taken care of nicely for the rest of their lives."

"And Inga?" May asked.

"Before I answer that," Kelly said, "what did you think of her— honestly?"

"Well, she was certainly skilled and efficient," May said.

"But . . .?" Kelly replied, encouraging May to finish her thought.

"But she was sort of odd," May said. "I can't explain why. There was a certain coldness to her. I guess I'd say she was aloof, for lack of a better word."

"That's what I thought you'd say," Kelly replied. "Still, Inga was pretty good for an AI, wouldn't you agree?"

"What?" May exclaimed. "Inga was a bot?"

"Sure was! A damned fine—and unbelievably expensive—humanoid bot with the most advanced AI mind on the market! Physically, Inga was built to be lifelike in every way, but she was definitely lacking in the personality department." He shrugged. "Money can't quite buy *everything*, it seems."

May's face took on a mischievous expression. "So did you and Inga ever . . .?"

"What? No! That would've been weird!" Kelly exclaimed.

I was horrified by her suggestion. "Bloody hell, sis! That's none of your business!" I said.

My outrage didn't deter May. "C'mon," she said, "you must've tried it at least once! I mean, just to see what it was like."

"Would you shut up?" I said, flushing with embarrassment on Kelly's behalf.

Kelly just smiled, then deftly changed the subject.

A new and different level of love was another welcome consequence of my imprisonment. Each time Kelly visited, my attraction to him grew. For a while, I dismissed such feelings, thinking that I was far too old for such nonsense. Still, I kept reminiscing about my attraction to Guiseppe during my brief time on Saraya, ill-fated though it was. Far too often my mind wandered and wondered about the possibility of an intimate relationship with Kelly.

On my seventy-third birthday, May and her family threw a lovely surprise party for me. That evening, Kelly, in cahoots with May's family, arrived with a bouquet of flowers as May's family went out for the night and May retired to her room to "make myself scarce," as she put it. Kelly and I had an amazing dinner by old-fashioned candlelight as he revealed how he felt about me.

After dinner he asked Pollybot to play a selected piece of music. It was a beautiful, slow, Mangorian composition. As it started, Kelly stood up and asked me to dance.

"But I don't know how to dance!" I protested.

"I remember you saying that at the university reception when you were seventeen," he replied. My cheeks flushed at the thought that he'd held on to that memory for so long.

Kelly extended his hand, which I took in mine. "Besides," he added as he pulled me close, "I don't know how to dance either. I'm just looking for an excuse to hold you."

As I rested my head on Kelly's chest and listened to his heart beating, I thought about how I had spent my youth fleeing every opportunity for love, focusing instead on my charitable work as I strove to atone for my misguided actions in my late teens. As Kelly held me, I accepted his love as a sign from the universe that my life had been well spent, and any debt I might have owed had been more than fully paid. I deserved love, I deserved Kelly, and I deserved to enjoy my remaining years.

When he kissed me, it felt as if all the stars in the sky came alive and danced with us.

Of course, we all followed developments on Terra with intense interest. At first, Kozoltoo claimed that my pa hadn't fallen from his headquarters and that anyone who witnessed the event was lying. At the same moment, vid was released from some of the more level-headed bystanders who, instead of rushing toward us, had used their Infotabs to record the scene as we pulled Pa from the moat. Shortly after that, someone provided a media outlet with evidence, in the form of Pa's detached clasper limb, that the crazed worshippers had fought over.

The Terrans were outraged at their spiritual leaders and were, as Tenisha had once alluded, "out for blood." Kozoltoo and Tenisha went into hiding, along with their top supporters in government. They were "rescued" by a diplomat who picked them up in an embassy transport. They raced to the nearest Alliance outpost where they hastily requested asylum. They are still living in exile, though not on the planet with that name.

At the request of the remaining Terran leaders, the Planetary Alliance sent a delegation to Terra. The Alliance held an emergency meeting and agreed to open relations with Terra, partly because the Terrans begged them to but mostly because the Alliance acknowledged the damage that isolation had caused. By cutting themselves off from other cultures and worlds, the Terrans filled the vacuum by turning toward mythology and superstition.

Isolation, as it turned out, is historically bad for humans.

The Alliance and the Terran government opened interplanetary communication. The Terran media was free to report the truth about Kelvoo and Kelvonism. Cultural exchanges were set up, with many delegations traveling between planets on goodwill missions. I do hope they're making good use of Pa's home when they're visiting Kuw'baal. I'm told that travel and free trade between the planets will follow in the coming months.

With that said, the people of Terra have been traumatized and have a long road ahead on their path toward healing. Sometimes I try to imagine how it would feel to base my life around an idealized version of a being who is presented as the pinnacle of wisdom and perfection, only to discover that I had been chasing a grand illusion.

I have been using my confinement to read and learn from history, especially human history from centuries ago when human life was limited to Terra and long before first contact with other worlds. I have been reading translations of ancient speculative fiction—stories of contact with "alien" species as humans imagined it would unfold. Sometimes those stories are disturbing, but they're also hilarious in their absurdity. Ancient humans usually portrayed themselves as peaceful and innocent, being forced to battle for survival against terrifying creatures who were invading Terra for the sole purpose of the violent annihilation or enslavement of humanity.

These stories, which were placed in a strangely contradictory category called "science fiction," were clearly a projection of humanity's flaws onto extraterrestrial species. These prejudices of early humans are rife with irony. Humans are the only known species that has ever committed mass murder through large-scale warfare. Only humans had become aware of threats to their home planet from pollution, climate change, or disease but failed to act when doing so would have required short-term sacrifice.

Humans are also the only species to embrace superstition. Certainly, mythology played a role in extraterrestrial cultures as they tried to explain natural phenomena, but as those cultures grew, learned, and unlocked knowledge, the myths became a historic footnote. In contrast, humans were willing to kill and die for their beliefs no matter how absurd they were on their very face. But that happened centuries ago, and until I became aware of Kelvonism, I would never have imagined that it could happen again, especially on the human home world.

I was in my teens when the anti-immigrant Human Independence Movement came to light on Terra and I was foolishly caught up in its propaganda. It was their rise to power that caused the expulsion of Terra from the Planetary Alliance. Now that they are emerging from their isolation, many Terrans have expressed a yearning for Terra to formally rejoin the Alliance. I wonder whether they are motivated by a need to *belong* to something bigger than themselves. Perhaps they look to the Alliance as a surrogate for the Kelvonist movement. No matter the reason, I don't see the Alliance accepting Terran membership any time soon, and frankly, I agree with the Alliance's "wait and see" perspective.

Kuw'baal, Perdition, Exile, and Terra are of great importance to the Alliance. Kuw'baal isn't a full member of the Alliance simply because the kloormari have not seen any specific benefits to joining. In contrast, the humans on Perdition and Exile have often broached the possibility of official membership, but since the Terran civil war, the response has been a polite but firm denial. My species is simply too unpredictable, at least for the moment.

Humans are, arguably, the most interesting and creative of all known sentient species. The reason lies in the diversity of our individual personalities and values. Some humans are as trustworthy as any kloormar, but others can only be counted on to serve their own interests above others. As a result, what we see as diversity is viewed by other species as a lack of unity, making humans too risky to trust. In my view, it doesn't matter much. We trade with the Alliance, and we cooperate in science, exploration, education, and so much more. For all practical purposes, humans are integral to the Planetary Alliance, even without official membership of the worlds we call home.

When I think about Kelvoo's place in history, I wonder whether humans will view the manner of Pa's death as unbefitting of someone with such a prominent role in history. A fall, followed by dying in a hospital, doesn't exactly fit the notion of perishing during an act of extreme valor as one might expect from a hero. On its surface, Pa's death may seem mundane. Still, my pa did not enjoy being labeled a hero, and in that respect, Pa's death was as fitting as any other. Perhaps it should serve as a reminder that death will claim us all someday as the great equalizer that it is.

Those are my thoughts about the lessons that we humans can take from my pa's recent experiences on Terra. These matters will be discussed ad infinitum by beings with far more wisdom and expertise than me. In the end, humanity will do whatever humanity does. I hope that knowledge and love will prevail as my species moves forward. I felt it was important to express my thoughts because people want to know what I think, as someone who was close to Kelvoo.

Today as May and I near the date of our release, I'm happy to reveal this story to the public. I hope my pa would have been alright with my decision to name it *Kelvoo's Teachings*. I wanted a title that fit in with Pa's previous autobiographies, *Kelvoo's Testimonial* and *Kelvoo's Terra*. I hope readers will understand that the irony in my use of the word "teachings" is intentional. Sometimes I worry that this story will be misinterpreted and used for malevolent purposes, but between Pa's section and mine, I can only hope our warnings and the lessons learned will be sufficient to prevent such misappropriation.

As for my personal life today, I'm overjoyed with the way things have turned out. That doesn't mean everything is perfect. Every day I think about Pa and mourn the loss that I share with my family and all those who knew or drew inspiration from Kelvoo—just an ordinary kloormar whose life was subjected to extraordinary circumstances. Just an ordinary being who was the most wonderful parent any human could ever wish for.

Also by Phil Bailey:

KELVOO'S TESTIMONIAL and KELVOO'S TERRA

Kelvoo's backstory, from the moment of human first contact

Kelvoo's saga starts with *Kelvoo's Testimonial*, when Kelvoo witnesses the arrival of a species from another world. With no prior knowledge of other planets or anything beyond the clouded sky of Kuw'baal, the kloormari are fascinated by the humans of the first contact mission. The humans are friendly and benevolent, causing the kloormari to trust them completely.

After the human expedition departs, Kelvoo's illusions are shattered when a scheming human deceives Kelvoo and eight other kloormari, abducting them and forcing them to aid a criminal gang on an interstellar crime spree.

Kelvoo's team must use their intelligence and limited knowledge of humans to survive their captivity and attempt a daring escape.

The second book, *Kelvoo's Terra*, begins seven years after Kelvoo's traumatic abduction and subsequent attempts to heal. Kelvoo's account of the abduction has sparked massive reforms throughout human society, with Kelvoo being revered as a legendary figure.

A remorseful professor, with the help of two human sisters in Kelvoo's care, convinces Kelvoo to move to the human home world. Once on Terra, Kelvoo is met with open arms by most humans, until a radical anti-immigration movement stages a murderous coup. Terra is plunged into chaos and civil war, threatening all extraterrestrial immigrants, and placing Kelvoo and the sisters in mortal danger.

Books one and two provide a gripping view into human nature from a true outsider's perspective, along with a fresh look at the eternal struggles of good against evil, love against hate, and knowledge versus ignorance.

Did you enjoy this independently published book?

Something you might have noticed about books from the large publishing houses is how alike they are. After all, the big publishers want to invest in books that follow a formula that sells. Apart from books written by the most famous authors, large publishers aren't always willing to invest in innovative, boundary-pushing stories.

As an independent author, I'm not subject to the narrower confines imposed by the mega-publishers. The downside, however, is that I don't have access to the huge marketing budgets or distribution networks of the major players.

Fortunately, you can enable me to keep writing and creating more books with nothing more than a positive online review or social media post. So, if you enjoyed my book, please support it with your review or post. Bonus points for social media posts with an image of the cover!

If you leave a review or make a post, please let me know where to find it and I promise to read it. Your feedback helps me to understand my readers and improve as an author for any future books I may write, and you may enjoy.

The same goes for my fellow independent authors. All of us appreciate your reviews and feedback.

You can visit my website to send me a message or find my social media links at:

www.kelvoo.com.

THANK YOU so much,

-- Phil Bailey